RIVER OF GHOSTS

A Mariner Adventure

Peter Tonkin

This first world edition published 2009
in Great Britain and in the USA by
SEVERN HOUSE PUBLISHERS LTD of
9–15 High Street, Sutton, Surrey, England, SM1 1DF.
Trade paperback edition published
in Great Britain and the USA 2009 by
SEVERN HOUSE PUBLISHERS LTD

British Library Cataloguing in Publication Data

Tonkin, Peter
  River of ghosts
  1. Mariner, Richard (Fictitious character) - Fiction
  2. Search and rescue operations - Fiction 3. Submarine
  disasters - Fiction 4. Treasure troves - Fiction
  5. Underwater archaeology - Fiction 6. Sea stories
  I. Title
  823.9'14[F]

  ISBN-13: 978-0-7278-6743-8   (cased)
  ISBN-13: 978-1-84751-128-7   (trade paper)

All Severn House titles are printed on acid-free paper.

Typeset by Palimpsest Book Production Ltd.,
Grangemouth, Stirlingshire, Scotland.
Printed and bound in Great Britain by
MPG Books Ltd., Bodmin, Cornwall.

For Cham, Guy and Mark, as always.
And for Muriel West. She loved a good story.

ONE

Trench

The glimpse of massive movement at the near edge of the utter darkness was so unexpected and so threatening that Robin Mariner screamed. She jerked her hands from the controls as though the little levers were suddenly electrified. Deep-sea exploration vessel *Neptune* began to drift sideways and downwards at once, the beams of her headlights sweeping across the steepening slope of the seabed valley. Her buoyancy balance was set so critically that only steady forward movement kept the sturdy little submarine explorer from sinking into the abyssal depths.

'Who's there?' snapped Richard, unconsciously echoing the opening lines of *Hamlet*, reminded of ghostly battlements on some deep subconscious level by the towering seabed cliff-top high above. His hands closed on his own controls more tightly as though he could force the vessel back up on to her course by sheer muscular force. 'Nay! Answer me . . .' His narrowed eyes searched the inky depths cut back by the brightness of the vessel's lights. Was there some monster of the abyss lurking in the nearest shadows, watching them? As though responding to his grated orders, something indeed heaved hugely at the edge of his vision, then turned to flee the light like the ghost of Hamlet's father.

Robin's hands tightened on her controls once again as the mysterious danger receded and the progress of the vessel steadied once more. The dangerous downward slide slowed. In sharp contrast to Richard's thoughts of Shakespeare's masterpiece, state-of-the-art readouts flickered across the multiple video screens at which he was staring as they showed what little could be seen ahead of the vessel, aft of her and to both sides, above and below. Half-focused details swirling against the utter blackness, registering on his mind at a level almost as deep as the castellations of the distant cliff-top that had made him think of Hamlet's haunted castle of Elsinore.

Complexes of bright green figures described tilt, yaw, pitch. Depth, speed and heading from both compass and GPS, the difference between them a function of local magnetic variables and the power of the deep-ocean currents. Ambient water temperature, hull pressure, disposition of equipment. And, most vitally, over-all power levels.

Richard glanced across at his intrepid wife and was shocked to see her face coloured pale green and slick with perspiration. Her near-purple lips were parted, still gasping with departing shock, looking as though she had been at the port or the plum jam. Elements of the disturbing colour must have come from the green of the readouts, he thought, but that was by no means the whole explanation.

The tension in the control room had been building for some time as Richard and Robin guided *Neptune* down the slope of the Ryukyu Trench. She was now nearly four full kilometres beneath the surface of the Yellow Sea in the only really deep water recorded on the admittedly sketchy charts between here and the Chinese coast. The hull-pressure figures were becoming simply terrifying. The water temperature was fluctuating as the faintest and most disturbing of red glows gathered like thunder clouds in the unplumbed deeps and warned of volcanic activity down there where the water was thickest and the skin of the world was thinnest, another kilometre below.

An hour or so earlier, when *Neptune* had swept so unexpectedly on to the massive serpentine monolith of the Okinawa–Guam submarine cable, lying like the tail of some colossal sleeping dragon along the upper slopes of the deep-water trench, Robin had screamed for the first time that day. But by no means the last. And Richard had jumped with shock. Their control of the craft had been less sure back then, and the way in which the massive fallen cabling, festooned with waving weed and alive with suspicious fish, had seemed to rear out of the darkness had genuinely frightened them both. To make matters worse, in her surprise, Robin had hit the button that released one of the vessel's emergency beacons. As he had wrestled with the controls, Richard had watched the priceless little piece of equipment streaking towards the distant surface like a rocket, surrounded by a surprisingly large cloud of star-bright bubbles. The distraction had nearly been fatal, for the light show was in the rear monitor and he had taken his eye off the forward screen for a moment. *Neptune* had actually bellied on to the somnolent monster of the cable. Only the fact that both the vessel and the cable itself were immensely strong had averted a disaster.

Even though Robin had settled quickly and was easily assured that there were several other emergency beacons left – for she had seen the design plans as well as Richard and knew that there were four – since that moment she had been focusing with all the terrified attention of a tightrope walker crossing Niagara Falls.

'It's all right, darling,' Richard said now, his voice a deep and reassuring rumble, only a little louder than the motors. 'There's nothing to worry about. I mean, what on earth can there *be* nearly four full kilometres down . . .'

The colossal squid hit *Neptune* then. It attacked from behind, though the rear-view screens seemed to show it coming head-on. Richard was astonished. He had supposed giant squid to be sluggish creatures that only ever swam backwards leading with their muscular bodies and dragging their tentacles behind them like weed. This one came in face first, its eyes gleaming briefly in the vessel's lights with the steely reflected brightness of old-fashioned metal dustbin lids.

As the monster hurled out of the blackness, it opened its tentacles like some unimaginable man-eating alien plant. The movement hid its eyes but revealed the beak-like gape of its mouth. The two longest tentacles whipped around the sides and closed across the forward screens. They were more than seven metres long, with wide paddle-ends like giant hands gloved in cratered mittens. In an instant they were pulling *Neptune* back as the six other tentacles closed around her in turn, each one the size of a giant anaconda.

The fact that in what was left of the overwhelmed light coming from *Neptune*'s shrouded headlamps the monster was coloured in the most delicate pinks shading to pristine whites like the petal of some exotic orchid only made the whole encounter more terrifyingly disorientating.

The weight of the monstrous cephalopod sent *Neptune* tumbling away down the vertiginous cliff. That, and the fact that both Richard and Robin, shouting in horrified surprise, had let go of the controls again.

The screens showing fore, aft, port and starboard were filled with the muscular writhing of the tentacles, the pulsing grasp of suckers the size of soup plates, slithering and smearing over the skin of the sturdy little vehicle. At the centre of the rear-view, the big black mandible of its mouth, every bit as hard, curved and sharp as a giant vulture's beak, yawned and struck, tearing at what the squid must have supposed to be soft, defenceless flesh.

'Power,' shouted Richard, his hoarse voice booming deafeningly in the constricted space of the control room. Working as smoothly as a pair of pistons in a Rolls-Royce engine, the perfect team that he and Robin represented reached for the controls again. The wildly flickering readouts showed all too clearly that *Neptune* and its un-welcome passenger were tumbling sideways down the cliff-face, and lucky not to be bouncing across the seabed like a runaway football. Even the water-temperature readout was racing as the tough little vessel sank all too rapidly through the last brightening kilometre of ocean towards the volcanic vents below.

But while *Neptune* came sluggishly back on to an even keel and her death-plunge began to slow, the red light from below gathered, shading the delicate orchid-pinks and roses of the huge squid's flesh to deep ruby-reds. As the first shock of that attack wore off it was replaced by an increasingly sinister and urgent tension deepened by what they were watching, as though the water through which they were sinking was turning slowly into blood.

'What have we got to frighten it off with?' asked Richard, scaring himself more than a little with the breathless sound of his shock-shaken voice.

'We could fold out the arms,' answered Robin, her own voice trembling with tension. 'That might frighten it.' She didn't add that the powerful arms were well equipped with pincers, probes, saws and soldering tools that might make them formidable weapons. Or that there were explosive charges available aboard as well. Richard and she had spent the whole of their lives protecting the environm-ent as best they could – so actually damaging this unique and endangered creature was the last of a list of options. Hopefully a fairly long list of options.

'Good. Try that,' commanded Richard, his mind still seeking alternatives. He had been adjusting the fins as well as racing the motors to steady the vessel – neither had frightened the squid. Folding out the arms probably wouldn't do much either, unless they used the array of potential weapons on the end of them. Or started reaching for the explosives. But he really did not want to hurt the creature if he could possibly help it. On the other hand, he wasn't about to risk *Neptune* just to save a squid – no matter how unique the monstrous thing might be.

'Time to call for backup,' he said, almost to himself. 'Or a bit of advice at least . . .' He reached out a finger and hit the commu-nications toggle – reminded quite poignantly, suddenly, of the paddle-gear selector on the steering column of his beloved Bentley Continental. He dipped his head as though the movement would bring the stalk of the microphone on his headset closer to his lips. 'You see this, Captain Chang?' he asked.

'I see.' Captain Chang's distant tones hissed in his left ear and dripped icy disapproval as always. 'It is on one of my bridge monitors, of course.'

In his mind's eye, Richard could see the Chinese captain standing squarely and impatiently in the centre of the command bridge of *Neptune*'s mother ship *Poseidon*, hands clasped solidly behind, face folded into its accustomed fearsome frown. 'Any suggestions?' he drawled, affecting sangfroid he was far from feeling.

'Kill it,' snapped the captain as though talking to a clumsy rating or an inept cadet. But then, the captain talked to everyone like that. 'Kill it at once!'

'You're a hard woman, Captain Chang,' he drawled, apparently even more laid-back as his mind raced. His eyes, unnaturally wide in the green gloom remained focused on the relentless tearing of that gigantic vulture's beak. Could the thing actually eat through the strengthened glass and special layers of composite, carbon and steel back there? he wondered. 'How do you suggest I kill it, Captain?' he enquired mildly.

The captain gave a dry laugh. Little more than a scarcely audible grunt. In Richard's earphone she might have been talking to him from another solar system. 'Any way you can. The risks you are running are far beyond acceptability, Captain Mariner, even as owner.'

'So much for backup,' said Robin wryly.

'Looks like we are to fend for ourselves, then!' Richard pushed the throttles forward, feeling the weight of the squid holding them back like a sea-anchor. He supposed the creature's mantle must be inflating like an underwater drogue. The squid obviously felt the gathering current and settled itself more securely. Richard saw the black beak bite and scrape higher and higher across the vessel's back. And at the same instant he also saw the best chance of escaping from the situation. 'Robin,' he said urgently, 'launch another rescue beacon. Launch them all!'

Without a moment's hesitation, Robin hit the emergency release. The three remaining compartments slid open immediately in front of the squid's face. Three beacons burst upwards, already shrieking their emergency distress calls. Richard had no idea whether the squid had anything like ears – or whether they could hear such things as the distress calls. All in all, he thought, it was most likely

to be the three explosions of bubbles that frightened the creature –
he just hoped that they would frighten it enough to make it break
its grip on *Neptune*. If they didn't, then the next series of compartments forward contained charges for use in demolition or seismic
testing, effectively powerful little grenades with remote-control
detonators. There were enough to blow the squid to atoms. The
triple-strengthened hull would certainly stand the shock.

But there was no need to put the explosives to the test. The
bubbles were enough. The massive creature vanished as suddenly
and silently as it had appeared. One moment it was clasping *Neptune*
to its working mouthpiece, the next it was a huge roseate mass
streaking towards the shadows that were darkened with a cloud of
midnight ink. *Neptune* leaped upwards as though jumping with joy.

'Right!' said Richard immediately, his spirits seemingly lifted
by the sudden buoyancy of the little vessel itself. 'We'd better bring
her home while the going's good. And check her over for any
damage.'

'Good thinking,' said Robin hoarsely. 'You want us to do it
ourselves or shall we hand over?'

Richard did not hesitate. He opened his mouth and drew breath
to answer, with his usual decisive quick thinking, that he would
like to bring *Neptune* back. He could learn a lot more about the
virtual sensing and remote handling systems as he guided her back
up through the five kilometres of ocean that lay vertically between
the remote AUV sub and the control room on the mother ship
Poseidon where he and Robin had been sitting for much of the
afternoon. But that he would understand completely if Robin wanted
a little R&R after the remote-control adventure with the squid.

Even so, his decision was overtaken by the speed of events.
Captain Chang's voice boomed into his earpiece a heartbeat after
Robin's question.

'Captain Mariner. You hand over control of the remote vehicle
to my men now. You come out of remote-control room. We need
you on command bridge at once. Big emergency here. *Big
emergency . . .*'

TWO

Up

Richard followed Robin along the narrow corridors on the lower engineering deck, where the remote-control room was located. The cramped little cabin with its swivel chairs, banks of monitors and pair of control sticks stood immediately behind the hi-tech sub-aquatic communications equipment located in *Poseidon*'s bulbous bow. It was joined to the more conventional engineering areas by the passage Robin was following now. Her golden curls seemed to sweep along the deck-head and only just manage to pass under the downward swell of the lights.

Richard walked in an uneasy, unaccustomed stoop, wondering whether the passage was so constricted because the ship's architects in Yantai, where she had been built by the recently reorganized and outward-looking management of the newly refurbished Raffles Shipyard, assumed that her crew would always be Han Chinese, and therefore relatively slight. He tried to think of all the tall Chinese he knew – but, even after some years as a Tai Pan in Hong Kong with a wide circle of Chinese friends and acquaintances, he could really only call to mind Fu Manchu and Dr No. One Mongol and the other Shanghaiese of mixed race – crippled indeed by the Shanghai triads if he remembered correctly. Both fantastically fictional. The thoughts were trivial enough, but at least they stopped him speculating as to the nature of Captain Chang's emergency. The feel of the vessel around him – made more immediate and intimate by the tightness of the passageway – assured him that the crisis was unlikely to concern this ship at least. It wasn't until they reached the main companionway that he felt he could stand upright.

The stairs led them swiftly up the four decks from the keel, if not to the truck then at least to the command bridge. Here Richard stepped out through a narrow door just behind Robin's shoulder into a disorientatingly vast and dazzling afternoon. It was not that the command bridge itself was particularly large. There was just room for a couple of big comfortable swivel chairs – accommodating the helmsman and one other – and standing room for perhaps half a dozen more. But *Poseidon*'s command bridge was walled on three sides with strengthened glass. Only the aft wall, leading into the chart room, the door, with a noticeboard on the inside, and the radio room were solid. Above the banks of equipment on the three other sides, clear clean glass sloped up towards the deck-head nearly seven feet above the deck itself. And the windows looked over the long deck and the stubby bridge wings out over the Yellow Sea.

It was only the Yellow Sea, thought Richard as he waited for his streaming eyes to clear, because they were facing north. Had he been looking south, it would have been the East China Sea, for they were somewhere on the notional line on the featureless ocean along which the two seas met, five kilometres above the Ryukyu Trench. Away below the eastern horizon on his right lay Korea and Japan. Away below the horizon on his left lay China itself; the nearest point of it, Dr No's dangerous Shanghai. Dead ahead – again hidden by the curvature of the earth itself – Bo Hai and Korea Bay. Due south, eventually, Taiwan. And south of that, Hong Kong.

It was a truly magnificent sight and one that could be bettered only two ways aboard – though Richard had tried neither yet. One was from one of the observation platforms standing like little bridge wings astride the big communications mast high above. The other was from the open bridge, the flying navigation bridge, that sat on the deck above, on top of this more formal and better-equipped command bridge. In many a vessel such as this one, on seas and days such as these, the upper bridge would be protected from the sun by canvas screens and open to cooling winds and glorious views while watch officers took some of the formality out of their duties. But not on *Poseidon*, he thought wryly. Not under the redoubtable Captain Chang.

Richard's thoughts occupied less time than it took for his eyes to clear. Even so, Captain Chang overrode the last of them impatiently, just as her square, powerful frame loomed surprisingly close between him and the hazy vastness of the afternoon. 'We have an emergency distress call,' she announced.

'You have at least four, I should think,' Richard answered frowning. 'All of them from *Neptune*.'

'No. Not from *Neptune*. From a submarine or rather vessels attempting to rescue the submarine. You know of Kublai Khan's treasure ship?'

'Of course. Its discovery has been on the news for weeks. The attempts to recover the treasure . . . You mean it's *that* submarine?'

'As you say. That submarine. It is trapped on the seabed. Too far down for anything but specialist access. *Neptune* – as you call it – is nearest. Men aboard die without help.'

'OK. Let's go. Where are they and when can we get to them?' Ever the man of action, Richard was sweeping Captain Chang towards the chart room even before he had finished speaking.

'Hold your horses, sailor,' said Robin, more thoughtfully. 'We have to recover *Neptune* first. We'll be of little use without her. And we'd better check her hull after that squid tried to make a meal of her.'

'We can do that as we go. But, yes, we need to recover her, of course. And that'll give me a chance to pick up those emergency beacons too before half the ships in the neighbourhood come rushing down to help *us*!'

'That's good,' said Robin frowning slightly as his mind raced. 'You go and oversee that – you'll enjoy a ride out in the Zodiac – and I'll do some planning with Captain Chang here and her navigating officers.' Now it was her turn to sweep the others along with her. 'You'll just catch the Zodiac if you hurry – I see they're about to swing it out. By the time you get back and we swing *Neptune* aboard, Captain Chang and I will have a destination, a course and an optimum sailing time all logged in and communicated to the authorities.'

Richard half ran on to *Poseidon*'s foredeck and immediately into the fleeting shadow of the little six-man inflatable sea boat as it was swung out over the side. There was a four-man recovery crew ready to climb aboard – their main function to attach the recovery lines to *Neptune* when she surfaced. They stood back amenably when Richard strode forward to join them, however; during the last few days he had won their grudging respect, for they were a good crew of solid seamen and they recognized one of their own kind. As a seafarer, if not as a Han or a resident of the Middle Kingdom. Robin, being a woman as well as a gold-haired *gwailo* devil, still had a way to go. And, courtesy of his days in Hong Kong, Richard spoke both Cantonese and Mandarin well enough to get by. Fortunately also, most of them spoke English – for they were an elite crew aboard an all but unique vessel. Which was why Richard and Robin wanted to buy her – when they had finished assessing her potential.

'It will be a while before *Neptune* surfaces,' Richard said as the

Zodiac slapped down into the oily calm. 'So we'll have time to get my distress buoys back. They're worth hundreds of dollars – thousands of RMB – each and I don't want to lose them if I can help it.' He swung his leg out over the gunwale and on to the first rung of the boarding ladder.

Also, he thought, as the sturdy little vessel slammed through the swell, I've a sneaking suspicion that those four beacons are the only ones we have. And we might well need them if this rescue lark starts getting complicated or dangerous.

Which, of course, it was almost certainly going to do.

The beacons were easy to find – they were designed to be, after all. They were easy to recover as well, but it was less simple to deflate their flotation rings, quieten their emergency transmitters and stow them aboard the Zodiac because they were sizeable and sturdy, designed to stay afloat and operational in the wildest extremes of wave and weather. Water-wise and buoyant though they might be, they were as unhandy as eels when they were dragged out of their element, and all five men aboard were soon soaking wet and gasping for breath.

Richard suspected acutely that he had used up his stock of goodwill before the first one was safely aboard and they were off in search of the second. By the time they had all four lying silently along the centreboard of the Zodiac, their flashing tops forming a complicated bowsprit so that the helmsman could reach the outboard without too much difficulty, Richard felt like Captain Bligh surrounded by four Chinese Fletcher Christians.

But before they could stage their own little mutiny on the *Bounty*, Captain Chang's voice came barking over the open channel on the two-way radio. 'Si Ji Shi Guan Xin,' she bellowed abruptly, '*Neptune* has surfaced on the starboard beam of *Poseidon*. It is time for you to stop playing around like children at the seaside and get down to some serious work.'

Richard was hesitant to get involved in the command structures aboard the vessels he owned; particularly if the crew were not directly employed by Heritage Mariner and therefore stood outside the company's personnel and recruitment systems. Especially if they were both foreign nationals and of the opposite gender. But the glances exchanged by the four men around him made him ask without thinking, 'Is she a good captain, Captain Chang?' He spoke in Mandarin as though this would keep the conversation more truthful and secret.

The leader of the little team, *Poseidon*'s boatswain, Non-commissioned Officer (Fourth Class) – as his captain had just called him – Xin, eyed Richard narrowly. He was one of the men Richard knew best aboard, for he doubled his duties as boatswain with those of reserve remote handler. His nickname, Richard knew, was Steadyhand – Steady for short. And the name was well suited to his short, square, deep-chested frame. And his strong imperturbable face. It was Steadyhand Xin who had taught both Richard and Robin the rudiments of handling *Neptune*. Fatfist Fu and Ironwrist Wan had helped too. They were the men currently employed in bringing her safely to the surface and getting her alongside on the far beam of the mother ship.

'Captain Chang is a fine officer,' Steady Xin answered at last, gunning the outboard and guiding the unhandily laden Zodiac in a wide arc designed to take her under the vessel's sharp bow. 'She passed out in the top of her year at Shanghai University and in the top five per cent of her intake at the academy in Dalian.'

'She would hardly have been given command of a vessel like *Poseidon* if she were not outstanding, Mr Xin,' Richard allowed, his Mandarin clumsy and formal as his mind strove to assess how much relentless extra work and almost unimaginable competitive pressure must have gone into these simply stated qualifications. For the family as well as the student. What agonizing sacrifices they must all have made – father, mother and child. Especially for a girl. More than twenty-five years of it, starting when she was four years old; perhaps earlier still. 'Have you served with her before?'

Xin shrugged noncommittally. Silence settled. Richard changed focus from the taciturn boatswain to the view wheeling past ahead of him. *Poseidon* sat high in the water, awaiting the weight of *Neptune* on her foredeck. The bulbous torpedo at the foot of her cutwater sat high enough to be awash with the gentle swell, like a little red sandbank. Above and behind the equipment-stuffed swelling sat a sleek, ultra-modern grey-painted vessel for all the world like a naval corvette – too big to be a patrol boat; almost big enough to be a frigate. She eased herself in the water with the authority of a battleship, however, never moving too abruptly, yet never quite at rest. Her lines were sleek, uncluttered. Her demeanour steady and graceful.

The only break in the elegantly geometric sweep of her busi-nesslike foredeck was *Neptune*'s cradle, flanked by the solid cranes designed to lift her in and out of it. She had no portholes and precious few windows at deck level until the determined grey thrust of her bridge house attained the stylish crystal rake of her command bridge. Above this, a thick communications mast reared, with a couple of observation platforms on either side and what looked like a radar receiver sweeping round and round at the top. Behind, the hull gathered up into the muscular thrust of the propulsion unit – grilles down the side but no funnel. Aft of that stood another square grey container shape for storage and accommodation. Behind that in turn was the helipad with the sturdy little chopper that had carried Richard and Robin out from Shanghai little more than a week ago. The latest generation update of the Chaig Z-11.

Downwind here, she smelt of hot metal, diesel and fresh paint. There was nothing about her yet redolent of rust or bilge. She smelt *new* – that exciting, indefinable odour associated with cars in showrooms. For all that her hull was angular and featureless, she had a sea-readiness about her; a satisfying combination of power and rugged grace. Like the *Neptune*, she was what ship-handlers from Shakespeare's day to the third Western millennium called *yare*.

Steady Xin brought the Zodiac under the bow. The cutwater whispered over Richard's head like a falling guillotine blade while the inflated gunwale under his hand slid up over the red thrust at its foot.

At once, they were upon *Neptune* herself, for Ironwrist and Fatfist had guided her to the pick-up point immediately on *Poseidon*'s starboard forward quarter. The AUV, or remote deep-water vessel, was the opposite of her computer-generated, mathematically perfect mother ship. She was organic, rounded and buttercup bright. But she resembled nothing so much as a giant crab, floating in the Yellow Sea awaiting recovery. Her carapace was deep daffodil yellow. It overhung the lower sections of her hull like the roof of a little house. Under the eaves clustered the majority of the lights and cameras. Below these, tucked safely away, the arms with their array of tools. Forward, she had a blunt, square face with the main headlamps looking for all the world like huge silver eyes. Aft were the propellers of the main propulsion unit – though these were supplemented by a range of manoeuvring screws and water-jets. The slick curve of the shell-back was marred by the four little hatches standing open, awaiting the return of the emergency beacons. And by the depressions where the loading rings sat, waiting for the lading hooks that would lift her on to her cradle on *Poseidon*'s foredeck.

Xin cut the power to the outboard and the rubberized black

gunwale nudged the slick yellow shell. Richard was out and up at once. He had overseen recovery more than once and was confident he could do so now. The submersible stirred a little under him, dipping beneath his weight, rolling because of his swift activity. In a moment he was on the top of the buttery slope, turning to catch the first of the four falls, stooping to clip the quick-release G-clip home into the lading ring. As he attached the rear two lines so his narrow eyes were busy completing the initial damage assessment.

He worked with that concentrated precision that marked much of what he did, focusing on the task in hand as well as on the assessment he was making, yet aware that Xin had backed the Zodiac away and was letting it fall back to the boarding ladder at *Poseidon*'s side.

By the time Richard stood up and waved to the crane crew, Xin and the others had passed the emergency buoys up and the boatswain was attaching the recovery falls to the Zodiac as well. Then, as Richard felt *Neptune* stir beneath him, swinging up out of the water towards the cradle on the deck – and the Zodiac did exactly the same with Xin also standing holding a fall as he flew – *Poseidon*'s powerful engine came up to power. With a deep-throated, grumbling roar, she swung away urgently on to a new heading east of north, churning the placid water to spray and foam behind her as she went.

THREE
Face

With four of them in there, the chart room was hot, crowded and even a little steamy. Captain Chang and the navigator, Senior Lieutenant Jiang, who the crew called Straightline, had already explained their destination, course and times to Robin and were grudging in their willingness to repeat them to Richard. But he was getting used to the taciturn, almost sullen demeanour of *Poseidon*'s officers and crew. And, until he could understand it and find some way of changing it, he was happy to ride over it roughshod. His time in Hong Kong had showed him that on occasion, properly exerted, apparently ruthless force could be of benefit to all concerned. It would establish his 'face' in the eyes of those he commanded – and save their face if anything went wrong, as the responsibility was so obviously his.

Face, he thought as he looked down at the chart to hide a wry smile. He hadn't thought of that peculiarly Eastern concept combining embarrassment, standing, respect and honour in many a long year. He hoped he was still good at handling it.

'Very well,' he concluded. 'I see that Navigator Jiang has laid in a direct course to the submarine's position – as usual. And I understand your desire to follow it as fast as possible, Captain Chang. Not only is time running out for the men in the submarine but that nasty little weather system Mr Jiang pointed out in his briefing could put a typhoon directly in our path . . .' And they don't call you Straightline Jiang for nothing, he thought, glancing up at their closed faces. If a typhoon crossed the course, *Poseidon* would simply charge straight through it. Xin said Jiang and Chang had been at the Naval Academy together. They seemed to share many characteristics. He could not see Chang stepping aside to let a typhoon divert her from her course either. He had characterized them both as the unexpected result of the 'One Child' policy inflicted on the Han. Spoilt 'Little Emperors' used to getting their own way without thought of parental sacrifices. But used also to working at levels and under pressures that would never be tolerated in the West.

Impatient, self-centred, unfeeling. Unlikely to back down in the face of typhoons of teachers, employers or earthquakes. Therefore, he thought, he had better get on with his own plans pretty sharply. He straightened. 'What are your plans, darling?' he asked. Robin looked at him steadily, silent for a heartbeat – just long enough to make him fear he had damaged her face in front of the officers. 'Captain Chang is about to do a full inspection,' she answered. 'It's her first since we came aboard. I thought I'd go with her.' The steady grey gaze held his own. Then it flicked away to glance forward.

Richard glanced that way also, looking through the open door, across the bridge and through the pristine clearview. The horizon dead ahead was a thick grey line and a series of cloudlets lay above it. They spread across the late afternoon sky like a sinister rash. As grey as if a series of artillery shells had exploded in the air out there. As though there was some kind of battle being fought just below the horizon.

He glanced back again to a frown so slight that only he would have noticed it. There was a secret message here. A worry? If he had been captain of a newly commissioned vessel still undergoing some final sea tests, with new owners suddenly heaving into view, who was called into an emergency situation – and likely to have to plough through dirty weather to get there – he would be going over every inch, plate and rivet too, he thought; Little Emperor or not. 'I'll maybe join you when I've finished,' he said brusquely. Robin gave a tiny nod: message received.

Although *Poseidon*'s forward deck seemed slick and featureless, there were actually a range of hatches between *Neptune*'s cradle and the solid lower frontage of the deckhouse. Two of these were open and as Richard arrived, the last of the emergency beacons were being lowered into them. He hesitated long enough to glance forward again, calculatingly. Down here, a good three metres below command-bridge level, the horizon seemed less threatening. But there was something in the air – something beyond the steady head-wind of *Poseidon* racing forward through a heavy calm – that raised the short hairs on his neck.

'Something nasty on the way,' he observed.

Steady Xin glanced up between releasing the top of the beacon and kneeling to close the hatch. His strong square face was closed, but he nodded his short-stubbled head once decisively. '*Tai-Fun*,' he pronounced, giving the weather its true Chinese name – Lord of Winds.

Side by side in silence they ran over to the A-deck bulkhead door and stepped into the bridge house with Xin leading. Without a pause, as though on critical business, they ran down the companionway and into the engineering sections. Immediately below the deck hatches was a big handling area that opened into the maintenance sections like an open plan kitchen-diner in a modern flat. Something worth several million RMB in the Shanghai Bund, for instance, or in fashionable Pudong across the Huangpu River.

The first of the emergency beacons was already on the electrical-maintenance bench with a young lieutenant stooping over it. A maintenance manual stood open on the work surface beside him but it was written in Chinese lettering and Richard had no idea what it said. 'Zhong Wei,' said Xin quietly, 'how long before we can get the beacons safely stowed back aboard *Mazu*?'

The young man glanced up, frowning, the lenses of his thick-rimmed glasses glinting. Although Richard knew well enough that 'Zhong Wei' simply meant lieutenant – as Xin's rank was 'si ji shi guan', NCO class 4 or chief petty officer – he thought of it as the young electrical officer's name. 'Why do you need to know, Si Ji Shi Guan?' Zhong Wei asked now.

'*Yu-qiang* is heading for a tai-fun, sir. We need to stow them in their right places or secure them safely down here.'

It was only then that Richard realized Xin was talking of *Neptune* and *Poseidon* – but calling them by the names of Chinese sea gods. The vessels' original names, no doubt – though both were still so new that there was nothing painted on bow or stern except their shipyard markings.

'They should be ready to take back topsides by the time you have assured yourself that your baby is lashed securely in her cradle, Steadyhand,' answered Zhong Wei. 'But only if you leave me to my work.'

Richard ran up the companionway on Xin's heels once again but as soon as they stepped out on to the deck he was back at the Chinese chief's shoulder. 'It must be hard for the crew to adjust,' he began. He was speaking English, far more confident of Xin's multilingual abilities than his own. Hoping also, as they approached the little team securing *Neptune* in her cradle, that they might not follow English quite as readily as the boatswain.

'How do you mean?' asked Xin, his accent thick with suspicion.

'Well, all the officers seem to have been navy trained . . .' Richard simply could not get his mind around the full proper designation, People's Liberation Army Navy. But Xin nodded. Although he had fallen to work checking and testing the first clip, he was paying attention. Richard watched as the strong, steady fingers settled the steel G-clip more neatly into the securing point on *Neptune*'s yellow side, then tightened the webbing strap that attached it to the permanent fixture in the cradle with a series of vicious tugs.

'And I assume the same is true of the enlisted men.' Richard glanced around the others who had been aboard the Zodiac with them, all busy and apparently deaf.

Another nod. Xin worked on, tugging with the almost brutal actions of a very worried parent stopping his child from running across a busy road.

'But since China opened her borders, what with the one country two systems approach in Hong Kong, the acceptance of the Internet, the liberation of the Shanghai stock exchange. Followed by earthquakes and the Olympics in '08 and so forth, there's been a great deal of movement out of the military and into the commercial arena . . .'

'Yes.' Xin completed his check of the first secure point. He glanced at the darkening horizon and proceeded to check the second even more forcefully still.

Poseidon gave a strange little corkscrew twist. She dropped her right shoulder for all the world like a rugby forward dipping into a hard tackle. A wall of water slapped up over her forward starboard quarter and soaked them all before it ran away off the slick deck. Richard glanced back at the Zodiac in time to see the waterfall sparkling off the black turtle shell of her inverted hull. They'd better secure that pretty well into the bargain, he thought.

But he didn't pause in what he was saying. 'So we have a half-military unit aboard this vessel testing it for the commercial market rather than for military applications.'

'As you say.' Xin went on to the next point, apparently satisfied. The headwind was supplemented by a little slap of counterdraught on Richard's right cheek. The Chinese boatswain glanced up, feeling it on his seawise skin as well.

'And just as you're all shaking down together and getting to know your shipmates and your vessels, a radio call comes out from the Raffles Shipyard that some *gwailo* businessman has bought her

out from under you and is coming out to join you for your final
series of tests. Tests which have suddenly turned into an emergency
which, if not precisely national in scale, will nevertheless pitchfork
you all into the public eye and on to the worldwide news services
– for better or worse. Better if we succeed in helping the men
trapped in the submarine. Worse if we fail them.'

'Just so. Worse if we fail them. Worse than you can imagine.
They and their search for the Great Khan's treasure have made them
heroes to the whole of China . . .' The pair went round to the starboard side and began to check the clips and fastenings there.

'Not only that,' concluded Richard thoughtfully, 'but the *gwailo*
barbarian has renamed both vessels in a thoughtlessly Western
manner. Thus damaging the face of all aboard from the captain to
the lowliest seaman. And bringing a great deal of bad fortune.
Something probably compounded by the fact that he brings with
him a *gwailo* wife with unlucky demon-yellow hair. Unlucky, even
though it is precisely the same colour as the Great Khan's missing
gold . . .'

'And doubly unlucky the fact that he is himself a giant with the
unluckiest blue round eyes the colour of the seas that swallowed
the Khan's yellow gold in the first place.' Steady Xin completed
Richard's sentence as he completed his check of the secure points.
He turned to face Richard squarely after giving the final one an
almost cursory tug, clearly happy to be speaking man to man. Though
Richard knew that in Xin's mind it was more likely 'man to
barbarian'.

Xin stepped right up close, still looking squarely up at him as
the other two went back to double-check the Zodiac. 'You have
lived in the Middle Kingdom if you understand this much and can
manage more than a grunt or two in Mandarin,' the irritable
boatswain continued. Raising his voice as the wind intensified from
the starboard quarter and blew strongly enough to make the chains
on the hoist that stood behind him like a gallows swing and groan.
'So you may be faintly aware of the methods by which our world
is ruled on every level. And consider. Since you came aboard, you
and your unlucky woman have watched as my baby here was
ravished by a devilfish. We have received news that the men sent
to rescue the Great Khan's treasure have not found it but have found
ill fortune instead. And now as we run to rescue them Tin Hau
herself, great Goddess of the Sea, is throwing the Lord of Winds
in our path.'

As if to emphasize his words, *Poseidon* gave that odd little corkscrew twist again and Richard saw that the waters ahead were beginning to break out of the ordered swells of the calm and into a sharper, greyer, nastier-looking sea.

'This is my ship, Steadyhand,' said Richard, stepping forward in his turn and switching to his most fluent Hong Kong-accented Mandarin. 'And this baby is my baby.' His broad hand slapped *Neptune*'s yellow side possessively. 'It is my face at risk and my luck being tested. By Tin Hau perhaps, or by *Yu-qiang* or *Mazu* or by any sea god, goddess or dragon you can name. And like any man in the Middle Kingdom – or in my own more distant kingdom – I will listen to the gods and hope for luck and make what sacrifice I can. *But I will do what I want to do in spite of them all.*' And as he spoke, the new wind that had brought the new grey seas also delivered the first cold fusillade of rain.

The rain was a good deal heavier fifteen minutes later when Richard and Xin employed the gallows-like hoist to move the beacons as swiftly as possible up through the hatches on to the deck. Then up again so that they could be lowered safely home into four compartments on *Neptune*'s back that stood open awaiting them. It was easily heavy enough to make the oilskins the men were wearing a very sensible investment – even for a potentially short and simple job like this. On the foredeck around them another little team of men, also in oilskins, were rigging safety lines in case anyone was forced to work on deck before they were through the gathering storm.

It was cold and tiring work for both teams – their main focus was to get it finished as swiftly and efficiently as possible. None of them had any inclination for further conversation; certainly not Richard or Steadyhand. The wind and the water were adding to the noise made by the hoist's motor and the creaking of its chains in any case. Any kind of conversation would have been difficult as well as ill timed and distracting. And to a certain extent there was nothing left to say. Richard would have to wait and see whether he had started a war with Boatswain Xin and the crew as well as with Tin Hau and the gods of the China Seas.

But at last the job was done. The lines were rigged and tested. The hatches on *Neptune*'s back and on *Poseidon*'s deck were all tight shut and the sopping team could escape into the dry security below. This time Richard went first, pausing at the raked grey corner of the sloping bridge house to look back at Xin as he gave a quick final check to the safe stowage of *Neptune*, the Zodiac and the hoists. The sky beyond the square boatswain was quite dark now and the sea beneath it almost the colour of granite. The rain was whipping from starboard to port with enough force to give an outline to the man and his equipment that picked up the failing light like a halo. For the first time, Richard noticed that in the distance, far beyond the gusty puffing of the wind, there was a deep, relentless booming. And just as he tensed to turn and run for the A-deck door where the last two of the little line-rigging team were waiting in the wind shadow of the bridge house and the wing, the first great fork of lightning pounced down, stark against a wildly whirling wall of blackness dead ahead.

FOUR

Typhoon

Richard left his sopping oilskins beside the A-deck door then went in search of Robin and Captain Chang. He found them in the engineering section. Although the three of them were navigating officers, they all lingered as the Shang Wei Senior Lieutenant Engineer Powerhouse Wang talked earnestly in broken English about his state-of-the-art lean-burning diesel powerplant with its special adapters designed to let it run on the new green biofuels. And its electrical alternative for steady cruising – switched off now because the weather conditions were already making demands on the engines far beyond what the electric system could provide. But Richard noted, with the satisfaction of a long-serving eco-warrior, that the electric system was powered by batteries automatically charged by the use of the main engine itself, independently of the generators and alternators that powered the rest of the ship and all of its equipment. The carbon footprint of the system must be little bigger than that of a sailing vessel.

Richard missed the introduction to the talk so he remained ignorant of exactly what type of engine was being described – but it all looked like Yamaha kit to him. The engine turned two advanced-style screws – no propellers here, not even the variable-pitch technology that Richard knew from his tankers. These were literally screws. Spirals of metal whose radius and profile ensured optimum forward power. Or, for that matter, reverse power. And they could run independently of each other. One on full ahead and the other on full astern with the helm hard over gave the corvette the tightest turning circle in her class. But this was as nothing, emphasized the engineer, to what she could do with both screws running full ahead. *Poseidon* was both impressively fast – as she was proving at the moment – and incredibly manoeuvrable.

Having indulged her engineer to an unexpected degree, Captain Chang continued with her inspection and Richard soon saw that there was an extra purpose to it. A glance at Robin showed that she too understood the frowning captain's real purpose here. And the increasing restlessness of the surging hull, coupled with the gathering roar of waves and weather, made her mission all the more vital.

Every door that Captain Chang opened then closed – to cupboard, corridor, work area or bulkhead – was secured with a determined *click* and then pushed hard again. And everything inside those cupboards, work areas, offices and cabins was checked individually to ensure that it was stowed – and in many cases secured – properly. As she proceeded, the captain ticked off item after item on her inspection checklist; but Richard was soon convinced that what was really important to the grimly determined woman was less what equipment was where and in what condition than that it was stowed safely and securely away.

Richard dredged something out of a literary memory fed by many long hours at sea where boredom had been relieved by voracious reading rather than watching videos, DVDs or satellite broadcasts with his crew. Something out of a story by Joseph Conrad. It was a vision of the dour spectacularly unimaginative Scottish captain of the good ship *Nan Shan*. Of Captain MacWhirr going round his new command checking all the door handles, locks and bolts, followed by a bemused young first officer. Ensuring that there was nothing aboard the vessel that might burst wide at a vital moment and do untold injury or damage to fixtures, fittings, officers or crew. Because MacWhirr and *Nan Shan* were sailing through waters only a little south of here – straight into the heart of a terrible typhoon.

Richard's literary thoughts took him up with Robin and the captain as far as the little galley where the cook was preparing the evening meal. The captain took one look round the neat but cramped facility with its glittering knives, gleaming choppers, smoking woks, boiling oil and flaring gas-burners and spat a string of orders.

'Cold cuts tonight,' whispered Richard to Robin.

'So I should think,' she answered equally quietly. 'If we're running under storm sails, the galley must be dampened down.'

In a surprisingly short time the steelware was stowed. Lethal carving knives slid into blocks as safely as King Arthur's sword in its stone. The choppers hung from big strong hooks and at once began to chime like discordant bells as the room began to heave and roll more violently. The gas range was doused at the turn of a knob. The gas itself was switched off at the top of the cylinder as well. The boiling oil poured laboriously but successfully back into a big tin drum that, like the gas cylinders, was secured in place with metal hoops.

And not a moment too soon, thought Richard. *Poseidon* gave that characteristic little corkscrew roll again. But this time she kept rolling until the four of them were staggering across the galley deck and the three visitors carried on out through the door, Robin clinging uncharacteristically to her husband's steady arm. Captain Chang slammed the fireproof galley door safely shut behind them and threw her weight against it while *Poseidon* swooped back up out of the roll. Then off they went together, staggering up towards the command bridge.

The motion of the racing vessel informed all of them that the time for captain's inspection was now past as an increasingly vicious see-sawing pitch was added to that rugby-tackle roll. There were almost no doors left to secure now in any case. All the other accommodation – personal or working – on this deck had curtains instead of doors. Cupboards, drawers and wardrobes may have had sturdy frames but they had moving parts made of MDF or light louvered slats. And they held little more than clothes and stationery. Chang passed these with hardly a second glance, therefore, for the risks presented by drawers sliding open or shirts and pens falling on to the deck were very secondary now to what was going on outside.

Captain Chang ran up to the command bridge first, but Robin and Richard were close behind her. As Richard arrived, slammed the door into the stairwell behind him and leaned back against the noticeboard on its inside, he saw Captain Chang waving the watch officer Zhong Wei Jiang impatiently back into the second seat. She preferred to stand between the two seats, holding on to the back of both, so that she could look down at the helmsman and check all the readouts, dials and displays in front of him. Thus it was that, for the time being, she found herself between Steadyhand and Straightline.

Richard spread his legs and rooted his feet as though he were an oak. He took firm hold of a nearby handle and looked out through the clearview dead ahead. The last of the light revealed a whirling wilderness of foam that seemed to be heaving from side to side as the ship rolled. The wind was whipping in from the starboard quarter at an angle that seemed increasingly fine as Straightline Jiang was forced degree by degree to face it, growling reluctant orders to Xin. Great sheets of foam and spray slammed and soared from side to side, exploding upwards in the middle of the slick deck, making

Neptune seem like a half-submerged reef. At the same time, *Poseidon* would drop her right shoulder and pitch forward so that the wilderness of dirty grey foam ahead could heave back up over her stiletto forepeak and break over the intrepid yellow vessel secured to her foredeck before hurling itself on to the clearview, seeming to stick there, thick as driven snow. Then, as the sluggish foam surrendered to a combination of gravity, clearview wipers and that tearing terrible wind, *Poseidon* would rear upwards and backwards, tossing her head like a runaway horse. Stabbing through the flanks of the waves, tearing them into yet more thick foam. The whole hull would jump up and back as though the bow, slim and strong though it was, had run into a safety net; as though the plucky and adventurous vessel had reached the end of some unimaginable bungee-jump.

It was this motion, Richard decided later, which made *Neptune* break free.

Steady Xin saw it first, of course, for he was dividing his attention equally between his duty and his baby. He shouted, a formless guttural that signified only shock and panic. Then, as the others gaped at him, he yelled, '*Mazu!*'

Richard arrived at Captain Chang's shoulder without conscious thought, having crossed the bridge in half a dozen strides even as she stepped forward to push her nose against the clearview. He found himself sandwiched between Chang and Robin. The three of them gaped down at the remote vessel through the streaming glass. They saw her rock restlessly in her cradle and jump threateningly back towards them. She had apparently grown a short tail of black webbing that lashed wildly behind her, stark against the foam.

'Somebody needs to secure her pretty quickly,' observed Robin grimly. 'If she breaks loose she'll come straight back through the clearview. She'd behead *Poseidon* along with all the rest of us as efficiently as a guillotine.'

'Captain!' shouted Xin. 'Let me go!'

For once she did not call him Si Ji Shi Guan. 'No, Steadyhand,' she said decisively, speaking as calmly and quietly as circumstances would allow. 'I cannot spare you. The rest of the team will go.'

'With your permission, I'll go too,' said Richard at once. 'Steadyhand, where are the spare retaining clips?'

It was Zhong Wei who met him at the A-deck bulkhead door, his thick-rimmed glasses reflecting the dim emergency lighting of the corridor. In one hand he held six black straps with G-clips at both ends and adjustable quick-releases in the middle. In the other he carried the harnesses made of identical webbing with identical G-clamps at their waists designed to fasten on to the safety lines outside. Richard shrugged his harness on, snapped the quick-release shut and checked the steel clamp. He thought – and not for the first time – that he was equipped much like a mountaineer about to scale a steep and deadly peak. Everest, perhaps – or as they called it here Qomolangma – he thought as he looked around the rest of Xin's little team.

Captain Chang's voice suddenly enquired calmly, 'Are you ready, Shang Xiao?' The gentle tones were surprisingly intimate, for he had tied the drawstrings of his hood tightly under the square jut of his jaw, crushing the little Bluetooth transceiver hard against his face from mouth to ear. Shang Xiao, he mused. She's calling me captain at last. Is that a sign of respect for my face – or a warning that it's all my responsibility now?

He gave a thumbs-up and showed it to his little team, raising his eyebrows to make it a question. They shrugged and gave a thumbs-up in reply. 'Ready,' he answered.

He held his hand out for the six spare straps and crossed the shadowy corridor towards his unhappy little team. As the electrical-engineering lieutenant wrestled the metal bulkhead door open, he handed the straps out – two to each of the other team members. He kept two for himself. Each man knew which straps he was due to strengthen. Richard had the one that had failed and the next one nearest to it, which seemed to be most at risk of breaking next. The straps that Xin would have gone for had he not been steering *Poseidon* herself through the storm.

Zhong Wei held the great metal door half open, allowing him to step out into the wind-shadow under the port bridge wing still pondering the full significance of Chang's last quiet words. It was the first time anyone had called him captain, since he and Robin had come aboard.

The typhoon drove all thoughts from his mind at once. It raved like a pack of rabid hounds, the noise shutting down higher brain functions as he fumbled his G-clip on to the line, snapped it closed and screwed the safety lock tight. As soon as he rounded the corner of the raked bridge house into the full power of the wind, his mind became almost subhumanly elementary, filled with simple and immediate things like breathing, walking, surviving long enough to complete his vital mission.

Breathing was difficult because the force of the wind would have left him breathless even had it not been filled with so much water. The power of it showed at once how wise he had been to tie his hood so tightly. For had there been any cranny large enough to allow the intimately invasive power of the blast in past his cheeks it would have ripped the thing from his head and burst it like a child's balloon. As it was, his jacket and trousers blew up until his lean frame seemed to be at the heart of a yellow Michelin Man. And where the wind went, so did the water. By the fourth step, his boots were full and sending icy fountains up his legs each time he took a step.

Not that taking a step was easy. The deck was slick with water that seemed to be sliding past with icy speed. Even the rough grey non-slip paint was overwhelmed. And the combination of wind and water attained both force and weight. The mass of foam, spray and occasionally solid green water was enormous. He was a man who understood the physical laws that dictated the weight of water – from ounces per drop to tons per wave. And he had to fight those laws every inch of the way. On his fifth step, he felt the hull beneath him dip and twist. The deck swooped down, sending him staggering forward until the lifeline stopped him. Then the wall of water came roaring up the deck and flung him bodily against the featureless grey metal wall where the A-deck bridge-house windows should have been.

But even in the heart of the deafening, overwhelming maelstrom, he heard *Neptune* screaming. So he forced himself erect and staggered forward again. And there she was, still trapped in her cradle but fighting like a wild thing to be free. He slopped across towards her, wading through knee-deep water, until he could see the first of the secure points he was here to strengthen. With eyes slitted against the icy invasion of the driving rain and burning foam, he put the second strap in his mouth and bit down upon it with all his strength. He laboriously loosened the strap in his hands, feeling his joints working slowly and painfully as though they belonged to an arthritic octogenarian. By the time he had set it to the longest setting he dared, his two reluctant companions were at their allotted places fighting to secure their straps before the whole thing tore loose. Getting groggy already, Richard fastened the lower G-clip in place on the cradle attachment before he realized how hard he would find it to get the upper one into place against *Neptune*'s restless stirring. With almost drunken determination he unscrewed the safety, folded in the articulated arm and slid the clip back out. Then he reached up and slammed the top clip home. Even so, it took all his strength to heave the vessel down that vital inch or two so that he could get the lower clip back in place. Then he tightened the first loosened strap before re-tightening the second, the one he had just fitted. And in the end, the tugs he gave the tightener on each one would have put Xin's most vicious wrenches into the shade.

By the time he had finished, the other two had secured and tightened both of theirs. So he gestured them back into the bridge house as he heaved himself round to deal with the last, the broken, strap. *Neptune* was now much quieter. Doubly secured and fully tightened on five of her six anchor points, there was almost no fight left in her. Richard stood with the worst of the weather pounding on his back, unlocked jaws he was surprised to find were frozen shut, pulled the strap out of his mouth and began to go through the laborious routine once again. His stunned brain somehow remembered that it was better to get the top clip on first and he reached up to do that. But he had calculated without the broken strap. The flaw in the system had not been in the webbing or the buckle of the quick-release tightener in the middle. It had actually been with the G-clip anchored to the cradle. The metal had yielded to the overwhelming power of the wind and straightened. What remained of the clip, therefore, was a surprisingly solid little steel bludgeon measuring nearly nine inches in length and weighing almost a pound. As Richard reached up to secure the uppermost G-clip, the wind whipped this round into his face. It hit him on the cheek and laid the skin open to the bone. Had he not been numbed by the storm as effectively as by a dentist's novocaine, the pain would have incapacitated him. As it was the blow laid him out, sending him tumbling full length on to the deck right at the outer edge where there might have been scuppers or safety rails on a more conventional craft. The safety lines strained and began to break apart. A massive sea swept over him, washing him back aboard. The safety lines held.

And because of all this, the Zodiac, which would have torn him overboard when it burst free of its lashings and whirled away bodily down the wind, missed him altogether. The three-metre length came tearing off its mountings, rearing upright like a bear. The solidity of its composite central section stood as tall as an attacking grizzly and the inflated sections made it bigger still, as wide as a black polar bear. The considerable weight of its Yamaha outboard held it erect, but, armed as it was with a sharp-edged claw of propeller, it also functioned as a formidable weapon. The whole thing drove through the point where Richard had been standing in an instant, the outboard skimming just above the wave-top, where it would have been perfectly placed to disembowel him had he, like it, been standing upright. It hit the gallows of *Neptune*'s derrick with explosive force. Then, with a bang like a cannon shot, it was gone.

Completely unaware of how near to death he had been, Richard dragged himself back on to his feet, as groggy as though he had gone ten rounds with Mike Tyson, but grimly determined to finish the job. He caught the metal spike in his left hand as it whipped in again, and reached up again to hook his own G-clip into place. Then, one-handed, he heaved until he could clip the lower one home. He unclipped the top of the broken line and turned to chuck it overboard. It was only then that he noticed that the Zodiac was gone. And there, immediately before his eyes, there was a scratch on *Neptune* deeper than anything the squid had made.

And, wondering how come he hadn't noticed these things before, he fell to tightening the last of the lines. Then, at long last, he staggered back to the port-side A-deck door where he surrendered to a scrum of hands all eager to unclip his safety so they could pull him into the bridge house. The dry warmth sent a shaft of agony into his cheek. He raised his hand, touched the place and looked a little dopily at the redness running on his fingertips. 'I seem to have damaged my face,' he said. And collapsed on to the deck and into a modest lake of brine and blood.

FIVE

Luck

Robin looked down at Richard's face. The choice was fairly simple, she thought. Either she stood here hesitating – in which case he would spend the rest of his life with a welt on his cheek like the tribal marking of an African chief. Or she got to work and stitched him up – in which case, with any luck, it would look more like the duelling scar of an old-fashioned Austrian count. But she simply couldn't stop her hands shaking. And until she did so any kind of fancy needlework was out of the question.

The deck team had carried him up here to the wardroom, whose central table was doubling as an operating table. With practised efficiency they removed his boots then slid him feet-first into the bench-lined alcove where the table stood secured to the deck. His feet hung over the far end, almost touching the plastic covering of the cross-bench at the foot. At the head was a chair which could be lifted away so that she had some room to move and work. They had given her the big first-aid kit and left her to it.

She hesitated at first, half expecting a doctor or a medical orderly of some kind to arrive, but the awful truth had dawned on her eventually. And the urgency of taking some action soon, for he was bleeding quite badly, and stirring and muttering in pain. So, she rolled up her sleeves, opened the box, slipped on some disposable latex gloves and went to work, comforting herself with the thought that she, like he, was a fully trained first-aider.

She wiped the Formica under his head with antibacterial wipes to soak up the blood and give her a clinically clean surface to work on. She injected his cheek with painkiller, then swabbed the wound and staunched the bleeding, though the price of that vital work was that his skin shrank under the astringent and the sharp edge of his cheekbone gleamed dully in the light. Even with the local painkiller, the pain of the antiseptic started him groaning again and rolling his head from side to side, so she injected a pre-filled syringe of painkiller into the side of his neck. Like everything else in the box, it was labelled in half a dozen languages, one of which was English, so she knew what it would do and how long it would take to go to work. Then she held his hand as he quietened. After five minutes or so he was deeply asleep and – apart from the rolling of the ship – lying still enough for her to start stitching the wound. But that was when her own hands really started shaking and she was forced to stop her work.

She was concentrating so fiercely that she did not notice that the ship was no longer rearing and pitching so wildly, nor that the roaring of the storm had fallen to little more than the grumble of distant thunder. Had she noticed these things, she would not have jumped and gasped when Captain Chang threw open the wardroom door and strode in carrying a blanket.

'You need to sew that up,' Chang observed, spreading the blanket brusquely over Richard's massive figure, her eyes busy on his pale face with its vivid wound. 'A scar or two might suit a man like this but nothing too large or disfiguring.'

'The spirit is willing but the flesh is weak,' said Robin, holding up her shaking hands. Chang was speaking English fluently and clearly understood the implication of the words if not the biblical reference. For she nodded once, decisively. The movement made her ebony pageboy bob swing almost girlishly. When she glanced up there might have been a glint of sisterly understanding in the depths of her black eyes. Just the hint of a smile. She looked down again, examining Richard's wound more closely. 'You don't faint easily, though?' she enquired.

'I've never fainted in my life!' said Robin. 'And I'm first-aid trained to Accident and Emergency standard. It's just that I've never had to stitch this bloody man up before!'

'Very well. Then you will be relieved to hear that the exposure of his cheekbone seems quite lucky to me – it allows me to see with a great deal of clarity that there is no structural damage. Nor is there softness when I press – you see? So, we can assume I believe that the skull itself, the jaw and the eye socket are all still intact. And, even without the benefit of X-ray, we can be fairly sure that once we close the wound, there will only be bruising to worry about.'

She straightened and glanced at her watch. 'We are in the eye of the storm,' she said. 'Straightline says we have fifteen minutes or so of relative calm before it hits us again from the opposite direction. With luck I will have time. Pass me the antibacterial wipes and assist me.

'Your captain made at least one friend when he saved *Neptune*,' continued Chang companionably in English as she went to work on Richard's cheek with a fish-hook needle. She also had clear suture and tweezers – all of which she kept dipping in the plastic kidney dish full of antiseptic Robin was holding for her. 'He said he had damaged his face as he came in. That was the kind of a joke the crew can appreciate. He is quite a man. For a barbarian.' She spoke quietly and easily as she worked, stumbling a little only over the unfamiliar Western sea god's name *Neptune*. 'And Steadyhand Xin is as grateful as if he had saved the virtue of his daughter.' She pulled tight a neat black X of stitching. Snipped off. Dipped in the antiseptic. Moved on.

'He was trying to save your command, not make friends,' answered Robin, a little more tartly than she meant. The hand holding the plastic kidney dish was still jumping as though she was being electrocuted while she stood there. She was finding it hard to keep the antiseptic from splashing all over the place.

'So he has made another. Me.' Chang glanced up. 'Because he *did* save my command. Both parts of it, I believe. And, more particularly, as I said, my crew have been impressed in many ways.' She snipped off. Dipped. Moved on.

Robin had no reply to that. She concentrated on keeping the liquid in the dish.

So Chang carried on talking, easing the little hook of the needle though the lipless gape of the wound and pulling the suture after it until the lips closed neatly together, hiding the last of the clean white bone. It distantly occurred to Robin that the uncharacteristic talkativeness was a way of covering stress. Better a tongue that moved too much than hands that refused to stay still, she thought wryly. 'I believe the crew will change his nickname from Giant to Goodluck,' continued Chang calmly. Tug. Snip. Dip. 'Perhaps most of all as everyone on the bridge observed how our vessels took such care to save him from Tin Hau's spiteful attack with the Zodiac. That indeed was good luck. And his face has been marked by it in many ways, you see?'

'What do they call me?' demanded Robin without thinking.

'Ah . . . They call you *Goldenhair*, I believe. Or something like it.' Chang glanced up at Robin's golden ringlets. That elusive trace of a smile was back. Robin spent an instant racking her brains for some obscure Chinese insult associated with gold hair. Nothing came. All she could think of was Siegfried's Kriemhilde. And, of course, Goldilocks and the three bears. She would check with Richard later, relying on his Hong Kong knowledge.

'And what do they call you, Captain Chang?'

'Shao Xiao to my face. Shao Xiao is my precise rank, assuming my command here equates to a corvette. Behind my back, I believe they call me Mongol.'

Robin gaped silently, nonplussed. She looked at Chang's broad, bland face with its square jaw, her full mouth, squat nose and long dark eyes emphasized by the straight fringe of the pageboy-bob haircut. Oriental, yes. Mongoloid, certainly not; not that Mongoloid was a term she would ever apply to anyone. She felt a yawning gap between her civilization and that much older one that Shao Xiao Corvette Captain Chang represented.

She glanced down at Richard. Something else to ask of him when he eventually woke up, she thought.

Chang snipped off the last neat stitch. Passed the suture, hooked needle and forceps to Robin. Glanced at her watch. 'I will return to the bridge now,' she said. 'I am sure you can finish this work, especially as I observe that your hands have stopped shaking. But I will send a team to carry him to your cabin. He may well sleep out the storm.' Again that elusive ghost of a smile. 'Lucky for him. There are many others aboard who would wish to sleep it out as well. But they will not be so fortunate.'

The team of four strong sailors turned up almost at once, so Robin packed away as best she could and followed them down to the poky little cabin they had been assigned, clutching the first-aid case. In the cabin she got two of them to help her remove the sopping, bloodstained oilskins. Then she sent them away before stripping off the overalls he had been wearing since he went down into *Neptune*'s control room. She soon regretted her sensitivity, however – for she was forced to use scissors in the end, unable to move his dead weight in the cramped cabin on her own. Particularly as she was working in the lower bunk, with its high sides and the ladder leading upwards at its head. When he was reduced to his underwear – damp though it was – she tucked him into the lower bunk and wedged him in as best she could with extra blankets and pillows.

As *Poseidon* really began to pitch and toss again, she covered the neat stitching on Richard's left cheek with disinfectant cream, then with a protective pad of gauze which she carefully taped into place. She wedged his head as securely as his body, using almost all the bedding from the upper bunk to do so. Then sat down in the cabin's only chair and kept watch over him as the dogged vessel fought her way through the madness that was the second half of the typhoon. And, as it turned out, through the watches of the long tropical night.

When the cook tapped on the wall half an hour later and lifted the curtain to enter, bearing a pile of perfectly prepared sushi, she was so deeply asleep that she did not stir. Nor did she do so when Steadyhand Xin pulled the curtain aside in turn at the end of his watch. He looked down at the pair of sleeping *gwailo* devils, his expression set and inscrutable as the deck pitched and heaved beneath his steady feet. Only when he was certain that neither of them could see him did he allow his features to relax into a tiny smile. His wise eyes looked from the bright riot of her hair to the white pad on the cheek of his lean, angular face. 'Goldenhair and Goodluck,' he whispered in Mandarin, so quietly that the words were lost beneath the raving of the storm. 'Perhaps it is not such a bad thing to have you both aboard.' Then he nodded the stubbled dome of his head once and vanished. A moment or two later the weather started to moderate and *Poseidon* began to ease her way out towards the calm and distant dawn.

Richard woke to blazing pain in his cheek and only the haziest memory of what had happened to cause it. He tried to move his head and discovered that it was wedged securely in place with pillows. He tensed his arm to move the pillow and found that his whole torso was equally carefully wedged into place. He opened his eyes and blinked in the brightness of cabin lights that told him *Poseidon* was back under normal power. He closed them again, without really registering any details, preferring to use his other senses for the moment. The easy way the ship was riding and the quiet bustle with which she was doing so told him that the typhoon was past. A gentle, familiar snore told him that Robin was somewhere close at hand. 'Robin,' he called, thinking wryly that he might well be wasting his time. The only thing guaranteed to rouse her in his experience was a cup of teak-dark English Breakfast tea.

But no. 'Richard?' she answered at once. 'Darling, how are you feeling?'

'My face hurts a bit. Other than that I seem to be fine. I'm absolutely starving, though. I'm afraid I've only got the vaguest idea of what happened. Is everything all right onboard?'

'Fine. We seem to have come through the typhoon but I think we only made it because of you. I don't know any details, I'm afraid, because I've been sound asleep. But I assume that it's "calm sea" if not "prosperous voyage", to paraphrase both Mendelssohn and Elgar. We seem to be making good headway.' She looked at her watch. 'Eight a.m. local time. Morning watch has just been replaced by the forenoon, if they're keeping standard schedules. And if there are any watchkeepers wide enough awake to take it after last night's adventures. I expect they'll be serving breakfast soon, though. Do you want to sit up?'

'Sit up? I want to get up! I mean I have a sore cheek, not a broken leg. Surely I can get up and out and be of some use?'

He suited the word to the action and sat up without even opening his eyes. It was only when his cranium hit the bottom of the upper bunk that he realized he was not where he usually slept. He opened his eyes and saw Robin's anxious face peering at him through the lateral bars of the ladder to the upper bunk. 'Ouch,' he said, with a rueful smile that he did not realize was boyishly lopsided.

'Oh, *darling*!' she said. 'That was bad luck!'

SIX
Shipshape

Richard at first announced that he was far too hungry to bother with any but the most basic ablutions. But then he caught sight of his reflection in a mirror. 'Good Lord!' he said. 'I'll need to look a bit more shipshape than this before I go out in public!' Then he invested the better part of twenty minutes in trying to make himself more presentable. He started, of course, with the directness of any child, by prising the bandages off his cheek to get a good look at the damage. When he saw the wound, with its neat X-stitches and deep, darkening bruising all around it, he whistled in awe, then winced at the discomfort the thoughtless movement caused.

Only reluctantly and at Robin's most forceful insistence did he agree to replace the gauze and have a flannel wash instead of a shower. She kept him company while he did this and filled him in on some of the night's highlights. She gave him particularly precise details about the bits he remembered least well. How he had cut his cheek open. How he had been knocked down and nearly swept overboard. How both of those things were oddly lucky – given how sore his damaged face was now – because had it not have been for them he would certainly have been killed when the Zodiac blew away.

Then, not a little shaken by her brusque description of his near death, he shaved while she tried to find him an overall that had not been either covered in blood or cut to shreds. By the time she returned with a complete change of kit he had managed to scrape away most of his stubble but at such a cost that he gulped down a double-dose of painkillers. Then, with his lean stomach imitating an angry tiger, he went out in search of breakfast.

Starving though he was, Richard was hesitant to join the one or two skeleton crew-members up and about in their traditional Chinese breakfast of cold rice and noodles when he and Robin finally made it to the wardroom half an hour into the forenoon watch. But a little negotiation soon produced wok-fried rashers of smoked pork and eggs, which satisfied them both, even though there seemed to be neither toast or marmalade. In the absence of English Breakfast tea, they eschewed jasmine and gunpowder, favouring good old-fashioned Javanese coffee. All served with a smile and eaten in companionable silence with the men.

'Things are looking up,' said Richard more cheerfully as they went through to the bridge. 'It was nice of those chaps to wish us good luck as we left. I don't suppose they realize I speak Mandarin, though.'

Robin nodded vaguely, thinking of the conversation she had had with Captain Chang while she was sewing up Richard's face. 'Is there a Chinese legend of a woman with golden hair?' she asked.

'Like Goldilocks?' he answered cagily, thinking of the range of golden-haired demons in Chinese mythology from the Tibetan Tamdin on down. 'I'm not sure! Why?'

'Nothing.' She followed him on to the command bridge. It was all but empty. An unknown crewman held the helm and an officer neither of them recognized held the watch.

'I was wondering, though, what someone on the crew might mean if they gave someone the nickname of Mongol,' she persisted, her interest suddenly piqued.

Richard swung his bandaged face round towards her dragging his gaze in from the scrubbed and stained-glass brightness of the morning. He raised one eyebrow quizzically, unaware just how lopsided his face still was after the painkilling injections and the basic surgery. 'Mongol?' He looked around the bridge. 'They call someone here Mongol?'

'Yes. I was wondering what it means.'

'Well, it doesn't mean what a Westerner would mean by it. There aren't any ethnic Mongols aboard. The entire crew seems to be Han. But even so . . . Look. You remember that film we saw years ago that was set in the Amazon? The hero goes into a bar and there's a bowl of nuts. He tastes one and tells the barmaid they're the best Brazil nuts he's ever tasted. And she says that no one local calls them Brazil nuts. Because they're in Brazil, everyone just calls them nuts! You remember that?'

'I suppose so. So what?'

'Well, a surprising number of these people – even Han – actually claim descent from the Mongols. Like people in England who say they don't like the French but claim that their family came over with William the Conqueror. The Mongols were the great warriors.

Conquerors and empire-builders. The Roman legions of the East. Half of the Chinese I've ever met trace their ancestry back to them. To the great Khans Genghis and Kublai who founded the Yuan Dynasty. Whose treasure, by the way, the guys we're here to rescue were looking for in the first place.'

'So,' she persisted, slowly, used to the way he could fly off at a tangent unexpectedly. 'If they call someone Mongol . . .'

'Chances are they mean that person is a good leader. A *very* good leader – particularly when the going gets tough . . .'

At that point Captain Chang came on to the bridge. She had Steadyhand Xin and Straightline Jiang in tow. 'Ah,' said Richard. 'The A Team. Shao Xiao Chang I understand I must thank you for preserving what little remains of my boyish good looks.'

'And I must thank you for preserving my command, Shang Xiao Mariner.'

'Your command, but my investment,' he answered easily, giving that lopsided grin, reaching out to shake her by the hand. An unaccustomedly Western gesture that she returned without a second thought, as the result of many expensive night-school classes in English and American language and culture.

'You have checked your wound this morning?' she asked solicitously.

'I have. And so has my nurse. I am very firmly under doctor's orders.' He smiled across at Robin, his expression taking any bitterness out of the words.

'Good. That is as it should be. I would hate to see my work wasted almost as much as I would hate to see your work wasted.' She looked meaningfully down at *Neptune* nestling safely in her cradle below.

'Ah, your baby, Si Ji Shi Guan Xin. It was my pleasure to look after her.' A more formal bow towards the sturdy boatswain. Returned again. With an inch or two of added depth that spoke of warmth, perhaps respect. 'Now the past is past,' said Richard straightening and turning. 'As to the future – Shang Wei Jiang, where is our destination and how soon can we get there if we stay at full ahead?'

'Straight ahead,' answered the lieutenant. 'And we should be there before the end of the watch if we stay at the top of the green.'

'And we won't be alone, by the looks of things,' added Robin. One of the bridge monitors had been turned to a satellite news channel and the screen was filled with helicopter shots of a modest fleet of ships, while a voiceover explained with breathless excitement where they were and what they were doing. Even when they switched over to the Chinese state broadcasting channel CCTV, the pictures and the commentary were still there.

'I had not expected there to be so many vessels,' said Straightline, his voice full of wonder.

'And I had not expected there to be so many cameras!' added Chang. She crossed to the salt-grimed clearview and looked down the deck. Her narrowed eyes all too clearly saw the damage done by the typhoon. Everything was shipshape, thought Richard sympathetically. But it would take a thorough scrub down to make it Bristol fashion. There was weed and what looked like seafood festooned all over *Neptune*'s cradle and fastenings. The long-departed Zodiac's fastenings lay around like more seaweed and the rings that they were attached to seemed to have picked up a profusion of plastic bags. The deck had dried quickly in the early morning heat, but the grey non-slip seemed specially designed to grab at salt stains and oil. In places it looked almost bleached. In others it looked like the floor of a bus garage. A couple of dozen seabirds, as exhausted as the rest of them, had settled on *Poseidon* and their droppings added to the general air of weary untidiness that hung about the vessel.

'Right,' decided Captain Chang. 'We just have time to make this ship fit to be seen! Lieutenant Jiang, get everyone up and out!' She swung round to face Richard. 'I will complete a quick exterior inspection so I can assign the work more efficiently. Would you care to accompany me?'

'I would,' said Robin, looking up from the monitor screen. 'It would complete the full inspection we started out on yesterday.'

'Good,' said the captain. 'Shang Wei Jiang, it is time to renew our contact with the shore and whichever of those ships is currently in command. Give them your best estimate of our arrival time, and get a detailed update of what is happening and what we are expected to do when we get there. Just as I do not wish to seem slack or untidy on television, nor do I wish to appear slow-witted or hesitant!'

Things outside were even worse than they appeared to be from the bridge. They already knew what a mess the foredeck was in, but Chang's inspection soon revealed twisted davits and a missing life raft on the starboard where the second half of the typhoon had hit with particularly vicious force. Things were hardly better on the port side, which had received the typhoon's first fury. Everything from safety lines to communications mast seemed to be festooned with rubbish of one sort or another. There were dead fish wedged in the exhaust grilles, half cooked by the engine fumes.

The Chaig chopper on the after deck was still there, its strong undercarriage bolted to the deck and its rotors firmly secured. But it would clearly need some of Electrical Engineering Lieutenant Zhong Wei's tender loving care before it was fit to fly again. Not least because of the octopus wrapped around the tail rotor. 'Those seagulls must be really exhausted,' Richard observed quietly to Robin, 'or they'd have had that for breakfast long ago.'

Robin gave a grunt in reply, but she wasn't really paying attention. She was watching Chang as the captain barked orders into a little walkie-talkie. At her staccato commands, the men of her crew came boiling out of doorways and hatches variously armed with brooms, mops, pails and hoses. After the first rinse-off, they would need to go over the ship again and assess how much paint and polish would be needed. Then again with screwdrivers, volt-meters and the kind of equipment usually kept in the electrical-engineering workshop beneath the forward deck hatches.

For there clearly had to be priorities beyond smartening up the ship. As Chang wanted to appear quick-thinking and decisive when they reached their destination under the eyes of the world, *Neptune* at the very least would have to be ready to operate. And, of course, the chopper if that was possible. But *Neptune* first.

And it was here that Richard's keenest interest lay. He left the women, therefore, discussing the Chaig on the poop deck and returned to the foredeck. Here he found Steadyhand and Zhong Wei going over the bright yellow submersible, the engineer's glasses up on his head like a hair-band as he inspected one of the arms.

'How is she?' Richard called, skipping over a soapy puddle and just avoiding a jet of water from the deck hose.

'She seems to have survived well.' Zhong Wei gazed up at him blindly. There was a smear of oil on the tip of his nose.

'She's immensely strong,' emphasized Xin with the simple pride of a father discussing the outstanding aspects of a beloved daughter. 'Nearly indestructible.'

Richard stood at Xin's shoulder and looked down at the arm the engineer was checking. Face-on the vessel looked unsettlingly human with the big headlights resembling eyes, the main camera like a button nose and the vent of the reverse-manoeuvring motor grinning cheerfully below. And the intrepid little vehicle had a steady, sturdy character all of her own as well, he thought. No danger was too great. No mission too complex. No depth beyond her. She would never let you down. It was easy to see why Steadyhand adored her. And not just Steadyhand. Richard tore his gaze away from that hypnotic wide-eyed grin and looked around the bustling deck for Fatfist and Ironwrist. He soon saw the pair of them up on the side of the bridge house, standing on a suspended platform, scrubbing away like a pair of window cleaners on a skyscraper. It was a bit Heath Robinson, he thought inconsequentially, but it looked safe enough, suspended as it was from the starboard lifeboat davits where the crews were working to repair last night's damage.

Zhong Wei pulled his glasses down and settled them on to his nose. 'We need to test the motors next,' he said. 'But we can't do that while she's in her cradle. If you will help me, Shang Xiao, we can release the lines you tightened last night and lift her up using the derrick here,' he said to Richard. 'Steadyhand, you can go down to the control room and run her through her main power settings on my command.'

'Yes, Zhong Wei!' answered the boatswain formally, reminding Richard that what he was using as the electrical officer's name was in fact his rank.

'Of course I will help, Lieutenant,' he replied as Steadyhand doubled off to go below. I really must check what his name really is, he thought. Or his nickname. Perhaps he's the one they call Mongol.

They used the quick-release catches and snapped *Neptune* free in a couple of minutes. Then Richard climbed up on to the cradle and reached for the falls as Zhong Wei swung the arm of the derrick round. The falls themselves were twisted and tangled. Richard could see that at a glance. He calculated that, tall though he was, he would not be able to reach them from here. So he stepped up on to the back of *Neptune* herself where a series of indentations made a serviceable flight of steps up between the little hatches to a flat area on top of the crablike carapace. He stood firmly on top of the little vessel, his eyes fixed on the falls as they swung towards him, arms raised to catch them. The crane swung smoothly round, still working, which was impressive, thought Richard, given how hard the Zodiac had apparently hit it, bouncing up off *Neptune* herself. Automatically, he glanced back to where the solid little sea-boat had been secured, on the deck between *Neptune*'s cradle and the starboard front of the bridge house.

And so it was that he, almost alone on board, was looking in the direction of Fatfist and Ironwrist's suspended platform when one of the lifeboat davits failed. The whole curved gallows of the pulley lurched out drunkenly. The lifeboat hanging from it swung one way while the plank the two men had been standing on went the other and the whole contraption came to pieces, pitching the pair helplessly out into the sea.

Richard's hand closed on *Neptune*'s falls and he used them to steady himself as he bellowed so loudly that he almost tore the stitching in his cheek, 'MAN OVERBOARD!'

SEVEN
Overboard

During the next few moments *Poseidon* demonstrated her ability to perform a tighter turn than any other ship in her class. All the cleaning was put on hold and the only people who continued with their duties as before were the men on the bridge and the teams trying to free the storm-damaged davits so that a lifeboat could be launched. Everyone else went on watch to see if they could make out their crew-members among the blinding gleams and heaving shadows of the wake.

Suspended by one arm from the *Neptune*'s falls, his feet spread and steady on the level section of her upper hull, Richard stood with his eyes fixed on the spot they hit the water. They were invisible at once. Most ships this size had Man Overboard poles that sat high in the water to guide them back – some even had transmitters attached. *Poseidon* either did not carry any or had none to hand. Even as the deck heeled beneath him while the nimble ship swung round, blessedly on the starboard tack, therefore, he stayed, turning in time with her, his eyes fixed. At first he was looking close behind the aft starboard quarter at the splashing hillock of foam that signalled their landing point. Then, more distantly, using his training and his imagination, through the edge of the bridge house as the widening rings they made in the water passed out of his line of sight. Then back on the aft quarter again and further still the ring of ripples and the foam both lost in the glitter of the wake. Then swinging round on to the beam, the forward quarter and finally, vanishingly far away, dead ahead.

As *Poseidon* steadied on her reverse course, he let his hand fall and stood there, eyes narrowed, refusing to look away from the place. Questions teemed through his mind. Had Fatfist and Ironwrist been wearing inflatable vests? They would have been on any ship he commanded – but he couldn't remember seeing the telltale orange brightness on either man. Had anything useful gone over with them? Anything big enough to hold on to? Anything that would float? Again, he couldn't be certain but he didn't think so. What bad luck it was that the lifeboat hadn't broken free. But it hadn't and it looked as though it was useless now, hanging in a mare's nest of rope from the tangled remains of the other sagging davit.

It struck him then. With the Zodiac gone and the lifeboats out of commission – for the time being at least – there wasn't anything they could put over the side to bring the men back to safety if and when they found them. And, as ever, his mind leapt forward again. Presented with a problem, running down a solution. 'Zhong Wei,' he called, still staring fixedly ahead. 'Stop watching out for a moment and get *Neptune* ready to go over the side.'

A moment later the electrical engineer appeared in his area of vision. 'Is Steadyhand still in the control room waiting to test the motors?'

'No, Captain. He has come up and gone on watch with the rest of us. Fatfist and Ironwrist are his team.'

'See if you can get him to go back down. And take my wife with him in case they need to use both controls. I rather suspect that unless Fatfist and Ironwrist have been very lucky indeed we'll have to send *Neptune* over to get them. And someone will have to go with her in case they're too badly hurt to pull themselves aboard.'

'I will talk to Steadyhand,' said Zhong Wei thoughtfully. 'And someone had better talk to the Mongol also. She will not like anyone other than herself making such decisions aboard her command. Can you see any sign of them?'

'No. And we're almost back at the point they went over. I can feel *Poseidon* beginning to lose way, so Straightline must think we're coming up to the same point too. Move yourself, Zhong Wei. There's no time to lose.'

Zhong Wei ran to obey, but Richard stopped him with one last call. 'Hey!'

'Yes, Shang Xiao?'

'Get me an inflatable vest, would you? I've got to try and keep my head above water. And now I think of it I'll need one each for the men I'm trying to help. Some rope, a lifebelt and a boathook if you can come up with one.'

Long before Zhong Wei returned, *Poseidon* had stopped. She sat solidly on the still water and everyone aboard strained their eyes for that one brief sight of their missing crewmates. Richard too had shifted his focus the moment they had returned to the vital spot and was searching the glittering surface for the least sign of life. But it was late morning now and the sun was high. It glittered off the water, making it impossible to see with any clarity. A gusty wind had sprung up too, just enough to break the big ocean swells into a confusion of wavelets, most of them seemingly the same shape as a shark's fin.

But then the sailor up on the port-side bridge wing who had the benefit of binoculars and a steady platform to use them on called out, 'Contact on the port beam. Bearing 270 degrees. Five hundred metres out. Man in the water.'

Had it not been for the typhoon, of course, thought Richard, the next order would have been something like, 'Sea-boat away!'

Instead, Zhong Wei reappeared at last, glasses flashing anxiously in the sunlight. He held everything Richard had ordered in an untidy bundle against his chest – and a headset. 'Xin says yes. Wife says you're mad but for heaven's sake take care. They have both gone down to the control room. Captain says good luck and stay in touch. It was the captain who sent the headset.'

While the engineer crossed to the little derrick, Richard held the headset in his teeth and slipped the life preserver gingerly over his head, lashing it securely into place across his massive torso and slipping the loop of rope safely over it. He put the lifebelt at his feet and piled the preservers on top of it. The boathook went on top of these and he held it in place with one foot for the time being. Then he fitted the headset in place. Luckily the stalk of the mic went down his undamaged cheek. 'You there, Captain?' he asked.

'Here. Good luck. Remember, *Neptune* is designed to work under water. She does not sit very high. But there is as you will have observed a well-protected little deck, if not quite a cockpit. Xin says there is also a series of hatch releases that will do as hand holds. They will not open unless they are twisted but you will need to be careful.'

'I know where they are,' answered Richard. 'I helped put the emergency beacons back in them yesterday.'

And that was all he said for a while because Zhong Wei engaged the motor on the derrick and *Neptune* eased up into the air. As soon as she lifted free of her cradle she seemed to come alive. Her motors purred. Her lights flashed. Her arms extended and retracted. Her rudders whined from side to side as though she was wagging her tail.

Richard held on to the ropes around him with both hands as *Poseidon*'s side vanished beneath him. Then *Neptune* swooped down, as eager to be in the water as a child. But she settled into the surface as silently as a stealth ship. As soon as he felt the water take her, Richard knelt on one knee, using the life preservers as a cushion, and took firm hold of the biggest hatch-handle. And not a moment too soon.

'Releasing now,' said a disembodied voice in his ear. The attachment points snapped open and closed. In the instant they were wide, the four lines that had lowered her sprang free. She settled a little further into the water, then began to rise and fall in time with the big rollers as she became part of the great ocean.

Richard reached up and pulled the toggle on his vest, hearing it hiss as it filled with compressed air. Then, smiling with quiet satisfaction, he reached down and took firm hold of the boathook. Feeling a little like an ancient harpooner looking for the nearest whale, he settled back a little as *Neptune* surged forward, beginning to smash her way through the waves. The sharp little wavelets of the wind-driven chop were higher than they had seemed from the deck, but even so Richard was out of their reach for the moment. They wasted their energy on the broad swell of the big round forecastle. The water slid up the vehicle as though over a sandbank and parted against a slight ridge that worked like a cutwater. Only spray came over the top and even that failed to reach his still-bandaged face. They might get a little wetter on the way back, Richard calculated. *Neptune* was designed to take a payload of more than 375 kilos, but she would certainly settle under the weight of two more men. The sharp-edged chop on the backs of deep-ocean swells became much more threatening as *Neptune* moved down here. The triangles of restless water all stood the better part of three feet high, a disorientating mess of sharks' fins. And increasingly they did not flow past with the distant rushing that was all he could hear from *Poseidon*'s deck. When *Neptune* moved out of the larger vessel's wind-shadow they hissed and bubbled, they shattered and exploded. The wind shouted over them carrying their spray on its breath like a drunkard's spittle. *Neptune*'s hull added to the restlessness, slapping through the water while her motors whined and her propellers thrashed the surface. And the long swells came past like Alpine fields, so long and green and tall against the sky that he might almost have expected Julie Andrews to come singing over their crests. Certainly, when he was briefly on the top of each succeeding roller he felt he could see for quite a distance, but as soon as he started heading down into the trough, all he could see under the hard blue sky was the next emerald mountainside.

*   *   *

It was *Neptune* who saw the danger first. As she rode the waves
like a big yellow cork, she settled steadily. The water came halfway
up her headlights putting her forward-facing cameras the better part
of a foot below the surface. After the storm, the upper ocean was
surprisingly clear and so, long before Richard saw either the men
or the telltale triangle among the sharp-edged waves, a voice in his
ear called, 'Shark!'

Richard tensed at once and strengthened his grip on the boathook,
wondering whether it would make an effective weapon. Oddly, even
over the noisy restlessness all around him he did not need to have
the warning word repeated. He heard it all too clearly the first time.
Images from *Jaws* flashed into his mind, replacing Julie Andrews
in a breathtaking instant with Sheriff Martin Brodie climbing the
sloping mast of the sunken *Orca* and feeding his boathook to the
monstrous great white a few scant feet below him. Richard's hair
stirred as his scalp clenched with tension. Only the fact that the
cool, clear warning had come from Robin herself served to calm
him a little. 'I can't see it,' he said. 'How big is it?'

'Dead ahead and it's hard to be sure,' said the steady voice. 'It
doesn't look all that big. I don't know enough about local sharks
to guess how dangerous it is.'

'How soon before I get to the men in the water?'

'Couple of minutes. Can't you see them?'

As Robin asked the question, *Neptune* crested a wave and there
in the next trough immediately ahead was Ironwrist. He saw Richard
at the same moment as Richard saw him and shouted with relief. As
Neptune powered down the back slope of the wave towards him, the
Chinese sailor began a clumsy crawl towards safety. He was swim-
ming strongly enough to make the lifebelt seem redundant, so Richard
concentrated on getting the boathook ready for him to grab. The first
priority was clearly to get him out of the water – then they could
discuss Fatfist while getting a life jacket safely in place.

But then Fatfist appeared on the crest of the oncoming wave
behind his companion, waving and shouting in turn. The wave was
a swell; there was no crest to it. But its angle up against the lower
sky made it go translucent for a moment and Richard could see
Fatfist's torso outlined like a fly in amber. Fatfist's torso and something moving in towards it. 'Look out, Fatfist!' bellowed Richard
in his foretop voice. 'Shark!'

'HOI!' yelled a voice in his ear. 'Watch it! You nearly deafened
me, you bloody man!'

'More power! Top of the green!' he ordered breathlessly. 'Steer dead ahead.'

Neptune swept past Ironwrist then and Richard leaned down to catch the sailor's reaching hand. Like trapeze artists they closed in the safe strong grip – each man's fist closing round the other's wrist. Richard heaved. *Neptune* swung round and sank a little as Ironwrist's weight and drag were added to her burdens. Richard heaved back, his eyes still on Fatfist who was sliding down the wave towards him, arms in the air, eyes and mouth unnaturally wide.

'There it is again,' said the cool voice in his ear. 'Shark dead ahead. Looks about six feet long. Two metres maybe.'

'I think it's after Fatfist . . .' he began, heaving at Ironwrist again without actually looking at the man he was helping aboard.

So that when Ironwrist jerked back and down he took Richard utterly by surprise. Teetering on the edge of his balance he swung round to see a shark's head fastened on Ironwrist's thigh. The attack was so sudden and unexpected that the sailor hadn't even had time to call out. The fish shook its head like a terrier worrying a bone. Richard heaved again, with all his massive strength and the added power of shock. The man and the fish lifted out of the water and began to slide up on to *Neptune*'s sloping deck. Suddenly there was an enormous amount of blood on the yellow vessel and in the green water. And now Ironwrist screamed. Richard drove the boathook down on to the shark's skull. It hit so hard there was a loud thump, and the wood of the shaft jumped and vibrated in Richard's hand. But the one blow was enough. The fish let go and slid out of sight. Richard heaved again and Ironwrist slopped up on to the deck.

Just as he did so, Fatfist crashed into *Neptune*'s bow. The head-lamps hit him in the chest. Head, arms and shoulders slammed forward, hands scrabbled desperately at the little raised cutwater at Richard's knees. 'Cut power!' he shouted.

'OUCH!' answered Robin. 'Too bloody LOUD!' But the way started coming off *Neptune* at once. Richard let go of the boathook and reached for Fatfist. He grabbed his overall by the scruff of the neck and heaved with all his might. He felt his fingernails begin to bend and break. He felt the tendons in his arm and shoulder strain and begin to burn as the muscles they were joined to tore. But Fatfist came up out of the water and slid over the ridge and on to the flat, square deck. 'Bring us home!' called Richard, but this time he managed to control his voice.

'That's better,' answered Robin. 'Bringing you home now.'

Richard swung round and hunched over Ironwrist. The sailor's overalls were torn and seemed slightly inflated, brimming with bright red water. But a quick inspection showed that the shark had failed to close its jaws. Ironwrist still had his leg and the thigh looked intact. Except for a neat semicircle of stab wounds. 'Better warn the Captain she's got more needlework coming in,' said Richard to Robin. 'And she'd better get Straightline to find out whether there's a qualified doctor aboard any of the ships we're going to meet up with.' As he spoke, he was wadding up a strong inflatable life-vest into a makeshift pressure bandage and using a jury-rig of straps to secure it over Ironwrist's wounds. Even as he did so, he felt *Neptune* swing round a hundred and eighty degrees and surge forward on the reciprocal course to the one she had just been following. Back to her mother ship and safety.

Then Richard abruptly became all too aware that *Neptune*, even as she was speeding back to *Poseidon*, was leaving behind her a thick red line of blood guaranteed to catch the interest of any hungry sharks in the vicinity. Starting with the one who had just done the damage. Whose mood was not likely to be much improved by a pretty vicious headache. Placing his hand gently on Ironwrist's shoulder and using the sailor's fainting body to steady him, he straightened, looking fixedly back along the little vessel's wake.

'Any sign of that shark?' he asked quietly, narrowing his eyes in the glare and trying to discriminate a fin amongst the triangular shadows of the wavelets following them.

'Not that I can see,' answered Robin, the voice of *Neptune* and her cameras.

'Right. Good.' Richard took a deep breath, closed his eyes and began to wipe his right hand down over his face in an unconscious gesture of relief. But the instant his sensitive fingertips touched the gauze on his left cheek he froze. And in that instant of immobility, Fatfist tugged at his left sleeve. It was not a forceful or a demanding gesture. But something about it caught Richard's attention as effectively as a scream. He swung round and looked down at the second sailor. Fatfist's face was the colour of ivory. His eyes were unnaturally wide, just as they had been when he had been calling from the wave-top. His mouth was still open, breathing slackly, as though he were some kind of sea creature filtering the currents on a coral reef. Under the bright globules of seawater there was an oily sheen of sweat. That one glance told Richard he was in serious shock.

Leaving Ironwrist to his own devices, Richard turned to Fatfist, his stomach suddenly churning. And it took him only a moment to see what the problem was. From the knee downwards the sailor's left leg was missing. The limb had been severed so neatly that the stump wasn't even bleeding. Fatfist's calf, ankle and foot, overall leg and sea boot had all been bitten clean off.

EIGHT
Race

Robin spent a fair amount of time with Captain Chang as *Poseidon* raced towards her destination at the top of the green with Steadyhand at the helm and Richard supporting Straightline on the bridge. While they did this, Engineering Officer Zhong Wei led a little team fighting to get the Chaig helicopter airworthy. As soon as he was satisfied the chopper was safe to fly, Zhong Wei was due to change hats – for the electrical-engineering officer was also the designated pilot. Radio Officer Shao Wei Broadband Dung in the meantime kept the nearest vessels appraised of their situation and tried to raise someone willing to send them a doctor. Someone with a helicopter which had survived the typhoon better than theirs had.

To begin with, Robin and Chang stood side by side in the ward-room working like a pair of surgeons – pushed far beyond the limits of their first-aid training as they fought to save Ironwrist Wan and Fatfist Fu. The shark bite was easy enough, if painstaking and time-consuming. The amputation terrifyingly difficult. Robin was at first simply relieved to discover that her hands only shook uncontrollably when called to operate on Richard. Otherwise she was as calm and decisive under pressure as the Mongol.

Because Richard and she had come out to China in such a hurry, Robin felt at a disadvantage – beyond those of her gender and her inability to get her head round the Chinese way of doing – and seeing – things. Under normal circumstances she and Richard would only have come aboard a vessel like this after careful vetting of officers and crew. She was used to knowing a dossier-full of information about every one of the crew-members she usually dealt with. There was often several volumes of information about commanders. Not so here. And she felt the loss of the information. Direct as ever, therefore, she began to probe the other woman's past.

As Robin did this she and Captain Chang sutured what they could of the blood vessels coming out of spasm in the surprisingly neat amputation point below Fatfist's knee. By the time they were engaged in getting some kind of pressure bandage in place to contain the rest, they had an easy two-way conversation going.

'What made you want to become a ship's captain?' Robin began as they settled to serious work after injecting Fatfist with enough anaesthetic to stun a yak.

'My father.' Captain Chang answered less abruptly than usual. Robin let the answer hang, knowing it would be expanded upon in due course. She had captained ships of all sorts herself. She knew how isolated any commander could feel. How difficult it was to open up. How hard it was to stop talking after the first hesitant steps had been taken.

'My father was the captain of a cargo vessel working the Huangpu and Yangtze Rivers, and the coast between Shanghai, Hong Kong and Macau.'

Robin looked at the woman, guessing her age to be forty or so. Her father must be mid-sixties, therefore. Statistically her parents – and even her grandparents – might still all be alive. 'Is that what your father still does? Or is he retired?'

'No. He has retired from that work, but not from all work. He was briefly the captain of a ferry working between Shanghai and Pudong. He works for the Shanghai Pilots' Office now. He is the Senior River Pilot for the Yangtze River itself – up the Huangpu into Shanghai and up the main stream as far as Nanjing.'

'And your mother?' Robin simply didn't know enough about the Yangtze to understand how well justified the pride in Chang's voice was when she talked of her father.

'My mother is an architect. She helped plan much of what you now see when you look across the river from Shanghai to Pudong. They still live in one of the few areas near Dongchang Road that have not been renewed under her plans.'

'Brothers and sisters?'

Chang gave a wry smile. 'Consider me a prophet of the famous One Family One Child policy.'

Robin did not have Richard's insight into the family structures of the Chinese races so it did not occur to her to ask about the older generation as well as the younger. Her own parents lived in blissful retirement in the South of France. It did not occur to her that three, sometimes four, generations of Chinese families might well live under one roof. 'So it was always the sea?'

'My father and my father's father were seamen, although Grandfather Chang was born in the year of the sheep and his yin was not strong. Neither was his luck. So it is surprising he did as well as he did as a captain. All through my childhood I was surrounded by tales of the great rivers and the sea, for my father's mother still lives with us – and it is only recently that my mother's parents have left the Middle Kingdom. These waters have protected our lives as well as our livelihoods since before the Second World War.'

Sometimes it was hard to make out the captain's quiet words, but Robin remained as fiercely focused on what she was hearing as she was focused on what she was doing. For it was a fascinating story. 'My father's father rescued my father's mother from the Japanese in 1937. She lived in Nanjing and the freighter he captained was working the Yangtze in those days. They met at the docks, where her father ran a warehouse. They were already in love when the Japanese invaded but his daring rescue of her family in the teeth of the terrible Japanese atrocities cemented their life-long love; and he remained unusually faithful for someone born in a sheep year. Almost all of her friends were raped and murdered. All of her father's business associates and her mother's friends were slaugh- tered or ruined. It was Grandfather Chang's support that allowed them to begin rebuilding their lives in the brief peace between 1938 and 1941, but they moved from Nanjing to Shanghai and set up business there. My father was born during this relatively peaceful period in 1940. His birth turned their luck around even further. 1940 was a dragon year. Dragons are much better suited to a life at sea than sheep. Father's sign was metal. His yang was great. As was his luck. Grandfather Chang was able to save the whole family from the Japanese army again in 1941, when they came back to Shanghai. At the same time, their air force was bombing Pearl Harbor and their war with America was beginning. Our family fled up the Yangtze once more, past Nanjing, past what is now the great Three Gorges Dam. The river kept them all safe once more. The river and the power of my father's dragon luck, even though he was only a baby then. It is a heroic story. The river is so full of our past and our history, sometimes we call it the River of Ghosts.'

Robin dimly sensed that Chang's tales of the more distant past were safer ground for her than the more recent past Robin had origin- ally asked about; there were different types of ghosts, she thought, and China was full of them. Not just the mighty Yangtze. But she pushed another question into the silence that fell then, while the pair of them tried to fashion a pressure bandage over Fatfist's stump that would hold things as effectively as the makeshift bandage Richard had put on Ironwrist's thigh.

'And since the war? During your own lifetime?'

It was a matter that almost went beyond the difference in their ethnicity and age. Robin saw the world and its history through Western eyes. Since 1945 there had been peace and prosperity – except for one or two little local difficulties. For Chang things were almost unimaginably different.

'My father's luck held Grandfather Chang safe. Or it did so for a time. After the Americans came in 1945, ships and ships' captains were still needed. Grandfather Chang flourished, and brought my father up as his apprentice, kept safe even through the days of Chiang Kaishek and the Liberation of 1949. Father was fully trained as a ship's captain by the time he was twenty-five, though he had not studied at the university or gained many paper qualifications. And this too was greatly fortunate, for when the Cultural Revolution gripped Shanghai and Grandfather Chang was taken from us by the Red Guards, they had no record that my father had any taint at all of the Four Olds. So he was able to stay in charge of his ship and use it as Grandfather Chang had done to protect our family from the terrible, seemingly never-ending typhoons of change.'

'The four olds?'

'The things that the Gang of Four wished to destroy as part of Chairman Mao Zedong's Cultural Revolution,' Chang explained, the tone of her voice showing simple shock that Robin should be so ignorant. '*Old* ideas, *old* culture, *old* customs, *old* habits. Old culture and ideas meant anyone who had any kind of learning. Old customs and habits meant anyone who had ever aspired to a bourgeois lifestyle. A whole class of people was wiped out. Including, unluckily, Grandfather Chang and the officers of his vessel.'

'But not your father or your family?'

'Because of Grandfather Chang's bravery, and my father's quick thinking and good luck. Everyone who could be saved was brought aboard his ship. And that included my mother, daughter of the ship's first officer, Seng, who was younger than father, and born in the year of the monkey. For them, of course, it was love at first sight.' Chang glanced up over Fatfist's stump. 'A match between a dragon man and a monkey woman is what you might call a match made in heaven. But for one reason or another they had no offspring for five years. Probably because of the political situation and their constant struggle for safety and survival. Thus I was born in the year of the dog. Unluckily for me, perhaps, for although dogs and monkeys get along, dogs and dragons find it less easy to do so.'

'Which is why you are not the captain of your father's old ship.'

'That,' allowed Chang with the briefest crinkling of her long, dark eyes, 'and the fact that my father's old ship died in the same year as Chairman Mao and was broken up for scrap at the same time as the Gang of Four. I am a child of Brother Deng.'

Fatfist was removed. Ironwrist replaced him. 'This is excellent work. Your husband is more than lucky. He is impressive.'

'I'll bet he was born in a dragon year as well,' said Robin drily.

'Or a tiger year, perhaps.' Chang agreed – Robin's mild irony was lost on the thoughtful captain, who took her words at face value. 'We can look at the astrological charts when we have time. I see your hands are steady enough to suture these wounds with me, but we had better paint them with anti-infectant first.'

They settled back to work. 'What did you mean, "a child of Brother Deng"?' asked Robin.

'I was still a child when Deng Xiaoping opened the economy. Everything changed, seemingly overnight. My parents were able to send me to school. My mother was able to attend the newly reopened university. My father was able to get his papers. By the time of Tiananmen Square I was at university myself, though we Shanghai students were not involved with the disastrous political movements in Beijing. My mother had graduated near the top of her class in architecture and was one of those earmarked to design the Special Economic Zone of Pudong, as I have said. After his ship was broken up, my father worked double shifts on the ferry to support the pair of us, but things were hard for all of us. It is not easy to graduate from Shanghai University with sufficiently high grades to get into Navy School at Dalian. However, things got easier when mother became involved with the Oriental Pearl Tower project and father was appointed as a river pilot. Especially as I was fortunate enough to win a scholarship.'

'And this is your first command?' Robin let slide any question about the unremitting efforts – of all the Chang family – that must have gone into that simple, modest statement *I was fortunate enough to win a scholarship.*

'Yes.'

'An interesting start to an illustrious career.'

Chang looked up. When she saw that Robin meant every word, she smiled. 'Let us hope so.'

*   *   *

Then, having discussed China's unique immediate past, Robin accompanied Captain Chang as she seemed to step decisively back into it. The comatose shark-attack victims were cleared away, and, while the wardroom was cleaned and tidied, the captain ordered all of her senior officers to stop what they were doing for a few moments. She summoned them down to a peculiar conference around the wardroom table that had so recently been an operating table that it still smelt strongly of disinfectant. None of the participants seemed to see anything unusual in the procedure – nor in Robin's attendance as expert witness. They talked in Mandarin but slowly enough that she could follow their conversation quite easily.

As Steadyhand Xin kept *Poseidon* on course, running at top speed, and Richard served a brief turn as watch officer, therefore, Shang Wei Navigator Straightline Jiang, Shang Wei Chief Engineer Powerhouse Wang, Electrical Engineer and occasional chopper pilot Zhong Wei and Shao Wei Radio Officer Broadband Dung all gathered purposefully for a conference in the wardroom. Captain Chang and her golden-haired guest sat side by side at the table's head while the others slid along the benches to the foot then filled up either side.

Chang called them to order as soon as they were settled. 'Although this vessel is technically no longer a warship of the People's Liberation Army Navy, it is time that we followed correct procedures. This meeting of the People's Control Committee of these vessels is therefore called to order. The agenda is to examine the actions of the ship's commander, Shao Xiao Chang Jhiang Quing, in three particular regards. Firstly as regards the deployment and recovery of the AUV *Neptune* originally named *Mazu*. Secondly as regards the conduct of this vessel *Poseidon*, originally named *Yu-Quiang*, through the typhoon, the near loss of *Mazu*, the loss of the Zodiac and the wounding of our guest Shang Xiao Mariner. And thirdly through the loss and recovery of Shang Deng Bing Seaman Fu and Shang Deng Bing Wan. Well, comrades, with regard to the first question, of the incident with the AUV and the devilfish, are there any comments?'

'The AUV *Mazu* suffered no damage,' supplied Zhong Wei, his glasses glinting earnestly as he looked around the People's Control Committee. 'Indeed, as matters chanced, the AUV's systems were given a thorough workout and her strengths and capabilities well established. Might I add at this juncture, Captain, that I have left word with my team working on the chopper that I be notified the instant they believe she is ready to go? At that point I will be asking permission to leave the meeting. Broadband has alerted the nearest ship with medical facilities that I will be bringing casualties to her quite soon.'

'Very well. We need to get our wounded into more suitable accommodation at the earliest opportunity. Broadband, thank you for your work in that regard. Now, back to the business in hand. Your thoughts on the first incident. From a radio communication point of view?'

'I agree with the lieutenant. The AUV's communication system also responded well to the test. Better than I could ever have imagined. Control was excellent. Every bit as effective as I have seen in equivalent vessels towing cables.'

'Five kilometres of cable is quite a handicap, though,' emphasized Zhong Wei. 'That is why the remote system is so liberating . . .'

'Just so,' agreed Captain Chang. 'Powerhouse? Straightline, have you anything to add?'

'Not at this stage, Captain,' said the navigator.

'Nor have I,' agreed the chief engineer.

'Captain Mariner? You were acting as handler during the incident. Have you anything to add – either about the attack itself or how *Neptune* or *Poseidon* and her command team reacted?'

'Nothing but praise for all concerned,' said Robin seriously. 'I was barely trained to handle *Neptune*. Had either Captain Mariner or myself any idea what was going to happen we would never have taken the risk. But once we found ourselves in the position we did, then we got all the support and guidance we needed to get *Neptune* safely home. And I hope these comments are being recorded.'

'They are,' said Chang shortly. 'Now, as to the typhoon. Straightline, I am sure you have some useful comments to add.'

'Well, I have brought a printout of the log, so I can take us through it blow by blow . . .'

It was at this moment that Zhong Wei's walkie-talkie began to sound. 'That will be the chopper ready,' he interrupted, rising from his seat nearest the head of the table, just at Robin's right hand. 'I must take Fatfist and Ironwrist now.' He turned purposefully, but hesitated before he took his first step. Suddenly hesitant.

'Yes?' snapped Chang.

'Captain . . . I have just realized. I cannot just load two badly wounded sailors into the back of a Chaig and take off hoping for the best. I will need someone to come and look after them. Someone with some first-aid experience . . .'

There was the briefest of silences as Zhong Wei's words sank in, then Robin said, in English, 'That'll be me, then.'

'Thank you very much,' said Chang flatly. Robin knew immediately that the captain had seen this coming. Had probably planned for it, indeed. That at least explained why her slightly redundant testimony had been so carefully sought at this strange little gathering. And, as if to confirm her darkening suspicions, using all the inscrutability for which her race was famous, Chang dismissed her with, 'You will report to the bridge as the lieutenant prepares to take off. Make sure your departure is recorded in the log. And ask Shang Xiao Mariner to step down here as well, would you? His testimony will be important in the committee's deliberations about the next two incidents, I believe.'

NINE
Luyang

The last thing Richard had said to Robin was, 'Remember what Jim Bourne told us at the London Centre briefing. *Don't go without your papers!*' And all through the flight from *Poseidon*, Robin's mind was a whirl of worry about her comatose charges and about the position she might find herself in. Not for the first time – nor, she suspected, the last – she found herself wishing most fervently that her calm and steady husband was seated massively at her shoulder. Ready to keep her safe from suspicious Chinese officers and agents as effectively as he had rescued her from African terrorist kidnappers only a couple of months earlier.

As the Chaig began to settle towards the flotilla of awaiting ships she blessed him fervently for that final reminder about the papers, however. She had been so bound up with her Good Samaritan duties that it had not really registered that she, a Western woman, was about to land on one of the most advanced – and secret – pieces of kit owned by the Chinese People's Liberation Army Navy. The destroyer in the centre. And that her recent conversations with Captain Chang had simply emphasized the massive differences between the Anglo-Saxon and Sino-Communist mentalities. It was something, to be fair, that the head of Heritage Mariner's Intelligence section had warned them about in his pre-trip briefing. There was even now a gulf of perception between the way she looked at the world and the way a Chinese citizen might. A gulf of perception into which she could all too innocently tumble. The least little gesture or glance might brand her a spy and have her down in the destroyer's secure accommodation and off to the Ministry of State Security in Beijing before you could say knife.

It occurred to her now, however, as the Chaig began its descent, and with such force that she all but forgot about the wounded men strapped each side of her. She found herself checking yet again through the bundle of documents so confidently caught up from the desk-top in her cabin a little less than an hour ago.

In Richard's absence, the only really positive aspect of her situation seemed to be the number of other vessels gathered in the area, she thought. Certainly, looking out of the Chaig's side window – stretching over the comatose Ironwrist to do so – her first impression was that there were half a dozen vessels on station. Lots of witnesses to watch her *come*, she thought; particularly important if she suddenly ended up unable to *go*. But then she registered the fact that they were all painted with the same grey radar-absorbent naval paint. There was one huge destroyer – their clear objective – a couple of frigates, two corvettes that looked a lot like *Poseidon* and at least one submarine. No one aboard any of them was going to do anything other than toe the party line as faithfully as the crowds bussed in to fill half-empty stadiums and cheer so televisually at the Beijing Olympic Games.

Robin may not have had the opportunity to bone up on the details of *Poseidon*'s crew, but, courtesy of Jim Bourne and Heritage Mariner's Intelligence section London Centre, she had been fully briefed on the People's Liberation Army Navy vessels that they were likely to meet out here. So she was able to tick off the classes of the ships below at least. All too easily, in fact. She had a memory as visual and almost as tenacious as Richard's. There was far too much for comfort in that section of her brain where Chinese navy warship specifications were stored.

The sub looked like a Russian *Kilo*-class – China had fifty or so of them, Jim Bourne had said. The corvettes were Type 104s without *Poseidon*'s adaptations and additions, though they were all of the same later hull design, influenced by the ultra-modern Turkish *Milgem* series. The frigates looked like old type 053 *Jianghu*s. But their destination was definitely the huge type 052 *Luyang* destroyer. London Centre had contacts all over the place – well outside the City remit. Largely because the Centre was filled with what the Americans still called 'spooks' and those that weren't ex-SIS or security were ex-naval intelligence to a man. Or, in most cases, to a woman. They had briefed that a *Luyang* had been undergoing extensive refit in Dalian, though she had originally been built in Jaingnan shipyards in Shanghai. This was probably her.

There was an aircraft carrier somewhere in Dalian too, Robin thought grimly. Thank God they hadn't sent that out as well. But a recently upgraded *Luyang* was bad enough. She would have to be very careful indeed where she looked. What she saw. And, perhaps most importantly of all, who saw her looking. Although *Poseidon*'s crew seemed all above board, there was likely to be a semi-independent staff of political-intelligence officers on board a ship like the *Luyang* destroyer. What Chinese Naval Security thought she might be secretly finding out would be reported to the commanding officer and via him to Fleet Headquarters. What the political-intelligence officers believed would go straight to the Ministry of State Security, Section Nine, Counter-Intelligence, Headquarters. The People's Republic version of the KGB's terrible Lubianka. Her mouth was dry, suddenly, and her hands were actually shaking as she triple-checked her passport, visas, IDs and permissions. She had read about the routine use of pliers, batons, ice-baths, rubber hoses, cattle prods and a range of electric-shock equipment in the HQ at East Changan Street in Beijing, and thoughts of such things really began to scare her now.

The *Luyang* looked huge – she must be the better part of five hundred feet long and about fifty wide. Zhong Wei was bringing the Chaig straight in over the stern, as confident with the chopper as he was with the electrics on *Poseidon*, and it seemed to Robin that the flight deck was slightly longer than it was wide – maybe seventy feet by fifty, ending in two-deck-high hangar doors. As the Chaig settled, these opened to reveal a swarm of sailors – hopefully medical orderlies – and a glimpse of the ship's chopper within. From memory, a Russian Kamov KA-28. But then the thought froze in her head. It was exactly the kind of thing she should not be thinking.

By the time the Chaig settled and the sailors surrounded her, Robin was every bit the solicitous nurse, ready to oversee the safe unloading of her charges. And just as well. Although Zhong Wei landed quite efficiently, he put the chopper down with enough of a jolt to wake the drugged men. So when the officer in charge on the flight deck jerked open the Chaig's door, Robin was fully engaged in calming and tending her charges.

'These are the men?' snapped the officer in rapid, heavily accented Mandarin, glaring at her. His epaulettes looked similar to Chang's, so Robin answered, 'Yes, Shao Xiao. Two shark bites. One thigh wound, one amputation. Both in need of more attention than the first aid they have received so far.'

The officer gestured and the Chaig heaved as men climbed in and passed Fatfist and Ironwrist down on to the flight deck. Zhong Wei climbed out to help them and the sight of his anxious glances at the strange officer's shoulder gave Robin a measure of relief.

'Papers!' demanded the officer. Robin handed over the blessed bundle Richard had reminded her to bring. Beneath the precisely squared cap, his hair seemed thick and coarse. Black as his suspicious eyes. But his hands were long, his fingers almost delicate, square-ended and strong like those of a concert pianist.

'Why did you bring this woman, Zhong Wei?' he demanded after a cursory glance at the papers. 'She is not a member of the crew. She is not PLAN.'

'She helped the captain tend the wounded, Zhong Xiao, she was the best equipped to help them during the flight. Our little corvette has no medical facilities like your fine destroyer. And, in furtherance of the People's policy on openness and economic cooperation, she is considering purchasing the vessel. It is she and her husband who gave the orders to come here.'

Better not let Captain Chang hear you saying that, buster, thought Robin wryly.

'Very well.' The grim officer handed Robin back her papers but he continued speaking to Zhong Wei as though Robin herself were invisible. 'You had better get her out of here at once.'

'I'm afraid I cannot do that. My chopper needs refuelling and I must double-check the tail rotor. It may have been damaged in the typhoon more severely than I had supposed. I'm afraid that we must stay for a little longer than planned.'

The officer turned away slightly, reached to a little microphone on his lapel and spoke rapidly into it. Robin understood enough to know he was reporting the situation to the bridge. After a moment or two he swung back and faced her fully. As he did so, he rearranged his face into a less hostile expression. He seemed actually to be seeing her properly for the first time. He gave a little bow. 'I am Lieutenant Commander Tan,' he announced in perfect American-accented English. 'You are welcome aboard our vessel, Captain Mariner. Our commanding officer, Commodore Shan, has asked that I escort you below so that you may be made comfortable while we see to your helicopter and arrange for your safe return. Perhaps, if your Chaig cannot be repaired and refuelled in short order, we will send you back in our ship's chopper. If the commanding officer and the political officer agree. It is a Russian Kamov with certain additions of our own. I am sure you will find it comfortable.'

'This is very kind of you, Lieutenant Commander Tan,' said Robin, falling in at his shoulder and following his purposeful stride across the flight deck. 'And please extend my thanks to Commodore Shan when you see him too.' She did not mention the political officer, though who he was and what his powers might be exercised her mind more than somewhat. Particularly the political officer's power over her.

The storm had gone completely, leaving an afternoon full of calm waters and light breezes. The sky arched above them like a blue porcelain bowl. The Yellow Sea might better have been named the Sapphire Sea. It was hard to imagine that a submarineful of men were trapped and dying far below the innocently dimpled cerulean surface.

Robin focused on these things. She did not look into the hangar where the Kamov lurked, even though Lieutenant Commander Tan had already told her about it. She did not look up above the big square hangar doors at the surface-to-air-missile housing there. Nor above it at the light grey sphere that contained elements of the Russian-made search radar, nor at the mast where there was more radar, nor at the top of the bridge house where there was yet more. Radar for searching, tracking, controlling guns and missiles. She looked at Tan's starched shirt sleeve, at the afternoon, at the door they were approaching, at her feet. Not at the funnel with its advanced heat-exchange and cooling system designed to cut the heat signature and outwit enemy gunners, even those using infrared and heat-seeking equipment.

'I expect the sonar systems on a ship such as this are perfectly developed to locate the missing submarine,' she said, as they stepped over the raised section and through the bulkhead door into a corridor.

'Indeed,' agreed Tan amenably. 'That is why we are in charge of the situation – our submarine-tracking equipment is the best in the fleet. That and the fact that we were the nearest to the incident. We were on our way from refit down to our station in the south. We have located the damaged vessel very precisely. But I'm sorry to say that beyond that we appear to be quite helpless. I am not an expert in undersea recovery, but the water is too deep for divers. Not that they would be of much use unless they had a wider range of equipment than we can supply within the time-frame. And even the nearest shipyards, at Jiangnan, Shanghai, do not have everything we might require. Or so it seems.'

The conversation was enough to get them along the corridor to a little wardroom. It was empty and dark. He switched on the lights and ushered Robin in. 'Please make yourself comfortable,' he said. 'What is it you say? *Captain's orders.* But in this case it is commodore's orders.'

'Are you sure there is nothing I can do to help Seaman Fu or Seaman Wan, the men I brought over in the chopper?'

'No. Thank you for asking. We have a full surgical team and a battlefield hospital aboard. Mr Wu and Mr Fan – is it? – are in good hands, I assure you.'

'Then perhaps you could allow me access to copies of any information you have on the crippled submarine. I'd hate to just sit here wasting my time.'

Tan's eyebrows rose fractionally. 'But what purpose would that serve?' he asked. 'As I understand matters, you are aboard *Yu-qiang* as owner. You will have nothing to do with the actual rescue attempt, surely? What purpose would it serve to show you this information?'

'I may be owner – or potential owner if everything goes to plan,' answered Robin laboriously. 'But the two men I brought over are the AUV remote sub-handlers. And they won't be handling anything for the foreseeable future unless your surgeons can work miracles. My husband Captain Richard Mariner and I are the only other two people aboard who have had any training or experience in handling *Neptune* – *Mazu* as you would call her. I am in a position to make a preliminary assessment.' She drew in an almost tremulous breath. 'And I may well, in fact, be part of the control team when *Mazu* goes down.'

'Wait,' said Tan. 'I will check on what you say. Assess what you suggest. In the meantime, would you like a cup of tea? We have English Breakfast and Earl Grey. As well as a range of China teas, of course.'

'English Breakfast, please. That would be most welcome. Milk, if you have it, but no sugar.'

While she waited for Lieutenant Commander Tan to return, Robin sat and let the bustle of the ship soak into her. It was familiar, almost restful. The grumbling of motors, the rumbling of alternators, the restless rustling of crewmen hurrying about their duty – the better part of three hundred and fifty if Jim Bourne could be believed. And he could. Sitting down at a long low table, she riffled through the papers she had brought with her until she found a blank sheet among all the official documents. Then she pulled a pencil out of her pocket and started making notes, thinking through the things it would be most important for her to know. Leaving aside for the moment the facts that had been broadcast on the TV and radio news networks, alert as always to the possibility of inaccurate reporting – either through sloppy journalism or calculated disinformation. She would need basic but absolutely accurate facts. Technical details of all sorts. Starting with the basics and branching into who knew what unsuspected territory. Whether they thought she was some kind of a spy or not.

As though she were making a shopping list, therefore, Robin started with random requirements, listing them as they occurred to her. She would put them into some kind of order later.

What kind of sub was it? How many crew? How many survivors? Any wounded?

What escape equipment was there aboard? Why could it not be deployed?

Communications? Current? If not, why not? Last contact? Distress calls? Clues?

What depth of water was the sub in? Currents? Tides? State of seabed?

Local flora or fauna? She shuddered, thinking of the squid attacking *Neptune*. Of the shark crippling Fatfist and Ironwrist. Then, remembering the Ryukyu Trench, she added *Volcanic/seismic activity?*

Cables?

Why wasn't the *Kilo*-class sub down there helping now? she wondered, scribbling a note that just read *Kilo?*

Then, remembering the trapped sub's original, widely publicized mission she added *Khan's treasure?*

TEN
Politics

The door opened and Robin glanced up, hardly knowing what to expect beyond a cup of tea. Surely a lieutenant commander like Tan would have far more important things to do than serve guests. She half expected a taciturn rating with a tray, therefore. What she saw was a slim, intense-looking Han wearing a shang wei or senior lieutenant's uniform, all except the uniform cap, and a pair of designer sunglasses.

The strange lieutenant crossed towards her, his movements precise and all but silent beneath the quiet bustle of the ship, the grumble of the motors keeping her on station. His loose-limbed almost casual way of walking was surprisingly un-military. Certainly it was in marked contrast to the way Tan moved – with something between a quick march and a swagger. He put down a tray that held a teapot, milk jug and cup, all of the finest porcelain, and looked up at her.

The Ray-Bans hid his eyes in a slightly unsettling manner, and their effect was intensified a thousandfold by his first quiet words, spoken in a perfect Oxford accent. 'I am Shang Wei Leung, ship's political officer,' he said. 'Would you like the milk or the tea in first?'

'The tea please, Mr Leung,' she answered formally, hoping the guarded tone would not betray the sudden nervous flutter of her heart. 'I'll add the milk myself.'

'Ah. You like to be in control of both strength and temperature,' observed Leung apparently affably as he looked down to pour the tea. 'It is to be expected in a leader such as yourself.'

As Robin added the milk and watched the pale clouds forming and swirling in the teak-dark liquid, Lieutenant Leung sat down opposite her and reached for her papers, then he sprawled back in the chair almost as though he was going to put his feet up. The bundle he lifted included the notes she had been making.

But Robin hardly noticed, for she was thinking a little desperately. Once again, his words were disturbing. Although he was checking her papers now, he seemed to be implying that he already knew quite a bit about her. She felt herself under pressure – perhaps even under attack. So she pushed back a little. Logic dictated that if he knew anything at all about her then he was most likely to know it from the associations she had already had with China – with Richard, through Heritage Mariner. 'So,' she said. 'You have worked in the Third Bureau?'

He looked up. He might have been amused or surprised – the Ray-Bans masked his eyes and added to his inscrutability. 'The Hong Kong office,' he admitted. 'Before I was assigned to *naval* duties.'

'Then you know that Heritage Mariner has always been a friend to the People's Republic. Particularly since the days of Chairman Deng.' She covered her nagging concern with a demure sip.

'Indeed.' He closed the papers and replaced them on the table beside the tea tray, leaning forward in that loose-limbed way then sprawling back again. 'Indeed. Is the tea to your taste?'

'It's fine,' she said.

The door opened with a brusque military snap. Shao Xiao Tan was back. He marched over to the table edge and almost came to attention, looking down at her. 'Commodore Shan wonders if you would do him the honour of coming to the bridge,' he said, speaking to her as though Political Officer Leung was not in the room at all. 'He believes that he can demonstrate to you the disposition of the vessel and explain our first assessment of the dangers most effectively up there.'

'I will accompany you,' said Leung, lounging up to his feet and picking up Robin's papers just an instant before she could reach them herself.

'Of course you will,' answered Tan as though speaking to himself.

The atmosphere between the naval officer and his political junior crackled as though they were a married couple trapped in a divorce lawyer's office, trying to carve up their past.

The destroyer's bridge was big but bustling. Feeling naked and threatened without her papers, Robin was careful not to stare around. She was all too well aware that she was under Leung's masked gaze. Instead she fixed her wide eyes on the plump rotundity that was Commodore Shan. He was a kind of anti-Santa, she thought. Big and round, but clean-shaven and brusquely efficient. Not the least bit jolly at all. Although his beautifully cut uniform strained a little at the seams here and there, there was no feeling of softness about him. And any Yuletide youngster throwing himself on this particular lap was in for a hard landing. But he was courteous and paid her the compliment of treating her, if not as an equal, then at least an intelligent and resourceful colleague.

'If you look out at the forecastle,' he said, in careful Mandarin that started out slow but speeded up as he saw how readily she understood him, 'you will understand the general situation at a glance. The bow of my vessel is precisely above the submarine. Precisely,' he repeated with some pride in the emphasis. 'If I let go my anchor it would hit it. Were the anchor chain of sufficient length, of course.' A ripple of courteous laughter filled the bridge. The commodore's face remained as still as a poker player's. 'The state of sea and weather are obvious,' he continued.

'Flat calm on a sunny afternoon,' she agreed. Her eyes took in the view through the wide clearview. They did not linger on the *Kilo* sub or the other vessels. They did not linger on the 100mm gun in its grey housing so much like *Neptune*'s butter-yellow carapace, only rounder, and split astride the long grey barrel. Nor the six-barrelled ASW rocket launcher beside it. She felt Leung's eyes burning into the back of her head and half expected him to be melting the Ray-Bans' lenses with the intensity of his gaze.

'Just so. Now, please be good enough to look at this.'

Robin crossed to the video monitor the commodore was pointing to, her tension beginning to ease under the increasing interest she was feeling. The screen showed a 3D schematic of the seabed immediately below, traced out in a grid of green contour lines. 'The sonar is mounted in the bows of the ship,' Commodore Shan told her. 'A computer enhances the scan and gives us this readout. I can give you a printout as you requested but it is not the same.'

Robin nodded in silent agreement, frowning a little as she concentrated. In fact, she thought, the commodore's pride in holding his ship precisely above the accident site was a little misplaced. The picture would be far easier to understand – would have far more detail and contrast – if he took angled soundings from either side. But what she could see on the screen slowly resolved into a picture she could understand. The outline of a submarine coalesced as her brain registered the familiar pattern. It rose above the undulations of the seabed all around it, strangely incomplete, as though a child had rubbed out bits of the outline at random. Really, only the familiar profile distinguished it. It looked like any child's drawing of a submarine. Cigar-shaped hull, bulbous nose, slim tail flaring into square propulsion housing. Fin. But then she realized that she was seeing the sub in profile. And, of course, from this vantage point meant that it must be lying on its side.

As her blood ran cold, Robin thought back a year or so. She had herself been trapped aboard a sinking Canadian sub off Cape Farewell at the southern end of Greenland for a while. The sub had been one of the old British *Upholder* class sold to the Canadians as their new *Victoria* class. Its name had been *Quebec*. She closed her eyes and went through *Quebec*'s escape systems, trying to imagine how well they would function if she was lying on her side. *Not at all*, she decided in no time flat. Well, that began to explain some of the crisis. And, she realized, that kind of disposition would be likely to put out the aerials as well. Unless the crew had managed to launch a buoy with a line to their radio, then they'd be out of communication into the bargain. It was only then that she began to wonder how many men were likely to be left alive down there. And just how far down 'down there' actually was.

'What is the name of the vessel?' she asked absently. She had heard it mentioned often enough but she couldn't quite call it to mind and was focusing on the picture – and the problem – too fiercely to be bothered with such distractions now.

'It is the *Huangpu*,' answered Commodore Shen. 'It is one of a series of diesel-powered submarines named for the great rivers. They would be familiar to you, perhaps, as *Romeo*-class vessels.'

Robin shook her head, genuinely ignorant. Jim Bourne had only mentioned *Kilo*-class diesel-powered subs in his London Centre briefing. Then the nuclear attack boats, the *Han*s, *Xia*s and things he called Project 93 and Project 94. 'Never heard of it,' she said. 'Is this some kind of scale?' She pointed to Chinese lettering along the side and bottom.

'Yes. Each of those marks represents perhaps a metre.'

'So *Huangpu* is – what? – seventy-five metres, two hundred and fifty feet long?'

Shan shrugged, Tan nodded. Robin risked a glance at Leung. Leung was going through her papers again, in very much more detail.

Then the two officers exchanged a brief glance and Tan turned abruptly, marching off the bridge.

'Do you have any way of knowing how many are still alive down there?' Robin asked, forcing her mind away from her worries and on to the job in hand.

'Our sonar has a limited infrared capability,' said the commodore. 'It is of course affected by the temperature of the water – there are gradients, warm and cool currents. And by the depth of water between us. Also by the thickness of the hull. As well as by the confusion arising from heat generated by motors and so forth. But . . .' He turned away and spat a curt order. Immediately the green schematic was overlain by red dots and pink clouds. The effect was oddly disturbing – almost sickening – as though the sunken sub had suddenly developed smallpox. It took Robin no time at all to understand that each of the red dots was a man. And she started counting. She simply couldn't help herself.

'I can save you the trouble,' said Tan crisply, stepping back in through the bridge door behind her. 'There are fifty red dots there. I counted as I was waiting for your helicopter to land.'

'Fifty men left alive,' whispered Leung. 'When will your vessel be here, Captain Mariner?'

'Not until tomorrow morning,' she answered. 'You must know that. I mean it took two and a half hours in the Chaig and that was at a hundred and fifty miles an hour flat out. They're coming as fast as they can but it's another eight hours' sailing time at least. They should be here before dawn with any luck. Ready for action at first light if Ton Hau's with us.'

Leung nodded. Glanced across at Lieutenant Commander Tin and Commodore Shan. 'Then I had better give orders for a cabin to be prepared for you,' he said.

And even as the full meaning of his words sank in, a helicopter clattered low over the bridge and swung away through the gathering evening, catching the light of the setting sun as it climbed the lower sky above the *Kilo*-class submarine.

And, with a shock almost as real as if Leung had pressed a cattle prod to her back, Robin recognized *Poseidon*'s little Chaig.

ELEVEN
Bridge

In the instant it took Robin to turn back from the sight of the departing Chaig and face the three officers ranked behind her, her mood had altered completely. All her nervousness had been burned away in a flash of white-hot rage. It was as though scales had fallen from her eyes and she saw all too clearly how these duplicitous creeps had fooled her.

They were all in on it. Even the tension between Tan and Leung was probably part of the act. In the accidental instant that Zhong Wei had announced his chopper could not whisk her back at once, she had become almost inextricably trapped.

Tan must have watched her trying so hard not to look at the all too secret equipment as he burbled with dangerous freedom about the Kamov helicopter. Freedom of information that should have rung warning bells deep within her already suspicious mind. Information she had accepted without a second thought – thus revealing her prior knowledge. No wonder he had sent the political officer in with the tea.

And then what Leung must have made of her notes beggared belief – *Kilo*-class, Khan's Treasure, all the rest. By the time Tan called her up to the bridge she must already have been doomed.

And then Commodore Santa Shan had played his own version of Tan's little game, giving her gobbets of knowledge that she already possessed, reading guilt into her lack of reaction. Only the *Romeo* class of the stricken sub had failed to fit into the neat little trap of trickery so sneakily closing around her.

Much of her anger and frustration was aimed at herself for falling so easily. But by no means all. Still, it would have taken someone who knew her very well indeed to read the danger signs in her honeyed smile. Her courteous words or her charming tone. 'That is very kind of you, Lieutenant Leung,' she said in her most fluent Mandarin. 'Please don't go to any trouble. I've a lot of work still to do up here on the bridge. If that's all right with you, Commodore Shan. Perhaps you will assign me someone who can demonstrate the way this sonar screen works. By the time my husband arrives in the morning I should be able to brief you all on how best to proceed. It will save a lot of time.'

'Lieutenant Commander Tan will demonstrate anything you wish,' answered Shan shortly, his eyes and expression equally unreadable. But Robin could almost hear the mental additions *within reason* and *unless it is secret* cracking through the air. Dumping the lowly babysitting duty on a senior navigating officer like this was surprising – but on the one hand, there was little for anyone to do but watch the weather and keep the *Luyang* on station. And Shan clearly didn't want her spreading the poison she represented any further through his command.

Shan turned on his heel and left the bridge. Leung ambled off in his wake. The ship's address system sounded – change of watch Robin assumed. She looked at her watch. 18:00 local time. 'Thank you, Commodore,' she called after Shan's retreating back.

Then she turned again. 'Commander Tan, the first thing I need to learn about is the radio. I must contact my husband and explain the situation to him. We don't want him becoming concerned and turning *Poseidon* off course to alert the authorities about my disappearance. That would harm the reputations of your commander and your country – as well as risking the lives of your fifty submariners, would it not?'

The carefully calculated *gwailo* barbarian yellow-haired devil's lack of subtlety raised the ghost of a smile at the angle of his lips, but he nodded once. Five minutes later she was talking to Richard. It occurred to her that she should continue the pretence of innocence but she was all too well aware that it was fooling no one. And in any case she was in yellow-haired demon mode. So she cut to the chase. 'The situation's fairly simple, darling,' she said. 'They have me, and they really don't want to let me go. At least not until you get here and we start sorting things out on the seabed. I don't know if I'm being held to make sure you get here quickly and do what they want when you arrive, or whether they're nervous I have seen too much aboard and might go charging off to reveal all to James Bond, if he's available. I really don't think I'm in any danger, though, and I've warned them that we can do some damage if we cut up nasty – as well as condemning fifty of their men into the bargain.'

'So, what do you propose to do?' His voice came like distant thunder over the connection. He was not a happy bunny, she thought.

Commodore Shan had better watch out. 'I'll be there in six or seven hours,' he continued, his words like gravel rolling over a big bass drum. 'What are you going to do in the meantime?'

'I'm going to do what we came here to do,' she answered brightly, given strength and determination by the simple sound of his voice. 'Get ready to rescue these poor men. I know what they're going through all too well myself, remember. So I'm going to use everything they'll let me near to survey the site of the accident and get a briefing paper ready for you and the rescue committee that will blow your socks off at breakfast time tomorrow.'

Both Richard and Robin had to be content with that. They were realists and widely experienced in facing apparently no-win situations. And rolling with the blows until it was time to counter-strike. Robin returned the radio mic and headset to the radio officer, who gave no sign of having understood a word. Then she went out to Tan, who gave no sign of having overheard any of the conversation. Robin smiled. She wasn't fooled by either of them.

'Right,' she said to Tan. 'You heard the commodore. Let's take a look at what this sonar kit can really do.'

It could do quite a lot, Robin discovered in the next few hours. And had Shan been more experienced in rescue and recovery or more willing to listen to the ravings of a *gwailo* yellow-haired demon woman – no matter what it did to his precious face – it would have done more still.

For a start, it could widen the area it surveyed in several different ways. It could change focus. The picture Shan first showed her was on the narrowest setting, pointing with laser-like intensity on the sub. The beam could widen to take in the seabed immediately around the site of the accident. And wider still – the laser becoming a torchbeam and then a searchlight. Or on the other hand the light, the beam or the laser could sweep in circles around the central focus, like the collision-alarm radar used to navigate the ship under power at sea.

'Does any other ship in this little flotilla have sonar anything like this?' she asked Tan.

'Similar. Not identical. This is the latest.'

'Just fitted at Dalian. Yes I know. OK. Is there any way we can patch their sonar readings into this? Get a wider reading, get better differentiation, a clearer picture?'

'I don't know. I am not sufficiently well trained. I am a commander not a technician; a watch officer, not an electrician. We are navigators. They are engineers.'

'I'm glad to hear that that distinction is maintained even in the People's Liberation Army Navy,' she said. 'It is one of the great social divides of the sea. However, it leads me on to ask – do you have an electrical officer who is trained and capable of helping me?'

'I must refer this to the commodore.' For the first time Tan frowned in what looked to her like genuine concern. He was beginning to see what she was trying to do, beginning to be drawn into the plan.

But the commodore's answer was curt to the point of rudeness and clearly in the negative. Tan seemed genuinely shocked by it. But their shared disappointment was the next step in a long road that promised to bridge the gap that yawned between them.

With Tan ever more genuinely helpful at her side, therefore, Robin started to exercise her considerable ingenuity in working out ways to get a really clear picture of the ocean bed immediately below. And they made progress. It was certainly a case of 'little by little' but they moved forward nevertheless.

Further out, along what looked like continuous lines from the trapped hull, the blank sections that looked like a child's eraser-work on the green-contoured schematic seemed to gain some contours of their own when the sonar signal could gain enough of an angle to show some resolution. 'This blank area,' said Robin, some time later, tracing one of them out across a wide-searchlight setting. 'Could it be some kind of cable?'

'If it is,' said Tan slowly, 'then that is worrying. For this looks the same. And so does this.'

'There was a Chinese sub trapped on the seabed not far from here a few years ago,' said Robin, her voice growing dreamy with fatigue. 'That accident was caused by fishing nets, if I remember right. These are too big to be fishing nets.'

Their silent study of the picture was interrupted by the chimes of the ship's address system. Robin glanced at her watch: 20:00. 'Is that the end of your watch?' she enquired.

'It is,' said Tan. 'But I'll stay as long as I can be of help.'

'And because the commodore ordered it.' Robin jumped. Had she actually said that out loud? She hoped not, for it would not do Tan's face any good at all. And she might need a friend. Sooner rather than later. 'That will be wonderful,' she said loudly. 'But don't you want anything to eat?'

'Yes. I am to take you down for food.'

'Can we have it sent up here?' she asked.

'Of course,' he answered.

As long as you keep an eye on me while I have my dinner, she thought. But this time she kept her mouth firmly shut.

The helmsman was replaced at the change of watch and Tan gave a brief order to the departing man. Then he fell into an easy conversation with the replacement helmsman and, when his own replacement appeared a little breathlessly, he dismissed him. 'Helmsman Qi is from Jinzhou, like me,' Tan volunteered affably. 'Like my family, his ancestors claim descent from the Great Khan.'

Qi glanced over towards her as Tan spoke his name and she saw the same dark skin, high cheekbones, sharp-drawn angle of jaw. But no light of intelligence in his eyes. No understanding of anything other than his name – for Tan was speaking in his New-England English.

'Good evening, Shang Deng Bing Qi,' said Robin in courteous Mandarin, and was rewarded with a fleeting smile.

'Another conquest,' purred Tan. 'I can see why Commodore Shan wants to keep you isolated. You are a one-woman revolution.'

'Perhaps he should have sent me back.'

'Perhaps he should. But he did not. Let us proceed. What have we learned so far?'

'That the sub *Huangpu* is *Romeo* class. What can you tell me about *Romeo* subs that is relevant and not too secret?'

'That they are ancient and mostly decommissioned. This one was on a treasure-hunt, remember, not on a naval operation. *Romeo*s are diesel-powered, basically equipped, based on the German U-boat design from what you would call World War Two. Complement of fifty-four including ten officers.'

'Four missing, therefore.'

'Or dead. Corpses have no heat signature.'

'No communications – or there would be a buoy bashing up against your sonar equipment in the bow.'

'No communications. Vessel lying on its side . . .'

'Trapped by some kind of cable, net or line. In water too deep to allow access by divers in anything other than very specialist gear. In a situation, by the look of things, that requires cutting equipment that won't be available in the time-scale we have.'

He nodded wearily. 'Even if we had it flown out here from Dalian or Jiangnan we wouldn't be able to deploy it.'

'Until Richard arrives with *Neptune*.'

A mess orderly arrived then carrying a tray. On it was a bowl of rice and a selection of dumplings, boiled, steamed and fried. A pot of China tea. Bowls, cups and chopsticks.

As they set to work with the chopsticks, Tan said, 'So. What next?'

'Survey the seabed,' said Robin. 'Do to the immediate area below us what we have managed to do to the sub itself. We need to know the position of every ridge and valley, boulder or clump of weed big enough to be a problem.' She stood up suddenly, and strode across to the clearview, teacup in one hand, chopsticks in the other. 'Hasn't the *Kilo* been down? Even for a look around?' she demanded, looking out at the submarine's riding lights. 'I mean what's the point of having another sub on station if it's just up here bobbing about like a rubber duck in a bathtub?' The submarine in question was sitting half a mile ahead of them several degrees up on the starboard, facing them so that her hull sat just above the surface with the blade of her fin high and narrow.

'Commodore Sheng has decided not to risk another submarine until we find out what happened to the first one.'

'And *Romeo*s are cheap, no doubt. Being the better part of sixty years old and mostly decommissioned. While *Kilo*s are very expensive,' she spat.

'That is a new-style *improved Kilo*,' he admitted. 'It is little more than ten years old. And, yes, it is very expensive. But I believe the commodore was swayed by the thought of putting another fifty men in immediate danger.'

'So, we work with what we've got.'

Just as Robin announced this, she noticed something. The *Luyang* was giving off enough light for her to see the nearby seas pretty well, and she had focused a series of searchlights on to the spot in any case. In the brightness, Robin saw a sudden gleam of white against the fin of the *Kilo*. There was a rogue wave running down on them. Not particularly high, but powerful enough to set the *Kilo* bobbing like the duck she had just described. She crossed to the sonar monitor, drained the cup with one swallow as though it was a shot of tequila, then set it and chopsticks on the plastic top and rested her fingers on the controls. 'Mr Qi,' she said suddenly in her most fluent Mandarin, 'tell me about Jinzhou.'

The helmsman glanced across at her, surprised at her sudden interest. She gave her most dazzling smile. His eyes lingered.

Then Tan was there. 'What are you . . .' he began. But he could have been speaking to either of them. He looked out of the clearview. '*Hell,*' he said.

The wave hit the destroyer. Distracted at the vital moment, the helmsman was taken by surprise. The *Luyang*'s bows swung off station, forced rapidly sideways by the rush of the heaving water. As is often the case with such waves, even small ones like this, the rogue was followed by something close to a squall. The big vessel heeled, swinging further to port while both Tan and Qi introduced Robin to a range of vocabulary that was utterly new to her.

But all of this went more or less over her head. Her hands working as fast as they could, her concentration undisturbed even when the cup shattered noisily on the deck and was joined at once by the chopsticks, she was scanning and recording, recalibrating, scanning and recording.

By the time Commodore Shan arrived with Leung at his shoulder, huffing and puffing, spitting orders and questions in rapid succession, Qi and Tan were back in control. The destroyer was coming back on station. The little crisis was past with nothing more to be done except to complete a radio check on the other vessels in the little flotilla and to make up the logs.

The other captains and commanders had been taken unawares as well, but no damage had been done. And once he was assured the destroyer had reacted fastest and most efficiently, Shan began to calm down. He was grudgingly accepting of Tan's brief report. He did not reprimand helmsman Qi. He was almost solicitous to Robin, giving orders that her food and crockery be replaced at once.

The only downside was that the watch officer was sent up with orders to do his duty properly and joined the three conspirators on the bridge for the rest of the night.

But the positive side more than compensated for the minor irritation. For Robin had managed to get her wide-angle survey of the wreck site and of the ocean bed surrounding it from half a dozen different points as the sonar-laden forecastle was swept away off line. And the picture she now had of the ocean deep beneath them was almost as detailed and accurate as anything she could have ever hoped for.

TWELVE
Echoes

At midnight the ship's tannoy echoed again, and the first night watch became the middle watch – if the People's Liberation Army Navy used such terminology, thought Robin distantly. Certainly one watch officer was replaced by another and another helmsman replaced Tan's countryman Qi. 'Richard will be here by the middle of the next watch,' Robin said. 'Say six a.m. We should be ready to deploy by the morning watch at eight.' She leaned back in the navigator's chair and looked up at her companion.

Tan grunted, but he did not look up from the printouts they had spread across the chart table beside the chart of the Yellow Sea itself, corners and curls weighed down with teacups and rice bowls; chopsticks supplementing dividers, pencils and rulers. 'You were correct,' he said at last. 'The extra angle shows much more detail.' But his voice was grimly unhappy.

With good reason, thought Robin. The most obvious thing that the new angle had revealed was the steepness of the slope at the foot of which the *Romeo* was lying. It was so steep, in fact, that the last sideways scan before Qi started swinging the destroyer back into line showed the cliff edge beginning to obscure the sub. It was little short of a cliff, in fact. This information not only aided the clear measurement of the slope, it also allowed an accurate assessment of the depth of the seabed at the cliff foot.

The slope plunged at this point to half a kilometre deep. A sheer drop down to where the *Romeo* lay trapped helplessly on its side. The sub lay on the wide bed of a submarine trench reaching into the Yellow Sea almost at the point where it became the East China Sea. Its keel was inwards towards the cliff wall, where it was lost in a lack of definition they were beginning to recognize as debris. And perhaps more . . . thought Robin, straining to see more clearly. They had come to see the straight-edged eraser marks as cables, but there was something about the definition of the keel. Its fin lay out, the thin line of periscope almost invisibly pointing away across the abyssal plain.

Robin's best guess was that the unexpected abyss was an offshoot of the Ryukyu Trench that she and Richard had been exploring more than five hundred miles east and south of here. The Ryukyu Trench was the better part of fifteen hundred miles long and between one hundred and two hundred miles wide for most of its length. So that wasn't beyond imagining. The scans showed the cliff-steep slope on this side – the southern, with *Romeo* at its foot. Then the undulating abyssal plain which swept away beyond the range of the sonar. It was by no means featureless, but neither of them had felt any serious inclination to study it. The stricken sub claimed all their attention – and hardly surprisingly, she thought.

But the dangerous little deep was not marked on Tan's chart, though it was a recently replaced one, the old Chinese naval chart updated with the latest Japanese hydrographic computer-enhanced diagrams. Which was as blank in this area as any of the others. And although Robin itched to get her hands on an Admiralty chart of the area, she couldn't remember anything marked on that one either. 'That's one hell of a hull,' she observed wryly, just for something to say. 'I hope I can hold together under that much pressure when I'm that age.'

'More than five hundred metres,' said Tan dully. 'Where did this valley come from? The average depth of the Yellow Sea is fifty metres and suddenly here we are with ten times that! It's incredible. Can *Mazu* operate at these depths?'

Robin was so tired it took her a moment to register that he was talking about the AUV *Neptune*. 'She certainly can. We were coming up to five kilometres down in the Ryukyu Trench when she was ravished by the devilfish yesterday. Or maybe that was the day before. Time flies when you're having fun.'

'But, even so – what can she do? Realistically?'

They were able to speak so clearly and bluntly because the chart room isolated them from the watch officer and the helmsman. And because, during their working time together, they had begun to build a grudging trust. The first seeds of mutual respect.

'You'd be surprised,' answered Robin now. 'Whether you call her *Mazu* or *Neptune*, she's a versatile little lady. It'd help if we could work out exactly what she'll be up against, though. Look at this area immediately up-slope of the *Romeo*. Does that still look like some kind of landslip to you? I mean I can see the cables she seems to be mixed up in. But that really doesn't explain how she got into problems in the first place. Is the slope steep enough for a landslip to have hit her? Can we check on seismic activity? Anything that might have triggered any undersea activity like that?'

'I can check with Fleet,' he said, willingly enough.

'Don't you have Internet access? Can't you Google it? The news services would probably . . .'

'Internet is down,' he said. 'But Fleet will know.' And off he went to the radio room.

Left all on her own in the chart room, Robin continued the conversation just as though Tan was still there. 'The next question,' she said quietly, 'is why she was sailing close enough to the cliff-face to get caught in an avalanche if there was one. What was she searching for in such a dangerous place. As if we didn't know . . .'

Robin couldn't see a ruler anywhere readily to hand so she laid a chopstick along the centre-line of the submarine's profile, the point sticking out of the rounded bow like a torpedo frozen mid-launch. And, taking that as a line, she added another. Then another, searching minutely along the course that the submarine would have taken.

Nothing.

But then she tutted. 'Silly girl,' she chided herself. And she went back to look below the line – at the floor of the ocean beneath the foot of the slope, at the flat seabed that the ancient *Romeo* would have sailed over had she not been trapped. She leaned forward until the chair creaked and traced the line with her finger, like a child learning to read. Her lips parted. The tip of her tongue settled into the corner where they joined. She jerked in a breath. The finger froze. The tired grey eyes widened. Blinked. Looked again.

And there it was.

Not obvious by any means; little more than a sketchy scribble that might have been done by a pre-schooler. A three-year-old from the desert fastnesses of Quingai, the endless Siberian steppe or the limitless plains of Arkansas. A three-year-old who had never seen the sea except in dreams and pictures.

A three-year-old who was nevertheless attempting to draw a boat.

Her tongue-tip vanished. Her mouth closed. She swallowed. 'Now that, if they actually saw it,' she said quite loudly, 'must have been a real bummer.'

'What must have?' demanded Tan returning with less military clatter than usual.

Robin's mind raced. She had formed a good working relationship with Commander Tan but it was only hours old. She certainly did not know – or trust – him well enough to go talking about the Great Khan's treasure ship with him. She had no intention of talking about it with anyone, in fact, until she managed to get Richard alone somewhere she was certain they could not be observed or overheard. 'You first, Shao Xiao,' she said, sitting back and lacing her fingers behind her neck making a headrest with her hands. 'Tell me what Fleet says.'

Frowning, Tan sat in the second chair by the chart table. 'There was something,' he said slowly. 'At about the same time as the sub's last contact, though no one has linked the two incidents. They came to different desks, of course.' He shrugged as if that explained everything.

'Yes?' Robin prompted.

'Not much. Not enough for an earthquake. Hardly enough to register. No one was willing to guess what it was. But they were willing to agree to an undersea avalanche when I suggested it. They'd probably have been willing to agree that it was Tin Hau sneezing. Or your devilfish belching.'

'Or Moby Dick farting. Yes, we get the picture. But there was something? Something big enough to register? Something big enough to trap them.' She leaned forward and pointed to the sub on the printout.

'What are you driving at?' Tan leaned forward in turn, frowning.

This was yellow-haired demon stuff, Robin knew. And this was the time of night when demons and ghosts were about.

'Even if they were keeping the most careful watch they were likely to have been simply overwhelmed.'

'And what have *you* just seen?' demanded Tan irritably. With your wide grey demon's eyes. *Had he said the words aloud?*

Robin reached over the half-chart, half tea-table. Took the last of the chopsticks and used its bamboo point to trace the outline of the echo on the ocean bed apparently immediately beside the sunken submarine.

Tan leaned even further forward as he fought to understand what she was driving at.

'I still don't quite see . . .'

'Why not?' she demanded, as though in the grip of frustration, flinging back again. 'Look at the depths. The commodore's insistence that we sit immediately above the accident all but hid it. The depths are different. There's some kind of anomaly, perhaps even

an overhang. The sub is part-way under that. But the depth readings from the later scans show that it's the better part of a hundred
metres higher than the hull! She may not be as badly trapped as
we thought.'

He gaped at her for an instant, then nodded in grudging agreement. 'There might indeed be more hope than we at first supposed,'
he said. 'This is the kind of discovery that makes tomorrow's mission
even more important than it seemed at first.'

In the face of his enthusiasm, Robin felt positively demonic.
It took all her strength of will to keep from looking back at the
chart – at that child's sketch that lay unnoticed a few scant inches
in front of the finger that was stabbing at the wounded sub so
hopefully.

'Are you going to report this to your commodore or your political
officer?'

Tan was silent for what felt like a very long time indeed. Then
he looked at his watch. 'Certainly not immediately,' he said. 'Not
at this time of night. It will give us hope for tomorrow, but there
is nothing we can do about it now.'

Robin nodded as though the weight of the world were on her
shoulders. 'What we need to do,' she said, 'is sleep on it.' She pulled
herself erect and gathered the printouts together. Tan watched her
dully and made no move to stop her. 'So . . . ' she said, using the
last of her energy to make her voice sound bright. To do her best
to cover up the guilt she was feeling at the depth of her deception.
'I need a cabin and a wake-up call at six. Six is when Richard
arrives with *Poseidon* and *Neptune* – and we can really get down
to business!'

THIRTEEN
Deep

A little less than four hours later Robin was awoken by a rapping at her door that sounded slightly less forceful than a military barrage. She sat up gingerly, mentally still aboard *Poseidon* and wary of occupying the bottom bunk with its limited headroom. 'Yes?' she called, guardedly, trying to cudgel her brain up to speed. Her cabin door slammed open and Lieutenant Commander Tan appeared with a Western-style cup of English Breakfast tea. He marched towards her holding the cup out in front of him, clearly more used to being served than to being a servant. The fragrance of the strong brew was all but overpowered by the aromas of soap and cologne. Tan was showered, shaved and resplendent in freshly pressed uniform.

'*Yu-Quiang* is coming alongside now,' he said. 'But you have time for a shower.'

She sat up blinking, reaching automatically for the tea, and was relieved to discover that she had tucked down half-dressed at least. She and Tan had started building something of a relationship in the chart room last night but she wasn't ready for too much intimacy yet. Especially in the face of the fact that she felt that she was lying to him every time she opened her mouth – lying by omission if nothing else.

The teacup linked them briefly, seeming for a moment to be hotter than it was. 'Thank you, Shao Xiao,' she croaked, sweeping a tumble of curls back out of her eyes with her spare hand. He stepped back. She brought the teacup to her lips, disdaining the fragile handle.

As Tan turned, the ship's tannoy sounded. She left her hair and glanced down at her wrist. 05:45 – no change of watches, therefore. It was the warning of *Poseidon*'s approach. The door snapped shut behind him. She swung out of the bunk, her body on automatic while her mind ranged elsewhere.

She extricated herself from bedding, stood up and crossed to the tiny en-suite shower cubicle and fold-down latrine while drinking her tea and without spilling a drop. With a practised dexterity that spoke well of her years at boarding school if nothing else, she slipped off her shirt and bra – once more without taking the teacup from her lips. She put the empty vessel down as she hopped out of her panties and stepped into the cubicle itself.

Ten minutes later and still steaming, Robin stepped on to the bridge. Her clothes were crumpled but serviceable; she didn't feel she was letting the side down too badly. Tan was there, standing at the side of a strange watch officer, behind an unfamiliar helmsman. But as yet there was no sign of Commodore Shan or Political Officer Leung. She dropped the bundle of papers and printouts on to the chart table, then crossed unopposed to the starboard bridge wing door and stepped outside on to the open wing itself. The morning was vast and cool, full of sea sounds and wind mutter all but lost beneath the throbbing of big ships' motors.

She looked back along the sheer side of the destroyer down on to the foredeck of the approaching corvette.

Poseidon was absolutely spick and span. As shipshape and Bristol fashion as though she had just steamed out of the shipyard where she had been built and first fitted. *Neptune* crouched in her cradle, but it seemed to Robin that she was almost ablaze with energy and anticipation. Then *Poseidon*'s clearview also caught the early sunlight, turning briefly into a line of dazzling gold mirrors. Robin narrowed her eyes, looking past the blinding brightness for the shadowy shape of Richard looming in the bridge house itself. She was overwhelmed, suddenly, with a desire to see him, touch him, feel the security of his massive presence. To tell him what she thought she had discovered and get a kind of absolution from him for having hidden the truth from Tan.

She shook herself. She hadn't felt as weak and mimsy as this when she was trapped alone on a sinking submarine, when she was being hunted through the rotting hulk of a supertanker in Archangel, when she was kidnapped and in the hands of African rebels. There was something about the Chinese and her inability to come to terms with them that really and truly frightened her. Of course, both she and Richard had come closest to a brutal death in China, which was all too fresh in her mind. The only positive thing that she could recall off the top of her head about her Chinese adventures was the friendship she had formed with the intriguingly mysterious Daniel Huuk. Daniel; a sort of souped-up version of Lieutenant Commander Tan. She wondered for a distracting instant where Daniel Huuk was now and what he was doing. And whether she would have dared to hide her secret truth from him.

Then the Chaig lifted off from *Poseidon*'s little helideck and Robin knew in her soul that Richard – at the very least – was on his way aboard. And, just at the moment it did so, the destroyer's Kamov lifted off the flight deck as though they were birds in a mating dance. She stepped back on the bridge to find Tan in the middle of a three-way conversation with Zhong Wei piloting the Chaig and Commodore Shan hurriedly preparing for his guests and passing on instructions to be relayed to the pilot of the destroyer's own chopper. Political Officer Leung was also in there somewhere, apparently suggesting where they should be accommodated for the briefing they needed to have at once. In among all this, Tan was also on to the galley, ordering tea, coffee and a range of suitable food to be sent to the ship's main wardroom.

The latter conversation succeeded the other two and ran over into Tan's determined progress back towards the destroyer's flight deck. Robin grabbed the papers from the chart table, gathered the Japanese hydrographic chart, wrapped the telltale wide-set scan in the heart of the bundle as though she were a smuggler and followed Tan as he marched through the ship like an invading army.

The pair of them came out of the bulkhead door by the Kamov's hangar almost shoulder by shoulder to find the Chaig just touching down while Shan and Leung stood waiting to offer a formal welcome aboard. The four of them stood in a little phalanx as the Chaig's down-draught battered them like a returning typhoon, then the side door opened and Richard folded himself out. Even stooping under the whirling rotors he was taller than anyone there and when he straightened he dwarfed them. But it was more than simply his height, thought Robin. It was his decisiveness, his determination, his air of command. In every way he seemed to fill the flight deck, and he swept forward, seeming to take control of the moment, the vessel, the flotilla and the situation all at once. Although he exchanged formal courtesies with Shan and Leung, his eyes never left Robin's and a huge weight seemed to lift from her shoulders as he gave the ghost of a heartbreakingly familiar smile.

Robin introduced Commander Tan, as Commodore Shan seemed to be too busy greeting Captain Chang and Leung greeted Straightline with a suspiciously familiar ease. Then Richard formally and a little stiffly embraced her. *Are you all right?* his dazzling eyes and mobile brows seemed to enquire as the deep growl of his voice asked, 'How are Fatfist and Ironwrist?'

Before she had to face the embarrassment of admitting that she didn't know, Tan answered in his best Boston accent, 'They are both sleeping comfortably, Captain Mariner. And thank you for asking.'

Richard nodded in satisfaction and hugged her with bone-crushing force, doing untold damage to the armful of papers she was carrying. As he did so, the Chaig lifted off to make room for the Kamov. This disgorged several people that Robin hadn't even begun to think of, but whose presence was obviously very much part of Commodore Shan's game plan. First, and most arrestingly, was the CCTV reporter Bridget Wang. Bridget's blandly pretty face, eager expression and unexpectedly intelligent gaze were familiar from the TV coverage of the treasure hunt – and the much more muted reports of the accident. With her was the inevitable pairing of a producer and a cameraman. Robin didn't catch their names because they faded into the background somewhat while everyone made a fuss of TV star Bridget. Robin felt Richard stir and step aside from the excited knot of media people and she followed him automatically, to be confronted by a dark-faced, wiry man in a battered, dirty, unfamiliar uniform. His crewcut hair was liberally sprinkled with grey but his Han face was round and young-looking, in spite of the fact that it was gaunt and exhausted. Tan was talking quietly to the man who was standing on the Kamov's step but still only reached the commander's shoulder. Richard dwarfed him. Or he did so physically, Robin thought. Mentally and emotionally the stranger held his own. There was a forcefulness about him, a burning restless energy that was somehow evident in spite of the fact that he was standing utterly still.

Tan looked up as Richard and Robin approached. 'This is actually the most important of our guests,' he said, speaking to Richard and Robin both at the same time. 'His name is Chen and he is the captain of the *Kilo*-class submarine. If you have any questions about the *Romeo* vessel *Huangpu* and what we can expect of her, then Captain Chen is your man.'

After this final introduction, they all went back to the wardroom to analyse those papers, consume a working breakfast as she gave the briefing she had prepared last night with Tan and hold the meeting that would determine proceedings for the rest of the morning at least. The briefing was terse and taciturn. Bridget Wang was allowed to film parts of it and she asked a question or two so that she would feature prominently in any report she broadcast later. Submarine Captain Chen asked one or two questions as well. Seemingly alone of the people there, Chen seemed to see the real importance of the point Robin was making about the relative heights as measured on the scan. His interest gave the little story she had concocted to distract Tan from the sketchy outline of the treasure ship seem much more substantial and important. That made her feel better about the duplicity, of course. And it made her feel much more positive about Captain Chen himself. 'It might well be crucial,' he decided at last. 'We will see when *Mazu* gets down there. But a rock shelf one hundred metres above the hull is a very different matter from a pile of rubble weighing who knows how many tonnes actually pinning her to the ocean floor.'

'We will have to wait until we can take a closer look,' said Tan.

'So let's get on with that now, shall we?' demanded Richard impatiently. And they all rose.

At 08:00 precisely, with the tannoy on the destroyer distantly sounding the change from the morning watch to the forenoon, the gantry aboard *Poseidon* creaked, lifting *Neptune* off her cradle. Robin stood on the corvette's crowded little bridge with Richard on one side, Chang immediately in front of her between Straightline and Xin who were seated and Tan on the other with Captain Chen like a slight ghost at his shoulder. As *Neptune* swung over the side and the lines lengthened, lowering her towards the water, Chang said, 'Captain Mariner, Seaman Xin, to your positions please and complete your pre-dive checks. Lieutenant Jiang, take the con until Xin's replacement arrives.'

Neptune's handlers exited, making the bridge feel very much more spacious. Xin's replacement, who had been waiting in the stairwell outside the bridge door, eased into the vacancy and took the con back from the navigator. The watchers on the bridge looked on as *Neptune* swung smoothly down until she was floating in the water. Sleeping still. Attached to the falls until the handlers assumed full control and opened the quick releases remotely from their crowded little workspace in the bows after they had gone through a series of checks almost as complex as the pre-flight routine on an airliner.

A moment or two later, one of the video screens came alive and was filled with what *Neptune*'s main forward camera could see – sea surface from water level, as smooth, as calm and as immediate as an early shot in *Jaws*. The same shot was repeated, each distinguished from the next only by a flicker of screen, as Richard ran though all the on-board cameras. Then back to the first shot – except there was a little bow wave now, gathering glassily up ahead of the camera. The handlers' communication channel crackled into life. 'Cameras checked,' said Richard in Mandarin.

'Propulsion all A1,' added Steady Xin at once. 'Testing ancillaries . . .'

'Robot arms, grabs, drills, cutters and so forth,' Robin explained to Tan, who nodded once, his eyes flicking restlessly between the screens and the wider picture through the clearview where *Neptune* bobbed, heaving, turning, dipping and rising as things folded out and in around her sides.

'Buoyancy control A1,' said Richard. 'Testing trim and dive controls during first section of the descent. Primary readings A1.'

'They can't test dive controls properly on the surface, of course,' Robin explained to Tan. 'But the control systems are all reading fine.'

He nodded again. '*Mazu* is larger than I had supposed,' he said at last. 'I can see how she might indeed be substantial and powerful enough to free the trapped sub.'

'In the right hands,' snapped Chang protectively, as though someone had taken the abilities of a favoured child for granted.

'She's in the best hands we've got,' said Robin.

No sooner had Robin spoken than the solid little AUV started moving in a much more determined manner. Thrusting forward to the agreed diving point and beginning to settle beneath the surface as she went. The bright daffodil yellow became the paler hue of Danish butter as the water closed over it, then the colour bled out of it as the elements of the sunlight's bright white spectrum were soaked up or reflected back by the water. Robin looked left, up at the bridge wing of the destroyer high above. Even at this angle she could see Bridget Wang speaking animatedly into a microphone and gesturing down to the AUV as her cameraman made heroic efforts to capture both the event and the lovely TV star reporting it.

When there was only a colourless, wave-distorted paleness to be seen, and even Bridget Wang had apparently given up trying to describe it, Robin left the bridge. Unable to contain her tension and excitement any further, she hurried down to the little control room itself. It was only as she passed the big electrical-engineering area that she realized that Captain Chen was right behind her.

The control room was almost filled by the shapes of Richard and Xin as they crouched in the chairs – their attitudes too tense and focused to be called mere sitting – but there was space for a third and even a slight-built fourth. And this was part of the ship's design. The back of the room, including the inside of the door, was effectively one huge pinboard. There was just room for Robin to pin the papers she had brought from the briefing into place and to work on them with Captain Chen beside her. Though the backs of her thighs and bottom occasionally brushed against the backs of the chairs – and of the men crouched in them.

For the first time in their brief and fraught relationship, Robin had cause to bless Commodore Shan. By placing the bow of his destroyer precisely above the point his sonar told him the submarine lay, he had ensured that the GPS readings for the *Luyang* were precisely relevant to the sonar readings for the wreck. Effectively, Robin soon found, the green contours on the 3D schematics were perfectly matched to the northings and eastings on the chart and the hydrographic diagram. They might not register the depth of the ocean bed but by God they pinpointed the place on the world's surface with all the uncanny accuracy of Google Earth. Even though it looked a lot more old-fashioned than the digital charts loaded into the computer-control systems above like the flight plans of modern aircraft, nevertheless Shan's dogged determination had rendered the paper readouts far more accurate than even the smartest modern technology.

And it was a function of *Neptune*'s control system that she could be located with equal accuracy. All Robin had to do was glance over her shoulder at the readouts on the control screens and she could trace *Neptune*'s progress across the large-scale charts towards the more precise schematics of the focused sonar readings. More, she could begin to dictate them, for as part of her briefing she had marked on the two charts she had to hand an archery-target eye of concentric circles. The precise locations of the searchlight scan, of the torchbeam detail within it – and of the laser-pointed bull's eye within that. Able to account for drift and flow, tide and current, therefore, she guided *Neptune* unerringly across the submarine ocean, discussing each move in Mandarin with the light-voiced, almost boyish tenor of Captain Chang, while Richard and Xin concentrated on moving her down through a vertical half kilometre of increasingly icy blackness.

Because of the urgency of the situation, and because of the utter steady stillness of the man, Robin found that she and Chen could work together with the kind of fluid understanding she shared with very few indeed. They became a team at once, each giving the other unreservedly the benefits of their learning and experience as they guided the AUV through the water. From the light-filtered upper reaches alive with fish of all sizes. Through the twilight deeps where the fish were fewer but larger and much more dangerous-looking. Into the black abyss where what they saw seemed either to be tiny things glowing like dancing stars or massive, threatening shadows looming at the edge of the light like the devilfish in the Ryukyu Trench.

Until at last there was something more than the restless constellations of underwater particles in the brightness of the searchlight beams, and Richard, finally, spoke.

'*There!*' he said.

FOURTEEN
Target

R obin tore herself around, frowning, at Richard's word. The mark she had just made on the chart was not quite on the bull's eye of her big round sonar-generated target. But then she saw what he was talking about. At the outer edge of the light thrown forward and down by the AUV there was a line of reflected brightness. It could have been the crest of a pale sand dune, the spume of a breaking wave, the apex of an iceberg. 'That must be the top of the cliff,' she said. 'You're still nearly five hundred metres south of the wreck point and nearly a hundred west.'

'And what are you reading – a hundred and fifty metres high?' added Chen, his eyes narrowed in thought.

'Nearly a hundred and eighty,' said Richard.

'Ten metres above the cliff,' calculated Chen steadily.

'Then a hundred and seventy – of cliff-face,' added Robin. Then, thinking back to their home on the cliffs so close to the White Cliffs of Dover, she added, 'That's a good deal higher than Beachy Head.'

'Let's hope it's not quite as sheer,' grated Richard.

'Captain Mariner has calculated that there may be an outcrop part-way down and the sub may be lying part-way under that, remember,' Chen emphasized in his quiet but forceful manner. 'It is that outcrop that may have been mistaken for a large weight of rubble. We need to keep careful watch for it as we get close.'

'What do you think, then?' asked Richard. 'Go along the cliff-top until we're above the sub, then look down – or go over now and follow the cliff foot to our target and then look up?'

Chang's voice answered over the intercom. 'Commander Tan says stay high.'

'Always keep to the high ground,' observed Richard drily in English. 'Tan's read his Sun Tzu.'

'So, Captain Mariner,' came Tan's voice, as smooth as a Boston lawyer's. 'You think this situation requires *The Art of War*?'

'Let's hope not,' answered Richard amenably, still in English. 'But top of the cliff it is.' On his word, both Robin and Chen stopped looking at the charts and schematics for a moment. Four pairs of eyes fixed on what the forward-facing screens revealed with utter concentration.

Neptune's light showed the edge of the incline in incredible detail as Richard and Steadyhand settled the AUV less than a metre above it. The seabed was rocky, dusted with deposits of sand and silt in variegated colours like the leaves on the ground in an autumn wood. There was a sparse outcropping of weed, but nothing like the overwhelming growths that sometimes choked the channels further north in Bo Hai and Korea Bay. But the weed gave them their first clue. Though what it was a clue *to* they could not at first guess. 'That weed seems to have been torn away there,' said Robin, craning over Richard's shoulder and still speaking English. 'Do you think the sub could have bottomed here then slipped over?'

'Possibly,' allowed Richard. 'What do you think, Captain Chen?'

'The scraping goes on along the edge,' answered the submariner so quietly and calmly that it took Robin an instant to register that he was also speaking in English. 'Look there – more damaged weed. And there, at the markings in that sand.'

'And on the bare rock beside it,' added Richard. He switched back into courteous Mandarin. 'Captain Chang, Commander Tan, can you see this? What do you make of it?'

'I see it,' said Captain Chang.

'I agree with your earlier observation,' said Tan. 'It looks as though something was dragged along here. But I cannot suppose it was the bottom of the submarine itself . . .'

'No,' agreed Captain Chen. 'These are not marks that a submarine would have made. Not that I can envisage a submarine grating forward along the bottom in that fashion in any case. The bottom of the *Romeo* class is extremely strong and well armoured against depth charges, collisions and so forth. But I cannot envisage a commander allowing his boat to scrape along the bottom like this no matter how well armoured his own vessel was.'

'Not at this depth,' emphasized Tan.

'Not at any depth,' snapped Chen.

'Perhaps,' said Richard thoughtfully, 'it's not a case of something being dragged *along* the edge. Perhaps it's a case of something *long* being dragged *over* the edge.'

'Like what?' demanded Robin.

'What was the first thing we came across in the Ryukyu Trench?' Richard asked. 'Before we met the devilfish?'

'The cable,' breathed Robin. 'That huge undersea cable!'

And even as she spoke, Steadyhand said, 'There is a place where the edge has been quite badly damaged.'

Robin swung round to the charts pinned to the wall and was not surprised to find Captain Chen was at her left shoulder. She glanced over her right shoulder and confirmed the readings on the screen. 'You're just coming precisely on target,' she said.

'But a hundred and seventy metres too high still,' added Chen. 'If Captain Mariner's briefing was correct – and I interpret the read-outs precisely as she does – then there will be an outcrop of some kind seventy metres down the cliff-face.'

'Then to hell with Sun Tzu,' decided Richard. 'Time to forget the high ground and take the low ground instead. Ready, Steadyhand? Right. Over we go!'

'WAIT!' called Robin. Her nose was all but pressed against the bull's-eye of her target. But the angle of her head allowed her to look across at the sonar printouts that gave the on-ground detail of what was actually there. 'Captain Chen, do you see that?'

'Ah. Yes. I see what you mean,' said the imperturbable submariner. 'It will bear immediate investigation, I believe.'

'Before you go over, come west, would you? Due west,' Robin ordered tersely.

'Heading left 270 degrees from your present position. One hundred metres or so,' confirmed Chen.

The AUV span on to her new heading at once, the machine, like her handlers, apparently utterly disregarding the questions and orders shouted by Captain Chang, Commander Tan and – via him – Commodore Shan. And probably Political Officer Leung into the bargain. Instead, angled slightly down by the head, *Neptune* hung above the damaged cliff edge. One sweep of her lights and cameras revealed an unexpectedly sizeable area of damage. There was even a kind of blast ring, thought Richard. A semicircle of shattered rubble thrown back on to the flat plain behind the cliff-top, almost as though there had been some kind of an explosion down here. *Neptune* moved over this stone-strewn area with gathering speed until she was skimming along the flat plain that reached towards the shallows of the Yellow Sea and the coast of China split by the great gash of the Yangtze's estuary beyond them. It was immediately obvious what had caught Robin's eye. There was a serpentine track here, as though a massive snake had come slithering through the submarine sand. And there, at the end of its track, precisely one hundred metres back from the damaged cliff edge, it lay. Headless. Inert. Dead. Like the corpse of the Kraken. A gigantic undersea cable that had been simply – if clearly violently – cut adrift.

Neptune rose. Steadyhand and Richard angled it with balletic precision and Robin thought it must look a little like a dragonfly come to sip at the surface of a pool. She could see it in her mind's eye hanging frozen in the water as though joined to the thing it was observing by a solid beam of light. The lights showed the lifeless monster reaching away back into the darkness as though at some unimagined distance. Its tail must rest somewhere on the east coast of China, somewhere near Shanghai itself. And on all three of the printed schematics, Robin confirmed, there it was, so obvious now that she could see the real thing, lying a little south of westwards until it vanished out of range – still showing no sign of ending or deviating. Seeming to reach unstoppably towards Shanghai. Chopped off at this end as absolutely as a felled tree. And the diameter of the square-cut end looked almost as thick as the trunk of a giant redwood, but that may have been an optical illusion, she thought. But the cut was not all that neat. The cable could almost have been blown asunder. Its outer protective skin was folded back. The inner weave of lesser lines and cables protruded in steel splinters that gleamed glassily in the yellow light. To Robin it resembled nothing so much as the top of a pineapple.

'What on earth could have done that?' said Richard, his voice awed.

'Seismic activity?' Robin hazarded. 'Fleet told Mr Tan they registered something . . .'

'Could be, I suppose,' he allowed. But he clearly wasn't convinced.

'Captain Chen?' asked Robin, but the submariner stood silent, his hand on the back of Richard's seat, his face etched in the strange light from the video screens, frowning with thought. And, perhaps, with something more.

'Devilfish?' asked Xin, still fixated on the submersible's earlier adventure.

'Wouldn't have thought so,' answered Richard. 'There are big sperm whales down here, though. Squid is their staple diet. Anyone think a sperm whale could have chewed through that?'

They all shook their heads like Muppets being worked by one string.

'It is of secondary importance,' Chang interrupted.

'True,' agreed Richard. 'Right, Steady, old fellow. Back to the job in hand.'

Neptune turned and retraced her course to the damaged cliff edge. Here the almost geometric angle had been broken back, as though some monster had indeed tried to eat its way through the rock. *Neptune* eased over the edge, following what looked like giant teeth-marks down a slope that looked steep but not quite vertical.

Richard and Steadyhand took it slowly, following the scored, scarred surface of the rocky slope. There was a combination of several sorts of damage here and their painstaking progress made it easy to see all of them. There were the snake-tracks of the retreating end of the severed cable up above. There was the length-ways scoring made by whatever had fallen or been pulled and precipitated over the edge. There was a scattering of scree from the avalanche spilling down below the bite-mark in the cliff. There had been some coral here – it was gone. The weed was gone as well, shaved off like a beard from a chin.

'Ah,' said Captain Chen suddenly. 'Congratulations, Captain Mariner. An inspired piece of interpretation. There indeed is your overhang. I would gamble a considerable fortune that the submarine is on her side and a hundred metres below.'

And, just as Chen observed, the analogy of a chin was suddenly entirely appropriate, for there, seventy metres down, with a hundred metres still to go before the bed at the cliff foot, was a jut of rock like a massive jaw. The outcrop formed an overhang perhaps twenty metres deep and the cliff-face retreated underneath it like the cavern behind a waterfall. Then the lower outreach of the slope spread out in a sloping fan of timeless rubble that spread away more widely and more widely still across the level darkness of the plain at cliff foot level.

And on that massive fan of rock lay their target. Captain Chen saw it first and hissed as though in sudden agony, crouching further forward still.

Everything – weed, coral, rock, boulders, tangles of cable as thick as tree-trunks – everything lay piled at the foot of the slope one hundred and seventy metres below the giant bite mark, one hundred metres below the unexpected overhang. Piled on top of the stricken submarine. Much less substantial than the outcrop had seemed. Particularly in the face of the submarine's surprising scale and latent power.

The submarine lay on its side, precisely as the schematics from the sonar showed it. But the schematics gave no indication of the size or the impact of the vessel. Perhaps only Captain Chen would have had any real idea of the power the sight of the wreck might have. Though Richard and Robin had both been involved with submarines before – and with sinking submarines into the bargain – they had never been in a nightmare situation quite like this.

Neptune settled down towards the seemingly massive wreck as delicately as a snowflake; as gently as one of the autumn leaves Robin had thought of, looking at the variegated sand and silt so far above. Richard and Robin gaped, alike awestruck by the nightmare sight of the thing, as though they had discovered the *Titanic*. It gathered in their subconscious and their imaginations like the ghost out of a hundred childhood comics, books, films.

Richard had always been a Western fan, a follower of Shane and Sudden, John Wayne and Clint Eastwood. But even he saw at once how absolutely this looked like one of the dreaded U-boats whose wolf-packs savaged the convoys in print and on celluloid, TV, video-tape and DVD from *The Cruel Sea* and *The Enemy Below* to *Das Boot*, *U-571* and *Enigma*. And it was so big. The schematic reduced it, but *Neptune*'s camera enlarged it until it seemed almost the size of the corvette they were in at the moment.

But Richard knew all too well that they could not afford the time to sit and gape. His eyes narrowed, seeking to put together the story of the *Romeo Huangpu*'s disaster from the clues that *Neptune*'s pictures silently revealed. The mess of coral, rock and rubble was on the top – had landed last, therefore. But it did not look anything like enough to incapacitate a vessel of this size.

'It must have been the cables, don't you think, Captain Chen?'

'The cables,' Chen confirmed dully.

The cables must have caught her and held her first. Those cables would bear closer examination, Richard thought, grimly, his mind racing away from what his eyes were assessing and what his hands were doing. At the very least it looked as though two cables had crossed at the top of the damaged cliff. One ran roughly north–south along the cliff-top and the other vaguely east–west across the slope. One from Taiwan to North Korea or thereabouts. The other from Japan to Shanghai.

Richard wondered silently whether the sub could have inadvertently got itself tangled in the Shanghai cable – which had pulled down the Taiwan cable from the cliff-top when it parted. The Taiwan cable plus all the rubble that went with it? Certainly, the Shanghai cable would have been simply hanging from the overhang.

'Would the systems on that sub have been capable of discriminating a dead-black cable hanging directly across their course?' he asked Captain Chen.

'Possibly. But probably not unless someone was keeping a very close watch,' Chen answered, trying to force some life and confidence into his voice. 'If the watchkeepers were paying close attention and keeping a careful watch they should have seen something . . .'

Richard nodded, his eyes almost as narrow as Chen's as he examined the picture on the monitor and cudgelled his brains for an explanation. But the only other explanations that occurred to him immediately involved the kind of coincidences and acts of violence that belonged in the world of James Bond.

'But what in God's name could conceivably have grabbed their attention so completely that they missed an undersea cable cutting right across their course and dead ahead?' Richard spoke the thought aloud without realizing it.

'What indeed?' echoed Captain Chen, his voice shaking with ill-suppressed emotion.

And, as Robin still had not mentioned the second vessel on the schematic of the sonar sweep at the briefing – or at all, in fact – the pair of them asked the question with genuine wondering ignorance.

FIFTEEN
Lie

Richard guided *Neptune* along the sunken submarine *Huangpu* about a metre clear of the hull as they studied the lie of the vessel's hull. They had come down on it a little less than halfway along its length, right aft of the fin. That first careful sweep covered the forward forty metres of its length, therefore. It established that what Chen hoped after his talk with Robin – the point he had made so clearly at the briefing – was true. And at first glance it seemed to be. Under the solid umbrella of the overhang high above, the rubble sweeping down across the fan of underwater scree covered the keel of the vessel up to the highest swell of her rounded side. But it was nowhere near as hopelessly overwhelming as the sonar scan had made it seem. The fan of rock, coral and weed scraped off the overhanging cliff ahead stretched from the root of the fin almost to the torpedo tubes. 'But it doesn't look too heavy after all,' said Richard. 'Do you think it would just slide off if we could find a way of pulling her upright?'

'It looks that way,' answered Chen. 'But getting the vessel upright in the first place might be more of a problem.'

'I agree,' said Richard. 'But the first step must be to work out exactly what is holding her down. And that means we need to look more closely at these cables . . .'

'I disagree,' said Chen. 'There is a higher priority than that.'

'What . . .' began Richard, simply not following the sub captain's train of thought.

'*Richard!*' spat Robin, shocked that he could be so insensitive. 'Your first priority must be to let the men aboard know that we've arrived. That help is at hand.'

'She is right, Goodluck,' Xin emphasized. 'As long as there is anyone still alive to tell.'

Tan's voice cut into the conversation. 'Lieutenant Leung is watching the heat signals on the sonar. He had just informed me there are still fifty hot-spots.'

'You're right, all of you,' said Richard, crestfallen. 'I was too wrapped up in logistics to think about personnel.'

'There will be a time when logistics are paramount,' Chen assured him, surprising Robin at least with the ready sympathy in his tone.

'But how will you get through to them?' Robin asked, her voice preoccupied as her mind whirled away to dangerous irrelevancies. Like whether the men they were trying to rescue had missed the cable hanging in front of them because they had seen the image of the treasure ship in the distance. Like whether they would tell the world about it if they had. Like whether she should be telling more open-hearted truth and fewer calculating lies herself. 'I mean they've been out of contact since the incident. No radio. No *nothing*, like as not,' she said a little weakly in the end.

'Easy,' said Richard. 'Steadyhand, will you switch on the sound system, please, then get her as close to the hull as you can. Commander Tan, get Leung to tell us when we're right above the densest concentration of heat-spots, would you? Now, where's that claw control?'

No sooner had Richard given his orders than the sound system came on and the control room filled with a weird watery whispering as the deep-sea currents flowed past *Neptune*'s microphone system like a river full of ghosts. The picture on the forward-camera monitor changed so that the clear metal side filled the shot like a smooth grey reef. Tan's voice broke the tense whispery silence. 'That's it! Leung says you're there.'

'OK,' said Richard. 'Here we go.'

A black articulated robot arm folded out into shot. A claw at its end opened and closed like a pincer designed for a metal lobster. The readout on the screen showed that *Neptune* was twenty centimetres from the metal and holding steady. Richard tapped the EXTEND button. The claw shot forward and hit the side. An echoey *clang* rang through the control room. Silence as the clang echoed on. *Neptune* lurched back a little but Steadyhand had been expecting that. Almost immediately she was back at twenty centimetres. Richard hit EXTEND once more.

Clang!

Silence.

Steadyhand had pushed the throttle as Richard pushed EXTEND so *Neptune* hadn't moved backwards this time.

The pair of them went through the same routine.

Clang!

CLANG! came the reply with desperate, utterly unexpected force. *CLANG! CLANG! CLANG! CLANG!* And behind the metallic noise there was another, far more distant and much more eerie. As though there were more ghosts down here – but these ghosts were cheering.

'It's alive! It's alive!' exulted Richard quietly to himself.

'We have lift-off!' said Robin and Captain Chen nodded, his hand closing on Steadyhand's shoulder.

Throughout the little flotilla a sigh of heartfelt relief seemed to fill the airwaves. Behind Tan's forthright 'Well done!' there was the sound of much more human, full-throated applause.

'Right,' decided Richard. 'That's enough personnel work for the time being. Back to logistics. Speaking of which, Captain Chen, how have those men managed to remain alive? From what I remember about old submarines like that the batteries were suspended in vats of hydrochloric acid or some such. Shouldn't they all have suffocated the instant she went over?'

'Like the tragedy in 2003 you mean, when we lost seventy men on a *Ming*-class upgrade of this same basic design? It happened when the engine malfunctioned on a dive and used up all the oxygen aboard. Everyone in the crew suffocated before they could surface?'

'Something like that, yes.'

'This boat is almost the last of her class. She has been adapted as a test bed for a new propulsion system designed to avoid accidents just such as the ones you mention. It is called the Air Independent Propulsion system. And, clearly, it works. That is why there was no leak of gas or loss of oxygen. That is why they are all still alive. But their time is extremely limited, of course, for even though the air aboard is clean, there is an increasingly limited supply of it. And it is dwindling fast. They will begin to die within the next six hours unless we can get them free.'

'No pressure there, then,' observed Richard, turning back to work at once. He and Xin span the little vessel through three hundred and sixty degrees and headed back towards the fin. Like the conning tower of the U-boats on which the submarine's design was based, it stood high and sat wide – no thin blade beloved of modern design here. It really did resemble a tower more than the fin on the back of a whale. It lay the better part of three metres from deck to safety rail, then it was extended another metre and a half at the forward end into something not unlike a funnel. Chen would have explained it in detail – form, function, precise measurements, the lot – thought Richard. But he didn't really care what it was for at this stage. Aft of it, nearly two metres long again, stood the periscope. And between them, at first glance like another piece of ship's equipment, lay a cable.

The cable reached in between the top sections on the conning tower then up over the safety rail that enclosed it like a battlement and on down the middle of the fin itself until it was lost in the pile of rubble on the lower section of the hull. Here lay the next part of the problem. One that they had not yet checked in any great detail either. A second cable.

The first cable was clearly the lower section of the great serpent lying beheaded a hundred metes back from the cliff edge above. The second was the one that had been dragged over the edge when the first one broke. It also lay on the submarine, lost under the pile of rubble at the base of the conning tower, but stretching in and out of the shadowy gloom right along the whole length of the cliff foot. It didn't seem as thick as the first one, but the weight of any great length of the stuff was bound to be very substantial.

'How long do you think it is?' asked Robin as *Neptune*'s light followed the second cable along the forward section of the sub and down on to the seabed immediately in front of the rounded bows.

'There's a cable,' answered Richard, 'that starts in London. It comes down the Channel, through Biscay, past Gibraltar and into the Mediterranean. Along the Med., then past Alexandria into the Suez Canal, down the Red Sea into the Indian Ocean. It goes round India into the Bay of Bengal, through the Malacca Straits, into the China Sea, then on up to Japan. This could be that one. It's in the right place.'

'Jesus Christ!' said Robin, shocked into blasphemy by the scale of the thing he was describing. 'What on earth is it for?'

'The Internet,' he told her.

'The *Internet*?' Robin's voice rang with simple disbelief. 'Don't they use satellite for that?'

'Satellite for phones. TV and radio – especially digital. Cable for the Internet. The cables in the eastern Mediterranean were cut a couple of years ago. Everywhere from Israel to India lost almost all their bandwidth. Nearly lost the whole damn system, apparently. Just think what that would mean. To close the Internet down. Cyber-terrorist's dream.'

'Let's hope we don't have to do it, then,' said Robin shortly.

'What do you mean?' asked Richard. Still in logistics mode, not personnel.

'Well, my dearest one, if it comes down to weighing the lives of fifty men against chopping the head off that second line, then I'm up for Dr Guillotine!'

Richard blenched. 'Let's not get ahead of ourselves here,' he suggested. 'We'll take it stage by stage and start with the one that's already cut. It looks pretty weighty. If we can move that then maybe we can get her to roll upright. Steadyhand, let's see what we can do with that big bastard there, shall we?'

The first thing they did was to follow the line of the cable back from the rubble on the sub's hull, over the horizontal conning tower and back along the seabed for a good few metres. It seemed to Richard that the cable must be almost half a metre thick. 'It's probably a huge fibre-optic bundle,' he mused. 'It almost certainly will be if it's actually anything to do with the Internet or telecommunications. And I can't offhand think what else a cable this size would be lying around down here for. Anyone have any ideas?'

No one had.

'Well, let's see if we can move it,' decided Richard after a while. 'Steadyhand, what do you think we should try first?'

'The cable is too big for *Mazu*'s claw to grip,' mused Steady Xin. 'She has a saw blade and an underwater oxyacetylene system. But they would take time. However, there are other alternatives which would do the job. It depends on whether we want to move it or cut it, I suppose.'

'Let's keep damage to a minimum,' decided Richard judiciously.

Spoken like a one-time Name at Lloyd's of London insurance underwriter, thought Robin wryly. But then she saw his point. Who would, actually, be covering any claims for damages arising out of what they did here? The cable she had just so blithely insisted they should cut must be worth millions of pounds sterling – perhaps billions. More even than the cargo of the Great Khan's treasure ship was said to be worth.

As Robin slipped into a brown study, Richard and Steady brought *Neptune* back to the upper edge of the rock pile on the submarine. There she sat, as still in the water as a hovering helicopter. One of the pieces of equipment stowed on the underside of her solid body was a grappling hook. They lowered this now, watching in the forward-camera's video screen as it dangled lower and lower. Like the grab on one of those fairground games where contestants select and try to retrieve appealing little prizes of all sorts – usually just out of reach – they tried to make the grapple catch the cable. But the snakelike trunk was festooned with a distracting array of seaweeds and as slippery as a rocky foreshore. The three times they actually managed to get anything like a sustainable purchase, they were frustrated by the weight of rocks piled on the loose end.

After fifteen increasingly irritating minutes, Richard said, 'Plan B, Steadyhand. Let's move some of this rubble and see if we can get a better grip, shall we?'

The grappling hook wound up. The lobster claw returned. Working with increasing speed and confidence, Richard and Steadyhand pushed the least stable rocks aside, starting little land-slides off the hull and back towards the cliff foot. Then they began lifting all the stones the claw could grip – and some of them were surprisingly big, for all they had to do was find a secure purchase point and *Neptune*'s buoyancy would do the rest, albeit at some little cost to her compressed-gas flotation-control system.

It took them half an hour to clear a valley in the rubble that un-covered the cable. But as they lifted away the last few stones it became clear that their problem was a little more complex than they had thought. The cable they had uncovered, leading in over the horizontal conning tower, met the other cable here – the one that had been pulled down off the cliff-top. And the first thing that the move-ment of the last few rocks revealed was that the two cables were tangled together. Then, as *Neptune* hovered just above the Gordian knot, its lights and cameras threw other potential problems into all too stark relief. For a start, what they had imagined as a simple T-junction where one cut cable came against a second relatively undamaged one was actually a jumbled mare's nest. Secondly, it looked as though the second cable – whether it ran from London to Japan or not – stopped here. For it seemed to have been broken as well. To make matters worse still, their clearing understanding of what they were examining so closely began to suggest that at least one of the cables, which had seemed to be a single line, was in fact double. Or triple. And perhaps both of them were.

But on the positive side there was plenty for Richard to grapple on to. Easing *Neptune* down and replacing the claw with the hook, he and Steadyhand secured a promising-looking strand. The AUV pulled sturdily and the whole mess shifted. The cable over the conning tower seemed to pull a little free. But then the whole lot snarled again. Without releasing the hold, Richard and Steadyhand reversed their angle and pulled the tangle down towards the trapped sub's keel. They had more success with this tactic, and the cables pushed a good deal more rubble off the slope of the submarine's side. The sub reacted by stirring. More debris slid off. Clouds of sand obscured everything and Richard closed down *Neptune's* propulsion until it cleared, but she remained attached to the cable like a balloon on a string. Readouts on the cloudy screen recorded a degree or two of movement, though, as the sub fought to pull itself upright. But then the cable tautened and their progress stopped.

'Right,' said Richard as the screens cleared once again. 'Let's see if we can slacken down that cable and give her a little more room still.'

Neptune danced over the top of the conning tower, which was now raised a good few degrees clear of the seabed and followed the shallow parabola of cable back out across the seabed. But it soon became clear that there was no hope of slackening it further out here. 'The force exerted by the sub trying to pull upright must have been pretty strong,' observed Richard thoughtfully. 'Looks as though it's tightened things up all round.'

Just his tone told Robin that he had thought of something. Probably something outrageous and dangerous, knowing him.

Captain Chen did not know him as well as Robin did, of course. 'That is the opposite of what we want,' the submariner said. 'We need to make things looser, not tighter.'

'Quite so,' agreed Richard. 'And how do we do that?'

There was a silence as they all struggled to follow his logic.

'If things got tighter when she came up,' he prompted, 'but in fact we want them looser . . .'

'You mean,' demanded Robin, thunderstruck, 'that you want *to lie her back down again*?'

SIXTEEN
Chop

'Yes,' said Richard. 'That's exactly what I want to do. The slack should let us slide that Gordian knot right off her altogether – like the rubble, down by the cliff foot.'

'Then what?' demanded Chen.

'Then there's only one thing you do with a Gordian knot,' said Richard, and made a chopping motion with his hand that Jackie Chan, Bruce Lee and Dr Guillotin would all have been proud of.

There was a great deal of lively discussion after that, but through it all – and fielding much of it – Richard continued to work. And Steadyhand Xin worked unquestioningly alongside him. *Neptune* had a detachable recoverable basket secured to her underside. Richard and Steady placed this carefully on the highest part of the chimney above the conning tower where the laws of physics dictated that the force exerted on their makeshift lever would be strongest. Then *Neptune* seemingly undid a lot of the work she had just spent the last hour doing. The lobster claw and the hook lifted rubble, coral, rocks and boulders, piling them on the basket. At first this had no effect at all, but then, after half an hour of work, and increasingly acrimonious discussion, the *Huangpu* settled a degree or two back down. The lessening slope meant that Richard and Steady could pull the basket further out and that too helped. The effect of the next few rocks was even more pronounced.

The bare bones of Richard's plan became immediately apparent. The cable reaching in over the falling conning tower was much slacker now. Before it could form coils on the seabed, Richard stopped filling his basket of stones and returned to the knot itself. Here he hooked the strongest of the grappling points and hurled *Neptune* at full power towards the cliff. Sure enough, the knot slid down. And the steepening of the underside round towards the keel helped the massive mare's nest past its tipping-point where its own weight would pull it down off the submarine's hull. If another couple of metres of slack could be eked out by forcing the vessel further over still.

Ten more minutes did it. And maybe twenty more kilos of rock piled precariously on the outer edge of the basket. The sub suddenly gave up the fight and rolled over hard against the seabed once again. Three more metres of slack appeared as the parabola vanished out of the cable above the conning tower. The knot scraped over the weed and barnacle encrusting the old metal bottom and slid free.

There was silence. Robin felt an unreasoning desire to cheer, but remained as silent as everyone else. Like them she really could not see what Richard's simple bloody-mindedness had achieved. 'Captain Chen,' said Richard, his voice full of the excitement Robin felt but did not yet understand. 'You said the keels of these vessels were particularly well strengthened. Against depth charges and whatnot?'

'They are armoured and strengthened to withstand charges as well as water pressure, yes. But this hull must be right at the outer edge of what it can withstand.'

'Right. So, two charges, I think, Steadyhand. We want to chop this thing free without disembowelling it.'

Light began to dawn in Robin's mind as Richard and Steadyhand guided *Neptune* back to the tangle of cable that now lay quite clear of the submarine's hull. The way the mare's nest had slid off the lower slope had cleared away all the rubble into the bargain. There was nothing there but a knot of cabling that reminded Robin irresistibly of disasters with kite strings and fishing lines. But on a giant scale.

The solid AUV dipped. The lobster claw crossed the video screen. For the first time it was putting something down rather than picking something up. It took an instant for Robin to recognize what it was. It was one of the explosive charges the remote vehicle carried for such things as seismic testing. And for blasting, if needed. Richard's deft fingers made the seemingly clumsy claw place it precisely on the cliff-side of the tangle. They made the sharp-pointed pincer angle the shaped charge carefully beneath the weight of cable until Richard was satisfied that the blast would chop through the cables without damaging the submarine.

Then *Neptune* jigged over the little hill of interwoven cabling and placed the second charge equally precisely under the point at which the lateral cable entered the mare's nest after having crossed the conning tower and the upper hull. Again, Richard angled the charge so that it would cut the cable by directing the majority of its power away from the ancient metal plates nearby.

'Richard!' called Robin, certain now she knew what Richard was planning.

'Yup?' he answered.

'Switch off the microphone!' she begged.

'Good thinking, darling! No sooner said than done. And thanks for the tip.'

Neptune skipped back again to the netting cradle with its pile of rocks. In an instant, even as Richard was speaking to Robin and shutting down the sound system, *Neptune*'s falls were attached to the anchor points at the corners and the remote was holding the whole crazy pile steady. 'Ready, Steady?' said Richard to Steadyhand Xin. Xin nodded once and Richard said, 'Go!'

Ready, steady, go! thought Robin. Only Richard. *Really . . .*

Both men's fingers moved with the precision of a Russian corps de ballet. *Neptune* lifted the counter-weight. Swung it free of the conning tower. The sub began to come upright immediately. And, just at the very instant that the cable sought to stop that upward surge once more, springing tight as a bow string, at its most powerful and yet its most stressed, Richard's fingers hit the DETONATE.

The two charges erupted at once. Together, they easily destroyed the tangle of cable. The knot was blasted asunder; the carefully placed charges even more effective than Alexander the Great's sword-blade at chopping through their own massive Gordian knot. The cable that ran along the cliff foot sprang apart, its ends lashing back like the end of the cross-cable at the cliff-top. And that cable also sprang free down here, its elastic retraction compounded by the victorious surge of the righting submarine. The frayed end blasted back, whipped up and reared like the head of a snake preparing to strike. But the strike never came. Instead the huge trunk of cabling recoiled across the ocean bed, collapsing under its own weight, until it lay as dead as its other half high above. And *Neptune*'s cameras were able to follow it as the AUV, even though she was anchored by the weight of stones in her basket, reared backwards and span like a cockle in a maelstrom under the power of the detonations.

By the time Richard and Steadyhand got *Neptune* under control again and refocused on the sub, the vessel was sitting upright, and even appeared to have lifted clear of the seabed. 'Good Lord, that was dramatic,' said Richard. 'I hope we haven't damaged anyone aboard.'

Steadyhand released the first two anchor points on the net below

Neptune and the cradle opened downwards like a trapdoor until the stones all tumbled free. Then, as Richard brought the buoyancy back under control, they retracted the falls and stowed the cradle back across *Neptune*'s underside. By now the Fleet was cheering, for the submarine was beginning to rise. The motors kicked into desultory life – but life nevertheless. The nose came up and bubbles oozed out of the ballast-tank vents as the crew regained control of the buoyancy systems.

Then the radio crackled into life, the crew of the sub trying to report in and give a preliminary assessment. But Commodore Shan joined reporter Bridget Wang, filling the airwaves with self-congratulation. They could hear Tan trying to get some kind of a status report from the *Huangpu* in among Shan and Bridget's publicity-conscious utterances.

Captain Chen was suddenly in motion, as though unable to bear the constriction of the tiny command centre any more.

In the silence after his departure, Robin said, conversationally, 'Richard, is there any way you can isolate the screens down here from the bridge? Stop them seeing what we see?'

'Steadyhand? Can we do that?'

'Certainly, Goodluck. These switches here . . .'

'OK, darling,' said Richard, intrigued. 'We're all alone and unobserved. Now what?'

'Just something I thought I saw on the sonar printout. Can you follow the cliff foot straight ahead for another couple of hundred metres?'

'I guess so. And I don't think anyone will be paying much attention to what we're doing either. Look at that TV monitor. The only one not showing *Neptune*'s pictures. What's that? Chinese public service broadcasting's CCTV? Looks like Bridget's just gone live to her devoted viewers in China.' As Richard spoke, he and Xin pushed *Neptune*'s throttles to the top of the green and the AUV sailed forward at full speed, following the beams of her headlights along the foot of the cliff above the meanderings of the slackened cable.

'I don't suppose Political Officer Leung will be following this on the destroyer's sonar?' asked Robin uneasily.

'Doubt it,' answered Richard glancing up from the hypnotic rush of shadow and whirling star-specks. 'Isn't that Leung beside Shan on the destroyer's bridge wing talking to Bridget as the sub comes up to the surface behind them?' Then he glanced back at the monochrome rushing of the deep-sea screen. 'Why?' he asked a little uneasily. 'What do you expect us to find out here?'

'I don't know,' said Robin, turning back to her schematic and her charts. 'What speed are you going? I want to double-check where you are.'

'Ten knots max, I'd say. Water's dead. No current or tidal movement. So we should be covering the ground at about that speed in a straight line. Why?'

'Just keep a careful lookout. If you find something you'll know the answer. If you don't I'll tell you later.'

'Jesus! Talk about cryptic! It's like working with Mata Hari!'

'You should be so lucky . . .'

'*Kebukeyi?*' whispered Xin. '*Is it possible?*'

Neither of them heard him. Neither of them saw what he saw – to begin with at least.

'*Bu keyi,*' he mumbled. '*It isn't possible . . .*'

'Not even a hint?' asked Richard, glancing back at Robin, playfully, still teasing.

'Not until I'm sure.' Robin's attention was caught by the CCTV broadcast of Bridget Wang turning to gesture dramatically at the surfacing submarine. *I wonder if those guys on that sub saw it*, she thought, not for the first time.

Then she looked down, still thinking, *I wonder what there actually is to see . . .*

Then Xin spoke for the third time, a little more forcefully; very formally. '*Mafan ni.*' I am sorry to bother you. '*Zhe shi shenme yisi?*' What does this mean?

Richard caught the tone of the words first. He swung back to focus on the screen. And the instant that he did so his attention became utterly riveted. 'I see what you mean, love,' he said in English. And it was his tone that captured Robin. Then, for the next few minutes, the three of them simply gaped as *Neptune* prowled round and about, her cameras revealing the detail of what the sonar had only hinted at.

As Richard had observed, the water here was dead. Such currents as eased across the Yellow Sea in and out of Bo Hai and the Korea Bay whispered over the cliff-top far above, and left the icy deep alone. And the deep was literally icy. Too cold for colonies of coral, sea-worm. Too lifeless to tempt the shoals of hunting fish and the predators that fed on them. Too inert even for much in the way of chemical reaction.

She sat at an angle, her back broken and her decking leaning in towards the cliff. High square poop just standing, walled with rotten stumps that must once have held a rail. Forecastle a lower echo, exploded on its after side where doors and the wood around them had swollen and burst apart. She was held in a slide of mud that half-smothered her but secured her timelessly in place. Her masts and sails were gone – long gone. Not even a stump or a papery rag remained. But the stump of a bowsprit pointed the way she would have been heading had she still been afloat.

Had she still been on the surface nearly a kilometre higher than she was. Had the year still been 1281 and Kublai the Khan on the throne; had his still been the chop, or royal seal, that ruled the Middle Kingdom.

And the chop of Kublai Khan suddenly became a thing of central importance. For on the slope of mud that swept down from the burst deck and the ruptured side above the broken back, the steady brightness of *Neptune*'s light picked out one of a series of sizeable boxes. The box itself was burst, and half out of it there lay spewed six or seven brick-sized ingots. Precisely what they were was by no means clear. But whose they were was obvious. The lid of the box was marked. A complicated rectangular seal had been burned deep into the pallid wood. Even eight hundred years and more of bloating in the icy water could not erase the power of the mark.

'That is *his*,' said Steadyhand Xin, almost breathlessly. 'It is the chop, the personal seal, of the great lord Kublai.'

And for a moment, Richard and Robin were so utterly overcome by what they had discovered that neither of them thought to ask how in God's name Steadyhand could recognize the chop of Kublai Khan.

SEVENTEEN
Fortune

'We have to alert the authorities,' said Robin.

'I agree,' answered Richard. 'But which authorities? There must be a fortune down there.' He glanced up to the monitor showing the local CCTV channel. Commodore Shan was explaining animatedly to Bridget Wang how he had saved the lives of the trapped treasure-seekers, through his outstanding skills of leadership and seamanship.

'We must inform the captain,' said Steadyhand.

'At the very least,' agreed Richard. He pushed the button that allowed him to communicate with the bridge. 'Would Captain Chang come to the AUV control room, please?'

This was the first time anyone had summoned Captain Chang in this way. She chose to respond surprisingly swiftly, alerted, perhaps, by something in Richard's tone.

Five minutes later she was standing beside Robin, staring wide-eyed at the screen. 'We have to alert the authorities,' she said.

And the importance of her words was suddenly emphasized by Bridget Wang. She turned away from Commodore Shan, suddenly, dramatically clutching her ear. 'I am in personal contact with the captain of the submarine,' she announced breathlessly. A small portrait of a man who looked surprisingly like Captain Chen of the *Kilo*-class sub appeared in the bottom left-hand corner of the screen. The ghostly whispering of an open line hissed quietly behind Bridget's nonstop commentary.

'Captain, are you there? Can you hear me, Captain? This is Bridget Wang of People's State Broadcasting here.'

'I hear you, Miss Wang.' The voice itself seemed thin and insubstantial, almost grey, somehow, like smoke, thought Richard.

'Congratulations on your miraculous escape, Captain. It is the best of good fortune. We will talk about that in a moment. But first I must ask you the question that all the world wants answered. *Did you find the gold?*'

'Sadly, no, Miss Wang. Our good fortune was not quite that strong.'

'No sign at all? Of either the gold or the emperor's treasure ship?'

'Nothing, I'm afraid.'

'Do you believe him?' asked Richard at once.

'What reason have we to doubt him?' demanded Captain Chang.

'None. And if he did know anything I guess now would be the optimum moment to announce it.'

'And yet,' said Captain Chang, 'we will be a little more circumspect. We will choose which authority we alert most carefully. In the meantime, recover the AUV, please. Bring *Mazu* home, Mr Xin.'

'But make an abso-bloody-lutely accurate plot of where she is on the chart before we do, please, Robin,' added Richard.

An hour later, they were all on the bridge. Captain Chen was gone, still ignorant of their discovery. The destroyer's Kamov was, apparently, doing one last circuit of the little flotilla largely for Bridget Wang's benefit. CCTV showed aerial photographs of *Neptune* being recovered and Bridget was explaining the AUV's importance in the rescue to her audience. Richard wasn't paying much attention to the broadcast but he noticed Shan's picture in the corner of the screen and assumed the commodore was getting the lion's share of the credit for the work that *Neptune* had done – as well as everything else. The benefits of command, he thought cynically.

'If we're going to pass this on up to any particular individual in the first instance,' he said, 'then I think it should be Commander Tan. All the footage has very precise location markers on it. If we're going to use it to back up our story then we run the risk of telling the world where the wreck is with the first frame we show. We need to start with the man we trust the most. And for my money that's Commander Tan.'

'You think we can get him over here before the destroyer heads back to base?' asked Robin. 'It's getting late and they'll want to pull out before dark, I should imagine.'

'I don't know. It depends on his duties and responsibilities. Robin, you were aboard. Was he effectively in command?'

'No. I got the distinct impression there was someone else actually in command of the ship, albeit under Commodore Shan's orders.'

'That would be logical. You'd want a full-blown captain in command of a destroyer. Not just a lieutenant commander. What do you think, Captain Chang?'

'A shang xiao. Yes. That would be the correct seniority. Why?'

'Well, that probably puts Tan on Shan's staff. Maybe even his staff officer. But even so, he's the most shipshape officer we've dealt with so far. And if Shan can spare him for half an hour he's the man I'd like to talk things over with in the first instance. If you agree, Captain Chang.'

'He was the only one interested in debriefing the submarine's crew, checking on hurt and wounded rather than getting his face on TV,' emphasized Robin. 'He's the one I'd go to.'

'And we do have to go to someone,' said Richard. 'We can't just hang around here and hope no one notices where we are or starts asking what we're up to.'

'In fact,' concluded Robin, 'we need some pretty sound and solid advice as to precisely what we *ought to* be up to.'

'Broadband,' ordered Captain Chang, turning to the radio operator. 'Get me Commander Tan on the radiophone. And make that what the Americans call *Person to Person*, would you?'

An hour later, as the afternoon began to gather towards evening proper, Commander Tan was seated in the wardroom with Chang, Richard and Robin. His intelligent Mongolian face was folded into a frown of thought. 'If what you say is true, then you have to alert the authorities,' he announced a little pompously.

'It's true,' Richard assured him. 'You can see for yourself; it's all in the computer's memory. And we agree we have to alert the authorities. But we need to know which authorities and how best to alert them.'

'Will the sequences we have stored in the computer memory be proof enough?' insisted Robin. 'Or will we need something more tangible?'

'I need time to think,' said Tan. 'Let's see what you've got.'

'You show him please, Captain Mariner,' said Captain Chang. 'I have a ship to run.' She could have been speaking to either Richard or Robin so both of them went back down with Tan.

The three of them stood in the control room a few moments later while Xin ran the footage once again. Tan literally gaped at the pictures. Date and time in the corner confirmed when the footage had been recorded. Location and depth markers corresponded precisely with what Robin had marked so carefully on the chart.

The final picture lingered on the burst box with its black-branded mark. 'How did you know that was Kublai's chop, Steadyhand?' asked Richard.

'From the television,' answered Xin, as though it was mind-numbingly obvious. 'Where else?'

'It's been on a lot,' added Tan, still absolutely transfixed. 'There have been countless programmes about the Khan and his treasure ships ever since the expedition first set out. And they were so close!'

'Are you sure they didn't see anything?' probed Robin. 'I mean I'd half thought that they might have missed the cable they ran into because they were all looking at the sonar signature of the treasure ship.'

'No,' said Tan shortly. 'That's not what Captain Chen reported at all.'

'*Chen?*' asked Richard. 'I thought Chen was captain of the *Kilo*-class.'

'That's right,' Tan told him. 'Right in both cases: treasure seeker and would-be rescuer. There are two Captain Chens. They are brothers.'

The screen went blank. Only the monitor showing CCTV remained live. Bridget Wang was gone. In her place three young women dressed in military uniforms so tight they might have been painted on were performing gymnastics in front of a panel of elderly men.

'The footage is impressive,' said Tan slowly. 'But it is very revealing, is it not? It will be worth a fortune all on its own.'

'Revealing?' For a moment Richard thought he was talking about the contortions of the gymnasts.

'If you show it to anyone with any nautical knowledge then you tell them precisely at what location and what depth the wreck itself can be found, for everything is up there on the screen. And if you try to tamper with the footage and remove the information you immediately render it worthless as proof of your story.'

'Good point,' said Richard. 'We had already thought of it, though. It's one of the reasons we wanted to talk things through with you. To find out what sort of approach you recommend.'

'A judicious element of secrecy is your strongest suit.'

'Which is why we have only told you.'

'And Captain Chang and Si Ji Shi Guan Xin here.'

'Quite.'

'Even so, you will find it very difficult to keep control of the information. This is a ship's company, not a silent monastery or a secret tong. Someone breaking the silence here is likely to get rich rather than disciplined by the abbot or chopped to pieces on the order of the Dragonhead.'

'We're in a black spot for communications,' said Robin thoughtfully. 'You couldn't get the Internet. We can get CCTV but only just and by no means all the time. And there is no mobile-phone service whatsoever.'

'Well,' said Tan after a moment. 'Let us go back up to the wardroom and continue our little conference there.'

Half an hour later still Richard was summing up when Commodore Shan interrupted with a message via Broadband Dung summoning Commander Tan back aboard to oversee the placing of a tow line aboard the battered *Huangpu* before dark so that Shan could pull her back to Jiangnan. 'We've all but settled things, anyway,' said Richard as Tan sent Broadband back with a message that he was on his way and a request that Zhong Wei get the Chaig ready to carry him across to the destroyer.

'We'll send *Neptune* down one more time and get some tangible proof. We can do that tonight or first thing tomorrow. Nobody's likely to disturb us before then.'

'We should go for that box with Kublai's chop on it – and whatever's in it,' suggested Robin.

'Then we'll set sail for the nearest mainland port. That'll be Shanghai unless anything unexpected comes up. It's, what, five hundred miles due west. We can make that in less than a day.'

'Twenty hours at twenty-five knots, standard cruising speed,' said Robin precisely.

'But still,' insisted Richard, 'who do you suggest we take whatever we bring up to? The authorities in Shanghai? Or should we be alerting the authorities in Beijing? We really do have to get this right. Heritage Mariner want to keep their offices in Hong Kong and expand into Shanghai as well. We need to keep all the authorities sweet there and in Beijing as well. If we were taking it to Hong Kong I wouldn't be needing to ask all these questions. I haven't been back in a while but I still know people who know people there. Shanghai's different, unfortunately.'

Richard was personally coming round to the view that he should be checking with his own people in London Centre at the earliest opportunity. They had their fingers on the pulse of who were the movers and shakers in everywhere from America to Africa to Australia. From Canada to Chile to China. Learning the best names to talk to in Shanghai and Beijing should be no trouble for them. Especially as they were already preparing the ground to open the new Heritage Mariner offices either in the Bund, if they could get hold of the real estate, or over the river in Pudong.

Except that the Internet was down and his mobile phone had no service and he had no way of contacting London Centre other than via Broadband Dung – and that, in his estimation, was about the same as using a public-address system.

'So,' he said again. 'What do you think, Commander Tan. Is there anyone in Shanghai I should talk to first? Anyone I should take the Khan's treasure to, whatever the Khan's treasure turns out to be?'

EIGHTEEN
Huuk

D aniel Huuk looked out of the window of the Shanghai Central Police Administration Building down on to People's Square. A group of locals were practising afternoon t'ai chi in Renmin Park. He could just see them through the trees. One of them appeared to be a Western tourist. She had devil-golden curls of hair that gleamed like guineas in the sunlight. He could have looked at individual faces if he had wanted to but that would have required binoculars. He was tempted. Had he really believed the blonde woman to have been Robin Mariner he would have called for them, but to do so upon an idle whim was far too indulgent. Had Robin or her husband Richard been anywhere in China at the moment he was certain he would have known about it.

He hardly needed binoculars to see the window of his room in the JW Marriott Hotel at the top of the elegant skyscraper on the corner in Tomorrow Square, however. Though he had enjoyed very little of the Marriott's luxury since he had arrived in Shanghai earlier in the day on the direct flight from Beijing, preferring to drop his cases there and come straight here. Then he had occupied the interim by making phone calls and arranging meetings, in refusing tea and all the other offers designed to add to his comfort that had been made by the anxious locals. Finally, deep in thought, he had come to stand by the window only to find himself distracted by the distant gleam of golden hair.

Instead of looking at either the leafy greenery of the ancient park or the beautiful silver blade of the ultra-modern skyscraper, however, he refocused his eyes until he could observe his own reflection in the pristine glass. He saw there a tall, gaunt man with long eyes, longer cheekbones and an unruly shock of black hair that almost disguised the academic breadth of his forehead. His face was an unsettling mixture of East and West, for he was of mixed race. The eyes and cheekbones were courtesy of his mother, the determined nose and square jaw from his father. His tall, thin body was clad in a black suit modelled vaguely on the universal uniform so popular under Mao Zedong; not that anyone had much sartorial freedom then. High collar, military shoulders, central line of buttons. Jacket falling far below the waist, apparently empty below the bulk of his deep chest. Plain black trousers of matching cloth. Big long bony hands matched, invisibly, by big long bony feet. Stripped, he was all curves and angles; whip-strong muscles not quite bulky enough to cover his surprisingly massive skeleton. Ivory skin clinging as gauntly to the rest of him as it did to his death-mask face. He wore no badges of rank or signs of power. Everyone who needed to know knew exactly who he was.

He still thought of himself as Daniel Huuk, though almost no one called him that nowadays. That name had belonged to an officer who had left the Hong Kong Coastguard at the handover a dozen or more years ago and vanished into the strange underworld that had existed in the aftermath of British rule. Where he had lingered almost invisibly, homelessly and aimlessly drifting through the bustling streets like a hungry ghost, hardly knowing where to go or what to do to find himself. Until, through Robin Mariner, he was reborn and redeemed. And more; much more.

Now he was more widely known as Deputy General Commissioner Huuk of the Institute of Public Security, appointed to the highest possible roving office after his outstandingly successful handling of security, particularly in Hong Kong and Shanghai, at the Olympics. He was also known, less widely, as Son of the Dragon Head Huuk, effective ruler of the Invisible Power Triad under the ancient but apparently immortal Dragon Head Twelvetoes Ho. Co-regent, perhaps, with the old man's daughter Su-Zi.

Both roles suited Huuk perfectly, even though he was of mixed race and laden with associations – not to say taints – of old colonialism and discredited law-enforcement; and they also fitted him ideally for the job in hand.

It was the task of the Institute of Public Security to evaluate policing experiences across the People's Republic. To study new issues – especially those arising from opening up to the outside world, in the Special Economic Zones such as Hong Kong and Shanghai. To introduce advanced techniques from around the world, including the Internet. It was the objective of the Invisible Power Triad to exercise power secretly by infiltrating and influencing the highest echelons of government – at local, district, zone, provincial and national level. And to do this by controlling the new technologies, including the media and the Internet.

So, when all Internet access from Dongxing in the south to Dalian in the north had collapsed without warning ninety-six hours earlier, isolating two complete Special Economic Zones, at least one international stock exchange and the complete east coast of China as far as Beijing and Baoding, Wuhan and Wuzhou, Daniel Huuk had been the man assigned to the case. And given carte blanche with regard to whatever he decided to do in the furtherance of his investigation. By both the chairman and the dragon head. Not that he needed carte blanche, to be fair.

Only the Dragon Head of the Green Gang could wield more unquestioned power on the streets of Shanghai than he could. And it was the Dragon Head of the Green Gang he had contacted first on arriving here. Only the Chairman of the People's Republic and the General Commissioner himself could wield more political muscle. And they were both in Beijing.

Deputy General Commissioner Huuk travelled alone, as did Son of the Dragon Head Huuk, though in both incarnations he could have surrounded himself with armies. He worked alone, though he was able to call on absolutely any aid he required; and from absolutely anyone, government employee or triad member – not that there was necessarily much of a distinction. Even the chairman himself would think twice about refusing one of Huuk's gentle and courteous requests. Which was why he had the best suite at the Marriott, though he had yet to actually step over the threshold, and why he had the commissioner's own office while the commissioner was engaged on a judiciously selected enquiry that would take him out of town for a few days – leaving the whole of his organization at Huuk's beck and call.

In the Marriott his unexceptional suitcase would have been unpacked already and his modest wardrobe housed in drawers, cupboards and wardrobes against his arrival. In the commissioner's office he carried only his briefcase with its state-of-the-art wafer-thin notebook computer – at the moment all but useless, of course – and one or two other necessities that he rarely let out of his sight. Everything else he needed was contained in the long skull behind that high, broad forehead.

There was a gentle knocking at the commissioner's door.

'Come!' he called, hardly raising his voice at all.

A constable, first grade, put his head round the door and bowed, even though his body was still hidden by the door itself. 'He will meet you at M on the Bund in an hour, Deputy General

Commissioner. He says to tell you that he has booked a table in your name. His name is not of sufficient *weight*...'

In the silence that persisted after the constable left, Huuk snapped open the case and looked at its contents. It was a courtesy, but one that he appreciated. His name carried no more weight with the concierge at M on the Bund than the dragon head's did. But the awarding of so much face was an unexpectedly elegant compliment. From a drug-dealer, a whore-master and a ruthless enforcer of bribery, blackmail and protection rackets. Or, of course, it could equally well be a subtle gesture designed to put him off his guard by a man who was planning to murder him.

After a moment or two, Huuk's long pale hands picked up a small, flat black leather box such as might have contained an exclusive personal grooming kit or even a set of expensive writing instruments. He opened it. And there, nesting almost invisibly in its black velvet, was a matt-black Rohrbaugh Stealth 9mm pistol. He lifted the gun out and laid it briefly on the palm of his left hand, marvelling as always at how much bigger his hand was than the pistol. It was a little more than five inches long and less than four inches high, and yet it held a magazine of six 9mm bullets with all the brutal stopping power of the very much larger SIGs, Glocks and Desert Eagles.

Huuk laid it on the table and neatly packed away its travelling case. Then he checked the movement – he had stripped and re-assembled it twice as the Beijing flight came in on its long finals to Pudong International Airport – and took out the magazine.

The little slide was loaded with Speer 147gr Gold Dot bullets with the new six-grain powder option for extra power. He checked it one last time and snapped it back home. He worked the action, listening with quiet satisfaction as the first round snapped into the chamber. He snapped on the safety. Then he took the black chamois speed-draw holster and snapped it to his belt.

Even with the loaded gun in place, there was no sign of anything beneath the skirt of his long jacket, no telltale pulling at the waistband of his trousers. He was supping with the Devil. The Rohrbaugh would lengthen his spoon.

NINETEEN

M

Huuk stepped out of the unmarked police car on the corner of Guandong Lu. He stood for a moment, seemingly alone on the thronging bustle of the pavement, facing Zhongshang Dongyilu – the Bund road itself – and, beyond its jam-packed multilane, the trees of Huangpu Park and the Huangpu River. But in the early evening, the greenery and the great brown swirl of the commercial waterway beyond were rendered insignificant by the thrusting brilliance of Pudong on the far bank. It had rained during the drive over here and the sudden vicious downpour had gone some way towards clearing the stultifying smog of a typical Shanghai evening. But the temperature still stood in the thirties and the humidity level neared 100 per cent. And the uncountable throngs of people and cars worked with unremitting energy to undo what little good the cooling, purifying downpour had achieved.

Huuk glanced right, across the road, to Number 3 The Bund. Last visit he had enjoyed a meal at Jean Georges there; but it was a while since he had visited M. It would be like seeing an old friend again. And of course it was an old friend who had invited him here. Well, not an old *friend*, precisely . . .

Huuk turned left and went in through the door, welcomed at once and guided up through the restfully familiar Art Deco ambience. 'I believe you have a table reserved on the terrace, Deputy General Commissioner,' he said as he led Huuk up. 'Your preferred table, of course. And your guest has already arrived.'

Zhang Tong, current Dragon Head of the resurrected Green Gang, had run to fat. He had indulged himself in more than excesses of food and drink, thought Huuk as he crossed the terrace towards his favourite table at the corner. One aspect looked over the Bund, the park, the river and Pudong. The other looked along the curve of the Bund up to Suzchu Creek, the double bridge of Waibaidu and Wusong Lu and the more restful Hongkou beyond. It was well positioned in terms of the passing dragon of feng shui and also seemed to catch the best of the evening breezes that cooled the airs up here.

Dragon Head Zhang Tong had positioned himself with his big broad back to the wall, doubtless so that his considerable bulk would obscure neither of these, the finest views in Shanghai. It also, Huuk noted, placed him in a secure position where he could watch the terrace for signs of danger. And it put Huuk with his back exposed, an easy target to anyone on the terrace or in the glass-fronted dining room behind. It might even be technically possible, he thought morbidly, for someone to hang out of the window of Jean Georges at Number Three and shoot him from there. Even allowing for the differences in height and the solid balustrade that walled the terrace like a battlement.

Huuk arrived at his chair and bowed slightly. Zhang Tong pulled himself to his feet and bowed back. Each gesture was courteous but minimal, as befitted kings and emperors greeting each other. Just enough to award the other face while carefully preserving one's own. It was only the desire to preserve face that had stopped Zhang ordering an aperitif and getting stuck in while he was waiting, thought Huuk as he eased his lean frame into the chair the maître himself held, and reached for the white linen napkin.

The maître summoned a waiter and then hovered while he asked, 'To drink, gentlemen?' M on the Bund had a famous cellar.

'I hear the 2004 Chablis is highly spoken of,' wheezed Zhang, losing a little face in his eagerness to be at the trough. But hoping to impress with his bon vivant knowledge, perhaps. 'Do you have a premier or a grand cru?'

'We have the La Forêt 2004 Chablis; it is by Vincent Dauvissat,' answered the maître.

'Bring the bottle.'

'And for the Deputy General Commissioner?' The maître bowed a little towards Huuk.

'Perrier. Five hundred centilitre.'

'Ice and lemon or lime?'

'Just a clean glass, thank you. The bottle will be well chilled, I know.'

As the maître gestured and his minion vanished, Zhang observed, 'The lamb is highly spoken of still, but I incline towards the suckling pig or the Bollito Misto myself.'

Huuk glanced up from Zhang to the maître. 'We will make our selection in due course,' he said. 'Perhaps you will bring the menu in ten minutes or so.' The maître bowed again and was gone.

As soon as they were alone, Huuk leaned forward. 'Brother

Dragon Head Tong,' he said gently. 'We are old friends. It is a pleasure to spend time with you. But I know the menu and the wine list here as well as you. This is not what we have come to discuss, is it?'

'No, Brother Huuk,' allowed Zhang Tong 'I have information. What do you know of terrorists?'

Huuk sat silently, turning the word over in his mind. Terrorists was a word with wide associations and many shades of meaning. It was a word that had been in its time applied to political opponents of one system or another. Half the people who had held the first meeting of the Chinese Communist Party in Sun Yatsen's house over on Xiangshang Lane in the French Concession in 1922 were calling the others terrorists before the year was out. Within five years, Dragon Head Du Yusheng of the original Green Gang was working with the Nationalists to smash the Communists – and they too became terrorists. After the invasions and atrocities of the terrorist Japanese, Chiang Kaishek's brief-lived Nationalist government became terrorists again when Mao Zedung and the Red Army marched into Shanghai. And when Mao was in power, and the Red Army was pursuing the Four Olds under orders from the Gang of Four, the whole country seemed full of terrorists and potential terrorists. Until Mao died and the Gang of Four themselves became terrorists.

While Huuk was turning these thoughts over in his mind, the wine waiter arrived with two bottles and an ice-bucket on a stand. He opened the Chablis for Zhang and placed the glass and the unopened screw-top Perrier bottle beside Huuk.

'Terrorists . . .' said Huuk, picking up his glass and polishing it thoughtfully with his napkin until he was certain it was clean and untainted.

'As careful as ever, I see,' observed Zhang. He took the bottle from the waiter, poured, placed it on the table and dismissed the servant with an imperial wave.

Huuk glanced down at his own busy hands. 'There was an emperor in the Western Roman world who died when he ate half an apple,' he said quietly. 'His murderer cut the apple for him and ate the other half in front of him. But he had painted one side of the blade with poison. The unfortunate emperor's side.'

'Men like us can never be too careful,' mourned Zhang.

'Just so, brother Tong, just so. But you were saying. Terrorists.'

'You crossed swords with some of them at the time of the Olympics.'

'Freedom fighters. Yes. The Tibetan monks who disrupted the route of the Olympic torch in England and America. Their supporters closer to home . . .' Huuk broke the seal on the Perrier carefully, listening for the reassuring snap and hiss. He angled the bottle and the glass towards each other. Began to pour.

'I had in mind the upsurge in terrorist violence among the Uighurs . . .' Zhang Tong swilled a mouthful of exquisite Chablis. Gulped it down like cheap rice wine.

'Our first recorded suicide bombings,' said Huuk. 'Well, we have opened ourselves to the West. We must expect Western-style atrocities, I suppose.' He sipped the Perrier.

The maître returned with the menus. Zhang Tong chose three things done with fois gras as his starter. Huuk chose the spring leaf salad. 'No Gorgonzola or walnuts,' he added. 'Bring oil and lemon. I will dress it myself.'

'Of course. And to follow?'

Zhang Tong chose the Bollito Misto in preference to the suckling pig. Possibly because there would be more meat in the combination of beef, veal, chicken, sausage and tongue. But that choice necessitated a big red wine as an accompaniment. Huuk chose the sea bass in herb crust. The maître promised that the sommelier would return with the red-wine list.

'So,' prompted Huuk gently. 'You refer to our own particular breed of Muslim fundamentalists . . .'

Zhong leaned forward. Something, possibly his woven cane chair, creaked. 'You say *our own particular breed*. I say there is no such thing. I say there may be, for lack of a better word, a *brotherhood*. Worldwide. Supported, perhaps, by the same powers that have supported the 9/11 bombers in America. The 7/7 bombers in London. The Madrid bombers. Who have supported the Chechyen rebels. The mujahedin. Al-Qa'eda. They may be in Afghanistan, the Gulf, North Africa, Pakistan. They may be opposed by the Western intelligence services when they target the West; but they might well be supported by the same people if they look east . . .'

'So,' said Huuk. 'You are suggesting that some Muslim Uighur freedom-fighters, who have just managed to organize suicide bombs in Xinjiang province for the first time, have taken a great leap forward. With the help of James Bond, Ethan Hunt and Jason Bourne. And have managed to shut down the Internet on the entire east coast of China?'

Zhang shook his head, clearly uncertain about the names Huuk

had thrown at him. But before he could reply the waiter arrived
with their starters and, at his heels, the sommelier. As Huuk sprinkled oil and lemon juice over his spring leaf salad, Zhang left his
pâté de fois gras unsullied while he discussed big red wines.
Eventually he settled on a 2002 South Australian Clare Valley
Armagh Shiraz which was, apparently, breathing up nicely in the
cellars below.

Then he turned to his food while Huuk returned to his conversation. 'I mean no disrespect by referring to famous Western films.
I simply mean that you seem to be suggesting involvement by the
CIA, the FBS and the British SIS in supporting Muslim extremists
here.'

'And the Pakistani ISI. Not to mention certain countries with
coastlines on the Mediterranean and the Gulf. But I'm not talking
secret armies here. Not what they call I believe black ops. Bay
of Pigs, Somalia or what not. I'm talking a little bribery to someone
in a local shipyard. Some explosives with a timer or a depth trigger.
A fast boat capable of sailing maybe a thousand miles at seventy-
five knots, with an extra fuel tank to cover the range. A GPS device
to reach the required location. A simple sonar kit capable of
tracking something big at depth. Some easily obtainable explosive.
A detonator.'

'You know of such an arrangement?' Huuk placed a delicately
flavoured leaf in his mouth and chewed carefully, the death of the
Emperor Claudius still somewhere on the fringes of his mind.

Zhang slid a telephone across the table. 'It is set. Press PLAY
and the video recorder will play back.' Huuk noticed for the first
time that on the smallest finger of Zhang's left hand there was a
tiny tattoo – almost like a ring. It was the character that signified
Green.

Huuk picked up the phone and pressed the button. He stopped
chewing. The telephone's screen filled with the unsteady picture of
a young man. His left arm was tied to a table in front of him,
stretched out with the hand spread flat on the wood. Angled almost
artistically between his spread fingers, the corner of its blade driven
deep into the tabletop, there was a meat cleaver. The background
was dingy, out of focus and cloaked in shadow but Huuk got the
impression it was in some kind of garage or warehouse. A boathouse, perhaps. He placed another leaf on his tongue. This one was
as bitter as endive.

'Yes,' admitted the man on the screen, so loudly that Huuk was forced to turn the volume down. 'Two men. Not Han. Dark skin. Curly hair and beards. Asking about boats. But I tell you I don't know . . .'

The picture jumped. Then returned as it was previously. Except that the cleaver was gone. On the other hand, the tethered man no longer had any fingers. 'A Cigarette,' the man yelled. Huuk was relieved he had the volume set so low. 'The Top Gun 38 GT.'

The screen flickered again. When it returned, Huuk automatically checked the fingerless hand. It was still in place. 'Twin Mercury outboards. The big 662SCIs. She should do seventy-five knots easy.'

The screen jumped. Cleared. The truncated hand was still in place. 'Fifty-five thousand American for the boat, cash dollars. Thousand-dollar bills. Then there was the extras.'

Zhang hissed. Huuk hit the PAUSE button and laid the phone face down on the table. The Bollito Misto arrived. The Shiraz accompanied it. The Chablis was moved into its iced bucket as though it was champagne. Apt enough, considering where the grapes came from, thought Huuk inconsequentially as the substantial remains of his salad were cleared away.

Then he noticed that in spite of the obvious swilling, there was only one glass of wine gone from the bottle. Zhang was being much more careful than he seemed. Interesting. He glanced up over the crusted sea bass that silently replaced the bitter herb salad. Zhong's red-wine glass was big; the serving of Shiraz in the bottom was modest in the extreme.

It was not until the waiters were long gone and his table partner was deep into the sizeable serving of tongue that Huuk hit the PLAY button once again.

For the first time the voice of the interrogator became audible. 'Extras?' It was a quiet voice, thought Huuk. A cultured voice. A professor's voice. A unique and memorable voice, with something about it that he could not quite place. He placed a sliver of the exquisite sea bass on his tongue as the victim gabbled his answer.

'Fuel. Obviously. Full tank and extras.'

'What range?' asked the inquisitor gently.

'Full speed maybe a thousand miles. Eight hours' sailing,' the victim expanded ingratiatingly.

'Any more?' the questioner asked.

'GPS. Garmin's biggest portable. Accurate to a few feet.' The extra detail again.

'And?'

'Sonar. Portable again but powerful. Gray DF2200PX.'

'For fishing, perhaps?'

'Too big for fishing. Boat, motors, GPS, sonar. Everything. Too big for fishing. Besides . . .'

'Besides?'

Just the way the word was said and then repeated stopped Huuk savouring the flavour of the perfectly cooked fish in his mouth.

The screen jumped again. Went black. This time there was no hand when the picture returned. The wrist was lashed with a thin woven-leather garrotte of tourniquet, but it still spurted weakly and oozed a little.

'American C-4 plastic explosive. Old but efficient.' The victim's voice was weak and shaky now. Huuk knew severe clinical shock when he heard it. 'Several kilos of C-4. Waterproof detonator. Radio-controlled. I told them they could set it off with a mobile phone if you could get a signal. But they were worried they couldn't rely on the signal.'

The screen jumped. Cleared. The forearm was still there – or half of it was. It no longer ended in the weakly spurting wrist. It ended in a bright red stump several inches below the elbow. The woven noose was as tight as it would go but it wasn't really stemming the flow of blood any more. 'Seventy-five thousand American all-in. Cash like I said. I can tell you where it is . . . You can get it easily. It's all yours. Seventy-five thousand American . . .'

'And what made you think the men were Muslim?' enquired that strangely unsettling voice.

'They were not Han. Their skin and hair. Round eyes with long faces and sharp bones. Their clothes were different from ours. Northern. I saw one of them wearing robes. Like what the men wear in Xinjiang.'

'How would you know what the men wear in Xinjiang?' purred the interrogator.

'Television. I've seen clothes like that on CCTV. In the cultural programmes. *Our Wonderful Country*. Bridget Wang the reporter did a series.'

The velvet voice thought aloud. 'It would be useless to ask you if you knew where two Uighur tribesmen would get seventy-five thousand American. But I can ask you to give me your best guess what they were planning to do with all the stuff you sold them.'

'I've thought about this a lot,' he said earnestly. His eyes were fixed on what was left of his arm. He did not look up at all. 'I've turned it over and over in my mind. I think . . . You know what I think?'

'Tell me,' said the gentle voice.

'You know that submarine? The one on CCTV? The one that's been searching for the Great Khan's treasure? I think they were going to track it on the sonar and drop a kind of C-4 depth charge on it.'

'Why would they do that?'

'Publicity,' he explained earnestly. 'Publicity for the cause. Like those Tibetan monks that went after the Olympic Torch. The hunt for that treasure was the biggest news story about China since the Olympics. They could easily make the People's Republic look stupid – and publicize their fight for independence. Like suicide bombers. But someone else doing the dying. Live on CCTV with Bridget Wang.'

'And how would they know where the submarine was?'

'Like I said. CCTV. Bridget Wang's been doing reports twice a day. All about the submarine. What it was looking for – the treasure ship. What it was finding – those undersea cables and so forth. They've been broadcasting pictures from the underwater camera they had rigged aboard. She even had diagrams on the screen. If those diagrams were halfway accurate then a Cigarette and a GPS could get you there. Sonar could find the sub. C-4 could blow it up. And that's what happened, after all, isn't it? The sub went down.'

'Yes,' said the gentle voice. 'That's what happened all right. The sub went down.'

The screen jumped. Went black. Flashed back for a second in a still picture. Huuk was so fixated on whether the arm was still there that it wasn't until after the screen went black for the last time that he realized this time the head was missing.

'Is that it?' he asked. 'Is there any more?'

'That's all,' said Zhang Tong.

Huuk switched the phone off and slid it back. His fish was hardly touched, but he was finished with it now. The plate opposite was almost empty. 'Your people?' he asked.

'Good God, no!' Zhang really sounded outraged to think that the Green Gang Triad might be associated with such brutality.

'Where did you get it?'

The Dragon Head shrugged. 'These things come to me,' he said.

Huuk nodded. 'You have given me,' he glanced down at the fish on his plate, 'much to digest.' He pulled out his phone and called his police driver. 'Where you dropped me,' he said. 'Five minutes.'

'Won't you stay for dessert?' asked Zhang Tong. 'The grand dessert platter . . . They have a truly legendary Muscat dessert wine . . .'

'Not dessert, I thank you,' insisted Huuk gently. 'Nor cheese. Or port. Though I understand they might still have some of the Taylor's 1948 squirreled away. Affairs of state beckon. And, of course, the information you have given me simply means I have more urgent matters to check up on. I thank you for your information and for your hospitality.'

Huuk stepped out on to Guangdong Lu precisely five minutes later. The pavement and roadway were thronging. His car had not arrived yet. He stepped forward towards the kerb and was immediately jostled by a young man in a designer suit who held a cellphone to his ear.

'Watch it, old man,' the young man snarled, pushing ruthlessly into Huuk's space.

Then he stopped, astonished, as the hand holding the cellphone flew up into the night sky. His head fell sideways on to his left shoulder, partially severed. A massive fountain of blood shot up into the air and fell back, thick and hot as monsoon rain.

Huuk stepped back at once, going down into a half-crouch as he drew the Rohrbaugh. The crowd on the pavement split apart, some of then starting to scream. He found himself at the heart of a clearing. The rude young man just had room to measure his length in the gutter, pouring life-blood into the drain. A tall man in black stepped over him holding a meat cleaver in his hand. The blade was dull and dirty. The edge was honed like a razor. Huuk shot him square in the face, point blank, knocking him back into the busy traffic as though he had punched him on the jaw. The gun jumped up in his hand, the tiny frame fighting to contain the kick of the massive load. Brakes squealed and something went *THUMP!* quite loudly. But Huuk was looking around for the next attacker. 'One,' he counted, tallying his shots with care.

Two came at him at once from either side, very fast indeed. He shot the one on the right in the middle of his torso, actually calling out 'Two!' as the gun kicked up again. The attacker sat down stupidly, surprised to find his legs no longer worked.

Huuk was down on one knee equally quickly, swinging the gun hard round. The cleaver hissed over his head. The attacker's legs collided with his shoulder, his stomach bashed into Huuk's ear.

Huuk pressed the Rohrbaugh's muzzle hard against the solidity of the pubic bone by his left cheek and ear, closed his eyes and pulled the trigger. This time the kick was lessened. Like sound and blast, it was soaked up by the attacker's clothing. But he was blown back as the bullet blasted in through the front of his pelvis and out through the base of his spine.

Huuk was up, his head ringing, but his hearing still clear enough to hear a familiar voice say, 'No!'

The professor/interrogator from Dragon Head Zhang Tong's brutal phone clip stepped forward, chopper at the ready. Huuk recognized the weapon as he recognized the voice – even from that one quiet word. And one glance at the last attacker cleared up the question that had lingered in his mind since the interrogator had first spoken to the fingerless – handless – armless – headless – informer. The professor was a woman.

'Four,' said Huuk and shot her between the breasts. She raised one hand – too late – as though to protect herself. The chopper span away. There on the base of the smallest finger was a tattoo that looked almost like a ring. It was the character that signified *Green*.

Huuk froze, his mind whirling. But only for the instant it took him to re-order his priorities. Then to make certain, 'Five!' he said. And shot her again between the eyes.

TWENTY
Treasure

Richard and Steadyhand guided *Neptune* across the ocean floor, their eyes riveted to the pictures transmitted back from the forward cameras. It was as dark on the surface as it was down in the depths but the AUV's headlights lit up the snaky line of the severed cable that they were using to guide them forward.

Poseidon's tannoy sounded quietly – so quietly that neither of the entranced men noticed it at all. Robin, standing behind them, glanced up briefly. Midnight, she thought. First officer to the bridge for the middle watch. That would be no hardship. No one aboard was asleep. Straightline would be on the bridge already, no doubt, standing at his captain's shoulder with everyone else aboard who could come up with an excuse to be watching the bridge monitors where *Neptune*'s video link was being relayed.

Captain Chang had briefed the whole crew at the start of the first night watch four hours ago after Tan had left to return to the destroyer and take the battered *Romeo* under tow. It had been a wise decision, supported by Richard and Robin. Keeping the discovery secret was clearly not an option. The alternative was trusting openness – which was in itself good leadership. And, as had been observed, they were in a communications blackspot – for the moment at least. As long as Broadband Dung could be trusted to keep a close eye on the radio then there would be no way news could get out.

Unless Shao Xiao Tan let them down, of course. But it was in the nature of things that news like this would run like water – there was no way of containing it for long.

The plan was simple, therefore; as agreed at the little briefing they had held late in the dogged afternoon watch. They would revisit the wreck, recover one single box containing enough treasure to support their story – together with the Khan's chop that would prove it – and return to Shanghai, contacting the authorities on the way. All they had done was to move the timescale forward. They reckoned on recovering their proof by the end of this watch and be docking in Shanghai at midnight tomorrow.

Or, in fact, thought Robin as the quiet chimes died and her watch showed the time as 00:01 local, midnight today.

'There!' whispered Xin.

Right at the outer edge of the creeping pool of brightness there was something pale and square. The two men automatically pushed their control sticks forward, making *Neptune* accelerate. The pale square seemed to rise up and come wavering towards them like a mathematical ghost. A ghost tattooed with a complex pattern of black lines. A ghost behind which the broken wreck of the sunken treasure ship loomed like something out of *Pirates of the Caribbean*.

When the Khan's branded chop filled the screen, Richard and Xin brought *Neptune* to a dead stop and let her hang in the still, cold water while they inspected the scene more carefully. What they were examining so closely was the top of a wooden box or crate that had partially exploded under the weight of the water and over the passage of time. Planks of wood drove down beneath it into the apparent softness of the silty mud that was the natural environment at the cliff foot. So different from the boulders that had been blasted down on to the submarine, thought Richard, still worrying somewhere deep at the back of his mind at the problem presented by the destruction of the cliff-top and the cables.

It was this, if anything, that made him unthinkingly tilt *Neptune* so that her lights shone up the cliff beside the wreck. And there, above the ancient vessel itself, right at the furthest edge of what the light could let the camera see, was the continuation of the overhang that had all but hidden the sunken sub. 'That explains a lot,' observed Richard. 'That overhang would hide the Khan's ship from everyone looking down from the surface.'

'No wonder she's been so hard to find,' said Robin.

'Until now,' murmured Richard.

As he spoke, Richard brought *Neptune* back down until the top of the Khan's treasure chest filled the screen again. On the soft mud beside it lay scattered the square objects that they had assumed to be ingots. Richard brought the first of these into sharp focus and a kind of sigh seemed to go through *Poseidon*. It was something subliminal but strangely audible. *Neptune*'s lobster claw moved smoothly down across the screen and reached gently out to touch it. The solid-looking cube slid back up the silty slope, then rolled over. 'That's not gold,' said Richard. 'Not heavy enough. Could be packing of some kind, I suppose.'

For a disconcerting moment he wondered whether the box might after all hold something like a washing machine. Or a refrigerator, factory-packed for transport.

'Well,' said Captain Chang's sharp voice, 'take what you can and get back.'

Richard and Xin moved *Neptune* back a little and released the cradle from her underside. The basket of woven wire netting settled on to the mud. *Neptune* flitted free and sailed back towards the box they had targeted. The second lobster claw joined the first. Steadyhand Xin held the vessel still while Richard slid the points of the claws under the branded lid. He closed them gently until the close-up showed the wood between them beginning to buckle. 'Lifting,' he said.

'Lifting,' echoed Xin.

As Richard retracted the claws slightly, Xin raised *Neptune* gently. The effect was to prise the whole wooden square free of the box it had guarded for eight hundred years or so. It came in one solid piece. Had there been fastenings or hinges they would have rusted or rotted to nothing centuries since, thought Robin.

Neptune swooped gently back to the netting basket and laid the wood in the corner. Then it danced back to the open box. The lights revealed a square of darkness reaching downwards like a little well. Or the mouth to a mine. Richard thought of Snow White. There would be room in this mine for a couple of her dwarfs, he supposed. 'Can we turn the brightness up?' he asked.

Xin touched a knob and the light intensified suddenly. The blackness was not vacancy. There was no mine shaft down here. There was more of the strange packing material. Richard reached a hesitant claw into the edge of the dark square. The packing yielded, seemed to be breaking apart. It lifted in the still water and oozed lumpily over the edge of the box. Richard shivered as though it was his fingers that were touching the strange material, not *Neptune*'s claws.

But then he touched something solid.

What sort of sensory magic was working here Richard would never know. But his hands on the controls felt quite clearly that the robot claws of a remote AUV the better part of a kilometre below him had touched something hard.

'Turn on the sound system,' he ordered. Robin reached in over Xin's shoulder and hit the switch. The ghostly whisper of the open channel echoed through the ship. Richard moved the claw again. A sharp metallic *clink*!.

'I think we're in business,' he said.

They deployed the water jet. The little hose was capable of pumping out water at considerable pressures, but they started on gentle. The strange rotting packing material lifted out and was easy to blow out of the way. Little by little they uncovered the shape of a bulbous football. Beneath it a long, squarish ridge. It was all black. Seemingly encrusted. Probably rusting or rotting, thought Robin, curbing her excitement by a sheer effort of will.

'I think I can get a half-decent purchase there,' said Richard after half an hour of painstaking work, when it became obvious that even on its highest setting the water jet wasn't going to move any more of the soft detritus out of the box. *Neptune* angled down. The camera gave a close-up of the strangely shaped football. Lobster claws reached down on either side of it to grasp firmly at the metallic ridge below. Richard closed them on to the metal, almost tempted to close his eyes – hoping to simply *feel* when the claws were closed tightly enough. But instead he divided his attention between the picture on the screen and the little red readouts that told him how much pressure each individual claw was exerting.

'OK, Steady,' he said, chickening out, when the red figures showed that the claws were exerting 75 per cent of maximum and the metal hadn't quite begun to yield. 'Let's go for a lift, shall we?'

Now his eyes flicked to some of the other readouts; particularly the one that monitored the load. It hadn't been worth checking with the box-lid because *Neptune* could handle a payload of 750lb. As he had himself proved by getting her to carry three grown men – albeit one of them was missing half a leg at the time.

Now, as Xin pushed the LIFT controls smoothly upwards, jettisoning water and filling the buoyancy tanks with compressed gas, the load monitor ticked past 500lb quite rapidly. It had reached 600lb before their objective began to stir. At 700lb the whole lot seemed to be lifting free and Richard had simply stopped breathing as he watched. But it carried on rising and it had just gone past maximum when the lobster claws failed and their objective settled back into its crate. *Neptune* went up like a balloon on a windy day and only Xin's quick reactions kept the AUV in the ball park. Still Richard got a close-up of the overhang above the treasure ship – from below and then from above.

'So near,' whispered Robin. 'So near and yet so far . . .'

'Go for it again, Steady?'

By way of answer Xin brought *Neptune* back down, trailing bubbles that looked like drops of mercury in the rear-view camera.

This time Richard set the claws to maximum grip. And they didn't bother getting fiddly or technical until the payload monitor was reading 700lb. Then Richard said, 'Easy . . .'

Steadyhand eased back on the lift and it seemed that the slowing of the exercise lent the AUV a vital element of extra power. Their objective began to stir again. At 725lb, it actually began to lift out of the box. As it came free, the monitor briefly maxed out. The figures froze on a bright red 750lb and for a moment Richard thought they were beaten. But then it eased back a pound or two and the job was done.

Working at the upper limit of its capacity, *Neptune* carried the contents of the box back to the cradle and placed it beside the black-branded lid. As soon as the lobster claws released their grip, the thing they had been carrying fell back. And there, on the black metal netting, lay a statue.

A frowning face glowered out from under a heavy war helmet. Squared shoulders were widened by overlapping tiles of armour. A deep chest and broad belly were contained in a massive breastplate. Armoured arms ended in gauntleted fists. One rested on the handle of a sword while the other held some kind of ceremonial mace. Metal skirts flared over mailed legs fearsomely booted. Richard was briefly put in mind of Snow White again. The statue stood perhaps a metre tall.

Without thinking, Xin brought *Neptune* down for a closer look at what they had recovered. The frowning face filled the screen. 'Do you think it's him?' asked Robin. 'Do you think it's Kublai Khan?'

'Looks more like Genghis,' said Richard. 'Fearsome little bugger.' But he spoke in a tone that told Robin he wasn't really paying attention to her or her thoughts. 'What?' she asked.

By way of answer, Richard's fingers moved. What had been at the edge of the screen came into the middle and the focus intensified under the added brightness of the extra lights. It showed the overlapping tiles of shoulder armour where Richard had closed the lobster claws twice during the lifting.

The black covering had been scraped away when the statue slipped on the first attempt. And underneath it there gleamed the bright, yellow, unmistakable sparkle of pure gold.

TWENTY-ONE
Genghis

'So,' said Robin much later as *Poseidon* raced through the last hour of the middle watch towards the morning and the morning watch – and Shanghai, which lay less than five hundred miles due west. 'Take me through this one last time. Genghis weighs as near as dammit seven hundred and fifty pounds.' They had decided to christen the statue Genghis when they discovered, as they lowered him on to the deck, just how much fiercer he looked up close.

'Maxed out the payload meter,' rumbled Richard from the top bunk. 'Damn near stripped the gears on the crane as he came aboard. So it certainly looks that way.'

'And seven hundred and fifty pounds is twelve thousand ounces.'

'That's right,' he answered with the certainty of an outstanding navigator used to doing calculations far more complex than 750x16 in his head. 'Twelve thousand.'

'And gold is standing at a thousand dollars US an ounce?'

'They use different ounces to weigh precious metals but not *that* different. So, again, yes.'

'So in melt-down value alone, Genghis is worth twelve million US.'

'Yup. Assuming he's pure gold. And that doesn't count the diamonds round the edge of his helmet and on his breastplate. The rings on his fingers. The pommel of his sword, which looks like a really big ruby. Or any of the other stuff.'

'Or the sheer incalculable historical value of the thing.'

'Agreed. Genghis is priceless.'

'Jesus! We'd better get him somewhere extremely safe and secure before news of what we've got gets out!'

'I know, darling,' he teased sleepily. 'These guys from the British Museum can be pretty cut-throat. And as for the Smithsonian Institute . . . I've heard *baaaaad* things. Not to mention the Chinese People's National Museum in Tiananmen Square! Now they really are frightening!'

'Sod off,' she said amiably. He answered with a snore that brought a grudging smile to her lips. 'Bloody man.'

But as she snuggled down, of course, her imagination was not full of museum curators armed with pens and chequebooks. It was full of cut-throat modern-day pirates and ruthless triad foot-soldiers armed with guns, knives and meat cleavers.

When her more gentle and ladylike snores joined his, Steadyhand Xin, who had been standing unobserved and unsuspected outside the curtain that served for a door to their cabin, smiled and started to make his way silently down the corridor. Goodluck and Goldenhair, he thought. They had certainly brought excellent fortune to the *Yu-Quiang*. And it was time to see whether some of it would rub off on him. The captain had warned them at her briefing that she was planning to collect all the mobile phones aboard at the start of the forenoon watch. He thought he would just see whether he could get his to raise some kind of service in the meantime. There were people he knew in Shanghai who would pay a great deal of money to know what they were bringing in.

Five hours later, at the beginning of the forenoon watch as promised, Captain Chang summoned the entire crew – except the watchkeepers – on to the foredeck. Everyone aboard surrendered their personal phone into a bag held, ironically enough, by Steadyhand Xin, who had spent a largely fruitless night made worthwhile only in the last few moments before he went on duty. Most of them were happy to do so. Shanghai was already only three hundred and fifty miles distant but most of their services would not be up and working for another fifty miles and more.

Genghis lay under guard, lock and key, in the main hold, surrounded by spare equipment, non-perishable foodstuffs and tins. The box-top bearing Kublai Khan's chop lay on a square of deck beside him, wrapped like a sandwich in wet paper. The security was frankly unnecessary. Both Genghis and his box-top were too bulky to be stolen by anything less than a crew of pirates. Genghis was too heavy to lift and there was no way to smuggle him off the ship. Only the jewels with which he was encrusted were any real temptation at all. But, given their size and provenance, rough-cut or not, they were nevertheless a potent temptation. And Chang, it seemed, knew her crew.

At least that was how it appeared to Robin as she watched the men in question exit *Poseidon*'s foredeck at a quarter past eight local time and go about their duties. She lingered, however, entranced by the way the morning was spreading out across the East China Sea. *Poseidon* was powering almost due westwards – the last heading Robin had seen was 265 magnetic, which was about right for these waters. Her preferred economic cruising speed was twenty-five knots but Chang had her running at more than thirty and she was kicking up a fine bow wave as she chopped ruthlessly through the lazy heave of the increasingly shallow waters. As she stood and watched, she saw the way in which the ocean's lazy movement changed almost imperceptibly as they crossed the hundred-metre line. In the last five hours they had run in from depths of nearly half a kilometre to less than a fifth of that. And between here and the entrance to the Yangtze, the seabed would shoal up until there were scant metres beneath *Poseidon* rather than tens or hundreds.

Robin went right out to the point of the forecastle head then, letting the wind tumble her hair as she drank it all in. The ocean heaved a little more restlessly, perhaps. There seemed to be a little more browny-grey in with the blue. The ship's whole demeanour changed subtly, as though she too felt how the bottom of the sea beneath her was sloping up with the steady inevitability that would eventually bring a shore. That might all seem very far away – *Poseidon* was still twelve hours out of Shanghai itself – but the shallows, the rules and regulations stood far out into the eastern sea. This wild, wide freedom had only a couple of watches more to go.

And as Robin wallowed indulgently in these thoughts she noticed something that was utterly and completely unexpected. A long, lean, powerful-looking launch came smashing eastwards through the gently heaving waters. When it saw *Poseidon*, it broke northwards in a long arc that brought it astern of the racing corvette. Then it fell into formation like a fighter plane, cruising easily off the starboard after quarter.

Robin went back on to the helideck to get a better look at the impressively sleek and powerful machine. On her way she met Zhong Wei, who was doing some maintenance work on the Chaig.

'Look at that,' she said.

'What?'

'That speedboat. It's following us.' It was only when she said the words that alarm bells really started ringing in her head.

'Where?' asked Zhong Wei, utterly unfazed.

'Back here.' She took him to the aft of the helideck and pointed down at the speedboat.

'Wow,' he said, clearly impressed. 'You don't see many of those around.'

'What is it?' she asked, her interest piqued.

'It's an American speedboat,' he answered. 'Just about the fastest money can buy. It's called a Cigarette.'

'It's bad,' opined Richard a few minutes later.

'I don't see how it can be anything good,' agreed Captain Chang. 'Shang Wei Jiang, what do you think? I've asked Broadband to try and raise him on the radio but he's not answering. We've tried all available bands and a couple of emergency channels. He doesn't want to talk to us.'

'Get Broadband to keep searching the frequencies,' said Richard. 'We may luck into him talking to someone else.'

The first officer looked down at the Cigarette, frowning. 'Word has got out already,' he decided forthrightly. He ran his hand back over the slick, shiny thickness of his hair. 'But I don't see how.'

'One Cigarette's not much to worry about, though,' said Richard bracingly. 'Even a big black silent one like that. I mean I know they were popular for running tobacco, cigars, cocaine and whatnot, but they're not all in the hands of the Mafia or the triads.'

'They cruise at about seventy-five knots and a big Top Gun like that can go faster,' observed Chang, still worried. 'Shanghai's the nearest port. If the Cigarette came out here at seventy-five knots, then she sailed, what . . .'

'Five hours ago, give or take,' supplied Richard. 'About the time we decided to bring Genghis home.'

'Shit,' said the captain. 'So it was a waste of time collecting the cellphones. Unless Broadband himself has switched sides. In which case collecting the cellphones was *still* a waste of time.'

'Looks like it,' agreed Richard. 'And in any case, you have to know that Cigarette is sending out locator messages to his friends and family at the very least. If he's on any kind of open channel then he's alerting the world and his wife.'

'What do you think we should do?' asked Chang, uncharacteristically indecisive.

'I think you'd better give the crew back their cellphones. That'll make them feel loved and trusted. Then, prepare to break open the gun locker,' said Richard roundly. 'You need someone trustworthy

who knows about guns to check your armaments, make sure everything is well oiled, fully loaded and in prime working order. Then
get ready to issue the guns at a moment's notice and start to repel
boarders. I think we've just sailed into pirate waters. And I don't
mean I'm expecting Henry Morgan, Long John Silver or Captain
Jack Sparrow, either.'

TWENTY-TWO
Pirate Waters

In spite of his last few words, Richard found himself humming the music from *Pirates of the Caribbean* during the next few hours. Lines half-remembered from the refrain and chorus that opened the third film ran irritatingly and all too prophetically through his head: 'Yo ho, haul together, hoist the colours high . . .'

Pushed to the limit, to the top of the green on the engine safety-monitoring system, *Poseidon* could run at a steady thirty knots, and with fuel to spare and the Cigarette relentlessly riding her wake, Chang saw no reason to slow. Richard agreed. He had faced pirates in the South China Seas when working out of Hong Kong and he knew they were ruthless, murderously violent and no joke at all. Both he and Robin had been lucky to survive their encounters and it was only the involvement of HK Coastguard Officer Daniel Huuk that had finally pulled their fortunes out of the fire. The Cigarette looked like a very bad sign to him, like the black spot Blind Pew passed to Billy Bones in *Treasure Island*. His inclination, like hers, was to run for cover with all possible speed.

Even so, it would take the better part of three full watches to bring *Poseidon* to safe haven, and the shallow seas ahead of her were complicated by more than the outflow of the mighty Yangtze River into whose wide mouth they were bound. For the better part of a hundred miles out, the charts showed complexes of routing measures, one-way systems, warnings, hazards, outright dangers and disturbingly variable depths littered with 'numerous wrecks'. None of which would affect the Cigarette – or any vessels choosing to join it with illegal plans in mind. Most pirate vessels here were small to medium-sized and very fast. The Cigarette probably drew less than eighteen inches. The largest he had seen himself drew a fathom at most; just under two metres. As he grimly observed, pirates could afford to work by pirate charts, not by the strictures of the Shanghai Port Authorities. But the directions on Chang's charts would slow things down and maybe foul them up for *Poseidon*.

Even so, at this stage Chang was still hesitant to call for help. If she had mistaken the intentions of the men in the launch, she would look foolish and lose face both aboard and ashore. Worse, she would make certain what she and Richard only suspected at the moment. For even a routine call to the port authorities or the coastguard would necessitate an explanation. And the only explanation she could offer involved Genghis – all $12 million-worth of him.

Captain Chang stood on her command bridge, therefore, and looked doggedly ahead through the still-crystal clearview. Richard for the most part stood at her shoulder, humming irritatingly, with the words of the pirate song circulating endlessly just below the surface of his subconscious. Unable to shake off a deepening sense of foreboding – and a strange feeling of unreality as the routines of the ship went on around him like the precision clockwork of his ancient Rolex Oyster Perpetual.

The crew went to breakfast. Neither Richard nor Chang ate, though Robin was careful to keep her energy levels high with a judicial intake of rice and fish. A routine Abandon Ship practice was held – but it stopped short of lowering what little they had left in the way of working lifeboats. At the end of it, the crew were invited to take back their cellphones as they returned to their duties.

At 11:00, three-quarters of the way through the watch, Chief Engineer Powerhouse Wang appeared on the bridge asking permission to slow the motors and check a bearing that was beginning to worry him. Chang just pointed to the big black powerboat that was bludgeoning through their wake like a triad footsoldier's meat cleaver.

He nodded and returned below.

Straightline Jiang, thoroughly in his element, checked his course every now and then, to ensure that nothing took it off its perfect plumb-line straightness across the Mercator-projection of his chart. After he came on watch at midday, he was able to check every fifteen minutes. And he had Steadyhand at the helm to make sure the sleek bow did not deviate by so much as a second of a degree.

At 12:30 the crew were sent down to lunch. Richard and Chang took noodle soup and sushi on the bridge, where Robin joined them. 'Get a grip, Richard,' she said bracingly – though she could as well have been talking to Chang. *Or to the wall*, she thought. 'One little pleasure boat jumps into your wake and you start to behave like this. What in God's name are you going to do if something really threatening appears?'

At the start of the evening watch she found out.

Robin came up on to the bridge at 16:00 carrying two cups of tea, determined to get Richard at least to relax a bit. She was all too well aware that he had spent a solid couple of hours in the gun locker with Zhong Wei, stripping, checking, loading and – where necessary up on the helideck – zeroing the corvette's modest stock of guns. She had bumped into him as he returned to the bridge after locking things up again an hour ago, wearing the aroma of gun oil as though it were an exclusive aftershave. It was then that she had decided on tea and a reality check – if not tea and sympathy.

But now she stopped in surprise, with the two teacups steaming fragrantly in her hand. Neither Richard nor Chang were on the bridge. 'Straightline?' she asked, for the first officer was lingering, making up the minimal logs of his uneventful watch.

The navigating officer pointed upwards. Robin nodded her understanding and rolled her eyes, then she climbed the last little external companionway up on to the open flying bridge immediately above the enclosed command bridge. Here, under the relentless thirty-knot headwind of a near calm, she found Richard and Chang with their eyes glued to binoculars.

'She's going at a hell of a speed,' Richard was saying to Chang as Robin arrived. 'Fifty knots? That's fast for a ship of her size. What is she? The better part of thirty metres long? Maybe a hundred feet. Looks like a British navy patrol boat or an American MTB. *Brave*-class vessels could run in excess of fifty-five knots. She's sitting high, too. Looks like she's drawing less than a fathom. Could she be anything official?'

'Not navy. Not coastguard or port authority. Not with those markings,' said Chang. 'Not that they'd be sending a pilot this far out – and without contacting us. How many would she have aboard?'

'As many as they could squeeze in, by the looks of things. She's as packed as a Philippines ferry,' said Richard. There was a little silence. Robin strained to make out with her naked eyes what the others were examining with their binoculars. And then with a start she saw it. Sleek, powerful, enormously fast-looking. Dead ahead and running exactly on a reciprocal collision course.

'What do you think?' said Richard, using that slow calm voice he reserved for when the going started to get tough. 'Think we should maybe break out the guns?'

'It's certainly time for me to call the authorities,' she said. 'You keep an eye on them. We'll decide about the guns later.'

Robin put down the teacups and picked up Chang's binoculars as the captain clattered down towards the command bridge. She pressed them to her eyes. The ship jumped into sharp focus, shockingly close at hand. Even head-on it was possible to see how long and sleek she was. The speed she was going was made all too obvious by the foaming wake she was generating from halfway along her length. Even with her foredeck crowded, her cutwater sat so high that she hardly had any bone between her teeth. 'He's showing off,' Robin observed, assuming automatically that the vessel was commanded by a man. 'He'll never be able to keep that speed up for any length of time. And if he's come from Shanghai with any plans at all to get back under his own steam then he's got to have extra fuel tanks stacked to the gunwales below. That's probably why the decks are so crowded.'

'What you see is what you get, you mean. Good thinking, darling,' said Richard.

'And you know that the reciprocal course is only showing off again,' she added. 'No way he's going to ram us with a shipful of friends more than two hundred miles from land. I mean, if these people are any threat at all – it's as pirates, surely. Not suicide bombers.'

'Good point again.'

'So he'll swing wide, cut speed, come up behind us past the Cigarette and try to get his men up over the stern or the side. Is that what you're thinking?'

'Yup. Unless he's got some kind of substantial weaponry aboard. Torpedoes, say, or rockets. Missiles.'

'Well, I suppose he could take out the command bridge with a missile and then hope to get his men aboard in the confusion. That might explain why he's charging down on us like that,' she said. Then, shocked at how swiftly she had been sucked into Richard's paranoid little world, she took a long, bracing draught of tea. But she did not remove the binoculars from her eyes. 'Still and all,' she continued, instantly revived, 'that boat must have left Shanghai at the same time as the Cigarette. It's just arrived later because it's slower. And the Cigarette must have left the moment we started heading home or a couple of hours later at the maximum – as soon as someone somehow raised the alarm. Not much time for planning or preparation. I can't imagine they'd just say, *Hey there's a boat with $12 million-worth of treasure aboard out there. Pass me the HJ-73 wire-guided missiles, would you? I'm going to get that sucker by teatime.*'

Richard had just given his characteristic crack of laughter, when the crowd of black-dressed men on the newcomer's foredeck suddenly parted. There was a sizeable puff of smoke, and a clear second later, a considerable *BANG!*.

By which time Richard had the hanging intercom hard against his lips and was yelling, 'Hard a-port. Hard a-port and clear the bridge if you can. We have incoming. I say again, *Incoming*!'

TWENTY-THREE
War

The instant Richard felt *Poseidon* heeling hard a-port, he dropped the handset to bounce on its suspended line and slammed the binoculars back against his eyes. He spread his legs to steady himself as he heard Robin stagger and the teacups crash on to the deck. They'd be lucky to escape with nothing more than some shattered porcelain, he thought grimly.

The automatic rangefinder readout on the bottom of his letter-box of enhanced vision showed the attacker's range as four hundred metres. But the closing speed was still nearly eighty knots so that was falling off rapidly. All of this went into his subconscious as he searched for the incoming missile, however. And there it was. Low above the water, coming at an incredible speed, leaving a trail of grey smoke to match the puff drifting away across the front of the opposite bridge. Maybe two seconds out from *Poseidon*'s own bridge.

But then, as *Poseidon* span on her heels, already going off-line, her motors screaming far above the top of the green and into the dangerous outer limits of the red, with her screws thrusting and reversing well beyond their original specifications, Richard glanced up. He didn't even have to move the binoculars. The attacker was turning port also, its course coming wide of *Poseidon*'s. The men on the foredeck were staggering and jostling each other. Between their legs he could see someone crouching over what looked like a black plastic suitcase. The missile operator, he thought grimly, trying to acquire control of his bird.

No chance. They had launched too late – with their target too close. Both vessels had reacted too swiftly and too violently. *Poseidon* particularly, with her instant alertness and her specially designed propulsion system. A seakeeper's dream. The controller needed a settled platform, a clear view and ideally some five hundred metres to get full control. None of which he had. Good enough. The approaching missile had all the electronic guidance systems of a moon rocket but they had been rendered about as effective as a

Neolithic spear. Even though the propulsion system was a little more advanced than a caveman's throwing arm. And the warhead, of course, would be just a little more effective than a flint.

So they just had to get out of its way. No trouble. Except that they had maybe one second to do so.

Poseidon heaved over a suddenly quartering sea, her heading running rapidly round to the south. Richard staggered and was surprised to realize how far he had also turned around. He had been so relentlessly focused on the incoming missile that he hadn't really registered that he was now facing starboard, not forward. And, he realized, starboard on the aft quarter, into the bargain.

That was Richard's last coherent thought before the missile hit.

After the shock-enhanced slow motion of the three seconds since its launch, the missile leaped aboard with ferocious speed. As Richard had observed, it was running low to the water, but it came up just before it hit – perhaps the controller had had a chance to pull it up to bridge height after all. It streaked in over the rails around the helideck and took the Chaig full on the angular glass-sided bubble of its cockpit. Richard had an instant mental flash of the short-bodied rocket with its four big tail fins in profile. It was one of those pictures that would linger in the memory like a photograph. Then the missile vanished into the Chaig and tore it bodily off the ship.

The Chaig and the missile together vanished sideways over the side, exploding into a considerable fireball about maybe twenty-five metres out across the ocean. The missile's momentum carried the whole thing further away from the ship so that the blazing wreckage fell like a crashing meteor, dragging its smoke tail with it down into the foaming sea. There was almost no backwash of force or flame to scorch *Poseidon*'s sleek grey side.

The same was not quite true of the sea, however. What fuel there had been in the chopper's tanks stayed on the surface and blazed briefly, giving the plucky little aircraft a kind of Viking funeral.

Richard staggered once again. This time collided with Robin, crunching porcelain shards to powder under his feet. *Poseidon* was twisting back hard a-starboard, leaving the puddle of blazing avgas like a submarine volcano erupting in their wake. He slammed the binoculars back under the overhang of his brows and brought the skimming profile of the pirates' boat into sharp focus. There was no sign of anyone getting ready to launch another missile.

He grabbed the wildly swinging handset and pushed the transmit button with his thumb. 'No sign of a repeat attack,' he yelled. 'Steady as you go.'

He released the handset and it jumped so high that it went over the top and came right round like some sort of fairground ride. But Richard didn't notice. He was still staring at the pirates. It looked as though they were planning to join the Cigarette in *Poseidon*'s wake and continue their attack by boarding over the side or stern. Just as Robin had suggested before starting to make jokes about pirates and whether they would have the time or the contacts to get hold of missiles.

'*Of course you realize,*' he whispered under his breath, still focused unrelentingly on the pirates, his voice pitched somewhere between Groucho Marx and Bugs Bunny, '*that this means war!*'

It was Richard's habit to say flippant things at serious moments. Evidence in all probability of too many youthful hours misspent in the celluloid company of James Bond and his ilk. But he knew just how serious this was. Even if the pirates did not have access to another missile, they certainly had access to a large number of ruthless and desperate men. And, as preparations for past and future Olympic Games had proved, the Chinese as a people had access to masses of unquestioning obedience simply undreamed of in the West. Chinese pirates, he knew from bitter experience, would quite literally *do or die*.

'We have to keep them from coming aboard at all costs,' he said to Captain Chang, speaking over the suspended handset that communicated between the flying bridge and the command bridge. 'They may be armed with knives and cleavers while most of us might have guns but they still outnumber us maybe two to one and if they get aboard it'll be all but impossible to stop them taking the ship.'

'But how do we stop them getting aboard? What weapons do we have other than the guns in the gun locker? We have no missiles on *Yu-qiang*, Richard.'

They were speaking English, except for Chang's use of the ship's Chinese name. This was the first time she had used his first name, however. A sign of desperation, he thought, if not of fear. Did she have a Western name, he wondered. Many Chinese took one as part of their English studies. He did not know hers. But he knew her Chinese name. 'I've been thinking about that, Jhiang Quing,' he said. 'And I think *Neptune* could fight an effective rearguard action.'

'*Neptune?*'

'*Mazu*.' He gave the AUV her Chinese name to emphasize his point. 'She is more or less indestructible, and she's armed to the teeth with a whole range of things that would make effective weapons even though they weren't originally designed as weapons.'

'But we are sailing at thirty-five knots. Not that we can keep it up for long. Powerhouse is having a heart attack and believes it's only a matter of time before his engines have one as well. The craft pursuing us are apparently capable of fifty-five and seventy-five knots. What chance does *Mazu* stand? She could not begin to keep up with any of us!'

'We have to slow things down, that's all,' said Richard.

The pirate boat settled in beside the Cigarette and hesitated in *Poseidon*'s wake ten minutes later. Whoever commanded her had clearly hoped the missile would do more damage, thought Richard. And now they were working on Plan B. As he watched them over the empty helideck from the height of the flying bridge he was aware that there was a bustle of activity behind him and below him. On the foredeck, *Neptune*'s crane was getting ready to drop her over the side, something they had never tried – or dreamed of trying – while sailing in excess of thirty knots. At the same time, the engineers, under the personal command of Zhong Wei, were bringing up cans of avgas – the now surplus lifeblood of the pilot's murdered baby. The immediate plan was simple enough. They would use one to cover the launching of the other. And, hopefully, to slow the pirates so that *Neptune* would have a fighting chance of doing them some serious damage. But they didn't want to make their actions too obvious. Richard swept the binoculars over the front of the foreshortened boat, all too well aware that someone back there would be watching him as closely as he himself was watching them. He pulled down the handset. 'Ready?' he asked.

'Ready,' came Chang's voice.

Richard hesitated, narrow-eyed, until Robin tapped him on the shoulder. She had left him alone up on the flying bridge five minutes ago while she had run down to get him one of the rescue flares from the battered lifeboats, and organize two lookouts to take position in the crow's nests halfway up the mast. 'Start pouring,' he ordered. 'And get *Mazu* ready to go over the side as soon as we slow.' He pulled the handset away from his lips. 'Robin, the captain will want Steadyhand at the wheel. That means *Neptune* is in our hands. Go down and get her fired up, will you? I'll be down when I've fired up the rest of this lot.'

Below on the after quarter of the weather deck, under the cover of the helideck itself, *Poseidon*'s crew were pouring avgas into the sea. At this speed, *Poseidon*'s wake started halfway along her length and ran apart quite swiftly. The gas being poured from that position flowed down the outer edges of the widening waves and spread rapidly across the sea behind them. But there was a central element to the wake, a foaming maelstrom churned by the racing screws. The gas poured straight over the stern into this was almost emulsified. It would take longer to settle out of the fizzing water and form a single flammable skin across the surface between the two wider slicks sliding down the outer edges and spreading relentlessly north and south of their course.

Richard felt the cool column of the distress flare along his lean cheek as he held the binoculars steady, his focus just in front of the pursuing vessels, searching in the white wilderness of water for that telltale oily rainbow.

And there it was. He dropped the binoculars to dangle round his neck. He aimed the flare, thankful that the target was so big that accuracy wasn't really going to be a problem. He fired. The ball of red fire soared lazily over the empty helideck, above the poop, across the stern, away out into the water behind *Poseidon*. And, guided by the good luck that had become his nickname aboard, it settled into the widest puddle forming there. In the dead calm on the warm water, it was still a foot above the surface when the sea exploded into flame. A wall of fire spread almost instantly across the central section of the wake – then, with no hesitation at all, it jumped to the north and south of *Poseidon*'s course, spreading exponentially.

Richard was in motion at once. He could feel *Poseidon* settle as the way came off her. When he pounded down the exterior companionway he could see *Neptune*'s yellow bulk being swayed out and dropped. He dashed through the command bridge, exchanging tense nods with Captain Chang. 'As soon as she's free, full speed ahead,' he said.

'As agreed,' she acknowledged. 'But only to the top of the green. The lookouts say the pirates have turned off course and are slowing . . .'

He was gone before she finished speaking.

* * *

Robin was ready and waiting in *Neptune*'s control room. The video
screens showed the familiar pictures with the water level halfway
up them. Richard settled into place and span the AUV until the top
half of the forward-facing screen was filled with fire. 'Full ahead,'
he ordered and the solid craft responded. As she surged forward,
her knot meter ticking up towards ten, he eased her under the water.
Just below the surface, the effect was very strange, for it seemed
as though the fire was somehow burning through the upper layers
of water. He went down a little further. The weird flame effect
swept over them. The forward screens began to clear. The pirate
boat was side-on immediately ahead of them. The profile of its
underside was disturbingly like the boat-belly breastplate that
Genghis was wearing downstairs.

Richard and Robin had been neither silent nor idle while *Neptune*
sped back along *Poseidon*'s blazing wake. 'We have to incapacitate them. Preferably both of them. But the big one at least,' Richard
insisted.

'Incapacitate,' Robin echoed. 'Not sink,' she emphasized. 'They
may be bad men but we don't want to turn them into roasted shark-
food.'

'If we get the chance to make that choice. Otherwise they're
toast.'

'OK. Best way to stop them without sinking them would be . . .?'

'Damage the propellers.'

'Agreed. But how?'

'We have jaws to bite and claws to catch . . .'

'*Neptune*'s not a Jabberwock, Richard. Grow up, for God's sake.
And if you're going to quote anything, try for something more
relevant than Lewis Carroll.'

'Sorry, darling,' he answered through gritted teeth. 'Just thinking
aloud. What would you like me to quote? I do a mean *Hamlet*:

' "For 'tis sport to have the engineer

Hoist with his own petar: and it shall go hard

But I will delve one yard below their mines

And blow them at the moon." How's that? Any better?'

As he spoke, Richard was bringing *Neptune* up behind the hesitating pirate boat. Twin screws filled the screen and behind them,
leading forward into the boat itself, two short drive shafts. The
propellers turned idly as the commander on the bridge tried to make
his mind up how best to get past the wall of flame. Between them
thrust a vertical rudder post with a hinge at the bottom in which

the rudder itself was set. There was a space of about six inches between the post and the blade of the rudder. The rudder hung as unemployed as the screws, also a victim of the hesitation on the bridge.

Richard did not hesitate, however. He had folded out the lobster claw during the first words of his Hamlet quotation and by the time he mentioned the moon he was holding one of *Neptune*'s shaped charges in it. Now he thrust the little high-explosive hockey puck unerringly forward. It wedged in between the rudder post and the rudder blade absolutely securely.

So that when the screws suddenly thrashed into life and the rudder blade went hard over as the boat leaped back into action, Richard's modern-day petar was even more immovably wedged in place. 'Count to five,' he ordered his gaping better half, 'then hoist the engineer – if not the colours. In the meantime, let's see if we can smoke that Cigarette, shall we?'

Five seconds later, the lookouts on *Poseidon*'s mast began to report to their captain the things they could see over the guttering wall of fire. The pirate boat was running at the better part of thirty knots along the edge of the thinning firewall, heading north and with only a few more metres to go before she could swing safely back into *Poseidon*'s wake. The Cigarette was behind her, on the same course and presumably with the same plans, but catching up fast. With her throttles wide, the speedboat was already at fifty knots.

Then a column of water shot straight up out of the sea beneath the pirate's stern. The boat leaped forward as though it had been booted roundly in the poop. Her forecastle plunged into the back of a wave, soaking everyone and everything on the foredeck, and washing several men overboard altogether. She spun helplessly aside and began to roll and flounder while the Cigarette roared past at sixty knots. But then, immediately in the speedboat's path, *Neptune* bobbed up like a floating reef.

Even had the Cigarette's driver seen the unmistakable, bright yellow hump of the hazard he would never have been able to avoid it. Instead he hit it, full-on. *Neptune* was bobbing up at full tilt, her ballast tanks blasted empty. The Cigarette was sitting at an angle of more than thirty degrees up by the bow. The two vessels came together at the very point where the wake began two-thirds of the way down the Cigarette's hull. She simply took off. Twisting slowly in the air like some kind of balletic projectile, she soared maybe ten feet up as she flew nearly a hundred feet forward.

It was just possible to see the figures of four men come flying out of the cockpit and go cartwheeling away into the sea.

The Cigarette hit the water upside down and tore herself apart in a great plunging mountain of foam that rocked her helpless companion on one side and extinguished the last of the floating fire on the other.

Then peace settled slowly on to the scene. And, just audible on the bridge as the lookouts completed their report and Powerhouse nursed his motors back to life, the sound of someone quietly whistling the jaunty theme tune from *Pirates of the Caribbean*.

TWENTY-FOUR
Authority

In the aftermath of the encounter with the pirates, Captain Chang gave permission to ease back on *Poseidon*'s speed. While she had no intention of returning and searching for survivors – not under the circumstances and not with a seaworthy if powerless vessel close by them – she did have several other priorities. And all of them necessitated slowing the ship dramatically. First, she had to recover *Neptune*. Xin took charge of this and remained almost hostile to Richard until he had swung her safely back aboard, gone over her with a fine-tooth comb and was certain that no real damage had been done to his beloved AUV. Next, Zhong Wei wanted to clear the helideck of the last remnants of the immolated Chaig and check the aft port quarter for any signs of blast damage. And, further, Powerhouse Wang was becoming really insistent over the matter of the overheating bearing – especially after the wild dash to the top of the red and the beyond-spec manoeuvring that had been going on so recently. And the revs had to be cut right back to allow him to work on that. Finally and most importantly, of course, Chang herself needed time to decide precisely what would be recorded in the ship's logs. And what would therefore be reported to the Shanghai Port Authorities.

'I had just raised someone at the Shanghai Port Office when you warned about the incoming missile,' she explained to Richard. 'So I never even finished identifying the ship, let alone passing any kind of message.'

'Possibly just as well,' he answered cheerfully, looking relentlessly on the bright side as *Neptune*, still in one piece, was swung gently back aboard. 'That means you can be selective about what you tell them now. I mean I doubt the pirates are going to file any complaints . . .'

'Not with the authorities at any rate,' interrupted Robin almost angrily. She was beginning to feel depressed in reaction to the overwhelming excitement of the action, thought Richard. 'But you can bet your life they'll mention it to someone.'

'They probably are doing just that as we speak,' Richard continued, crossing to the clearview and looking down on the sight of Xin bustling about securing *Neptune* back into her cradle. 'So we'd better get our story straight and report in ourselves ASAP.'

A little silence fell on the bridge. The three of them looked across at Straightline, who had been on watch for at least part of the adventure and would have to approve anything they recorded. But he was marking the line along the ruler's edge that would take them directly into the northern, west-bound section of the eastern lane of the Shanghai approaches routing-measure labelled A3 on his chart.

'I will have to reassess arrival time, allowing for our new speed,' he announced, as though he had heard nothing of their conversation. 'But, shipping aside, the channel is clear, thirty-four metres shelving to twenty-five in the danger zone where all six lanes of the first system come together. Then up again to thirteen metres if we follow routing-measure B2 into the next system. And nine point five metres if we continue along B1 into the mouth of the Yangtze itself. But by that time I expect we'll be under the direct control of the authorities if not of the pilot.'

Robin glanced across at Chang, suddenly struck by Straightline's words. What were the odds that the man who piloted them into the mouth of the Yangtze would be Captain Chang's father? Could she, in fact, request that her father come aboard and pilot them safely home? The idea was suddenly very appealing indeed.

By the time a slightly hangdog Xin had come up to report that *Mazu* was undamaged and to observe that Goodluck and Goldenhair had actually handled her well, the log was made up.

The discovery of a very elderly looking wreck and the recovery of some unremarkable items was all but glossed over. The Cigarette was mentioned only briefly. The sudden appearance of the larger vessel was described in more detail. Their utter amazement to find themselves being pursued, under fire and observing the loss of the Chaig was detailed almost exactly – 'Someone's going to pay for that chopper,' Chang insisted. 'And it's not going to be me!'

'So that bit's got to be accurate enough to stand up in an insurance-claims court, is that it?' asked Richard.

'You bet!'

'Shouldn't be too much trouble getting supporting evidence,' he told her cheerfully. 'I'll bet a couple of the guys will have videoed it on their phones.'

She went pale. 'Would they have videoed *everything*?'

'Shouldn't have thought so. Things got hectic and hairy after that, didn't they? But that rocket. It has YouTube and MySpace written all over it.'

'When the Internet comes back up,' added Robin. 'I think it's still down. How long is that now?'

So they were confident enough to agree that the fire in *Poseidon*'s wake started when the blazing wreckage hit the water. And it was easily sufficient to make pursuing vessels turn aside in wild confusion. Leading to the collision that crippled the larger vessel and destroyed the Cigarette. Problems with *Poseidon*'s own engines – in particular concern over a badly overheating bearing – prevented any rescue attempt, but *Poseidon* was able to observe everyone back safe and sound aboard the crippled but seaworthy vessel. Shanghai Port Authority alerted. Coastguard asked to assist the marooned men.

'Think they'll buy it?' asked Robin, still looking on the dark side.

'I would,' said Richard bracingly. 'In fact I'd probably give it the Booker Prize.'

'Well, it sure as hell wouldn't get this year's Pulitzer for accurate reporting!' she snapped back.

'Probably deserved the Nobel for Literature,' he answered so airily and childishly that she was forced to chuckle.

'Shakespeare couldn't have done it any better,' she allowed at last. 'Though he'd probably have put it in blank verse.'

Captain Chang walked away from this as soon as she realized it was neither very serious nor even slightly relevant to the making of her report. Which she had better do post haste as it was already logged as having been done. She looked into the radio shack and said to Broadband, 'Get me the Shanghai Port Authority, would you?'

The person who took Captain Chang's call was called Bing Yuesheng – Big-Eared Bing. As with so many Chinese he was named for his attributes. And there is no doubt at all that his ears were big. As indeed were his buck teeth and his Adam's apple. Bing was also known as Chatterbox, because it was one of the absolute given rules of the Port Authority Building that anything that Big-Eared Bing learned became public knowledge with uncanny rapidity. As the call from *Yu-qiang*, also known as *Poseidon*, came in, Bing was sitting at his desk in the new Port Authority Building on Dongdaming

Lu, just down from the International Passenger Terminal. He had headphones positioned extremely uncomfortably over about three-quarters of his ears. He had a microphone stalk that kept bashing unsettlingly against his lips and teeth. And he had in front of him a computer screen filled with contacts, maps and diagrams that had been piped through the system, saved and updates. He hated his earphones, he mistrusted his mic and he truly missed his Internet access.

Big-Eared was lowly in almost every way. He was among the most junior of the Port Authority officers. He had passed out of a lesser university with an almost mediocre upper-second-class honours degree. He had failed to achieve his objective of going to Jiatong University because he had been doomed to a lesser school. And he had been robbed of a first-class secondary education because his parents were second-generation farmers from that area east and south of Yongxu that had been flooded by the Three Gorges Dam. In Shanghai they had found only the most menial of employment and, although they had worked their fingers to the bone, all they had achieved in life was to fail their only son. The room he worked in reflected his lack of face and standing. It was shared with several others. It was physically low within the tall new building. It had one high window which looked over the Huangpu at the lower stories of the architectural fairyland that was Pudong. But as there was usually either river mist, city smog or rain beating against the dirty glass, Bing and his co-workers had long since stopped looking at the view.

In fact the only thing that gave Big-Eared Bing any real hope of making progress towards the power and respect he felt he deserved was a little tattoo that was still so new it was itchy. It was on the last section of the smallest finger of his right hand. It was the character that signified *Green*.

Now, suddenly, his screen lit up, his earphones chimed and he said, 'Port Authority,' into his microphone.

'Shanghai Port Authority,' came the distant contact. 'This is Captain Cheng Jhiang Quing of the vessel *Yu-qiang*, also known as *Poseidon*. Identity number . . .'

As Chatterbox Bing punched the details of identity number, position, course, speed, heading and destination into his computer, so little red flags began to light up on the screen. He continued to feed in Captain Chang's report of her adventures with the unnamed but apparently hostile vessels, so more red flags lit up. By the time he had taken down the full details and assured the worried captain that he would alert the coastguards on her behalf and get the stricken vessel and its strangely armed crew some kind of help, the computer was directing him to do a fair amount else besides.

Shanghai Museum would need routine notification about the incoming artefact. That was standard procedure. Even though the captain made whatever she was bringing in sound almost worthless and of little historical interest. But even so.

And, next, in one of the offices more elevated than this one in the building above him there was the Commissioner of Wrecks. He would need to be notified of *Poseidon*'s discovery. Though again, the wreck she had discovered seemed to be of little interest and no particular value. And lay too deep to bother either the coastguards or the chart-makers in the hydrographer's office.

Thirdly, there seemed little doubt that some type of weapon had been fired, leading to the destruction of a Chaig helicopter. It was standard procedure to contact the relevant section of the Commissioner of Police's organization in their offices overlooking Renmin Park. They would probably want to spread their nets wide, and Bing would not be surprised if he was soon contacted by someone from Army Intelligence.

There was a duty to be done that was prompted by something beyond the little red flags on the screen. Bing had not been accepted into the resurrected Green Gang until recently. The ceremony had been simple – little more than drinking the blood of a black cockerel and swearing an oath. And, of course, holding his hand still to receive the tattoo. But his position in the triad had been set and his duties clear. He must report all ships' movements to Flatface Ang, who owned a boat-rental business down in the Shanghai dock area. It was a duty that must be fulfilled in spite of the rumours that Ang in fact was an undercover operative for another triad entirely – and that he had recently been discovered floating in the Suzhu Creek with most of his left arm missing. But he would report in nevertheless, and the message would be received by someone – and, no doubt, go on up the ladder of power towards Zhang Tong, the Green Gang's current dragon head.

Next, there was a favour to be given. Even as a Green Gang Triad member, Bing did not yet enjoy so much face that he would willingly pass up the opportunity to add to it. A request had come in from the Pilots' Office. The nearly legendary Yangtze River Pilot Grandfather Chang had asked to be notified of any information concerning the vessel *Yu-qiang*, which everybody knew was the command of his brilliant but amazingly ugly daughter.

And, finally, there was a tiny circular request that the office of Port Authority Director Lu should be notified of any incident that involved one of those strange American super-fast powerboats they called Cigarettes.

In his mind, Chatterbox Bing put all of his duties in order. He would call the director's office first and Flatface Ang or his two-armed Green Gang replacement next; he would call River Pilot Grandfather Chang last.

He reached for the phone and dialled.

'Yes?' came a curt voice on the other end of the line.

'Port Authority Officer First Grade Bing,' he said formally. 'I wish to report an incident regarding a Cigarette.'

'Wait! Transferring you now.'

'But . . .' The telephone buzzed at him sufficiently loudly to hurt his ears. But before he could react the connection was made.

'Director Lu speaking.'

Bing gobbled a little like a turkey. Took a deep breath and repeated, 'This is Port Authority Officer First Grade Bing, Mr Director,' he said. 'I wish to report an incident regarding a Cigarette.'

'Where?' barked Director Lu.

Bing gave the coordinates that Chang had given him. There was a short silence. Bing strained his ears and was just able to make out a muffled conversation. Director Lu had put his hand over the mouthpiece of his phone. Then he was back. 'Transferring you now . . .'

This time the buzzing in his ears was loud enough to hurt. He grabbed at the headset and bruised his lip between the mic and his incisors as he moved it. 'Ow!' he said. 'Shit! That really . . .'

'Who is this?' snarled a new voice. Just the way it spoke sent shivers down Bing's spine. In his worst nightmares this is what he had dreamed that the voice of a triad dragon head like Dragon Head Zhang Tong would sound like. A very angry dragon head. But no, he thought, sucking blood from his lip. This was actually worse.

'This is Port Authority Officer First Grade Bing,' he said formally, as soon as he could. 'I wish to report an incident regarding a Cigarette. Who is this?'

'This,' said the terrifying voice at the far end of the line, 'is Deputy General Commissioner Huuk of the Institute of Public Security . . .'

TWENTY-FIVE
Management

*P*oseidon entered the Shanghai Approaches Routeing Management system at 31 degrees and 7 minutes north latitude, 123 degrees east longitude as the bridge chronometer clicked up to 23:00:00 hours local time, ten hours later. She was heading due west, 270 degrees, allowing for magnetic variation, and proceeding at twenty knots as requested by the Port Authority standing orders for the management system.

It was the fag end of the first night watch and the third officer should have been in charge of the bridge but both the captain and the first officer were there as well, as were the owner and his wife. They entered the northern, inbound channel of the leg marked A3 on the chart, and registered their course, speed and position with the relevant authority, as though they were an airliner coming on to its long finals before landing.

'The only drawback to having gone for the Nobel Prize for fiction with our log entry and report,' observed Robin, 'is that they don't know where they should be putting us. We really need to be going into a secure anchorage with severely limited access and lots of armed guards, especially as guys with missiles are likely to have equally well-armed friends. But as it is they could well just stick us down in the Luhuadao anchorage and leave us hanging out to dry.'

'That's possible,' allowed Richard. 'But it's not very likely. They'll read between the lines at the very least. Look what we've done, even according to the edited version. We've helped rescue a trapped submarine crew. We've found a wreck in the area they were treasure-hunting. We've been attacked by missiles, possibly by pirates. And we've brought home some artefacts of unknown provenance. They're not just going to let us hang in the wind. At the very least they'd be worried that Bridget Wang would get to us, even if they didn't think pirates or triads were much of a threat.'

'I agree,' said Chang. 'Straightline, watch your course.' She turned and called into the shack: 'Broadband, stay in contact with those ships as well as with the management team at the Port Authority.'

Robin glanced out of the clearview. She could see Captain Chang's point. After their experiences in the empty vastness of the eastern Yellow Sea, the bustle here was deeply unsettling. Especially since the only vessels they had seen since the People's Liberation Army Navy left were enemies. They had come on to the management system close behind a big freighter. Another vessel had already settled into their wake. If she looked left, she could see the lights of ships coming out of port, looking like a huge freight train being pulled relentlessly eastwards.

Robin had always considered herself the practical one and Richard the romantic. And yet she was vaguely disappointed that the big ships coming past her were the faceless universal tankers, freighters and container ships that would have been just as much at home in the ship-management systems of the Channel or the Strait of Hormuz. Where were the great square-ended junks with their rice-paper sails strengthened like kites with bamboo struts? Where were high forecastles and fortified poops, the four-, six- and eight-masted monsters of legend? Where were the living descendants of the dead wreck they had found so recently?

Long gone, she decided sadly, turning away at last. Suddenly exhausted she said to Richard, 'I've had it, darling. I'm off to my bunk now.' And when he turned to look at her it seemed to her that he was gaunt with fatigue. His cheekbones looked unusually sharp – even with the bruising and scarring on one; emphasized by the hollowness of his grey-stubbled cheeks and the dark rings under his eyes.

'Yes,' he agreed. 'There's nothing but routine ship-handling for the next watch and more. I think I'll get my head down too.'

Down in their cabin, as Richard was tugging his clothes loose and getting ready to climb into the upper bunk, Robin suddenly took his face between her hands. 'Are you all right?' she asked, allowing some of the worry that had plagued her so much for so long actually begin to show.

'Fine.' He gave a lopsided grin.

'Really? The face doesn't hurt too much? I was worried your cheekbone was cracked.'

'Smarts a bit sometimes,' he admitted. 'But it's nothing really. I say, I think the scar'll look a bit dashing, don't you? Very Henry Morgan.'

'Oh that's all we need,' she said wearily, giving up at last and dropping her hands to her sides. 'Another bloody pirate.'

*   *   *

While Richard and Robin grabbed some well-earned rest, Captain Chang oversaw her command's first hour or so of passage through the A3 leg of the Shanghai Approaches. Then she handed over formally to Straightline, who was born for this kind of work. 'Call me at the least sign,' she ordered as she pulled the bridge door open.

'Yes, Captain,' he answered, flinging the words over his shoulder with no intention at all of obeying her order. Then, with the bridge to himself except for the helmsman, he guided her through the middle watch into the hazard area at the inner end of leg A3, across and down leg C2 with his heading religiously 240 degrees after having checked the current local magnetic variation. For the next few hours he guided *Poseidon* as directed by the managers at the Port Authority, between Changjiang Anchorage Number 2 to the north and Changjiang Anchorage Number 3 to the south. Just before the end of his watch, at a little north of 31 degrees north and 122 degrees west, he swung on to 283 degrees, carefully double-checking the magnetic variation once again.

When Captain Chang returned to the bridge at the beginning of the morning watch, she found him proceeding with caution against a falling tide along the channel to the north of the wall of warning lights and buoys, with his echo-sounder checking the all too variable depths beneath *Poseidon*'s keel.

'The forenoon watch should find us entering the narrower management lane of Nancau Hangdau, Captain,' he announced by way of greeting. 'But there'll be more buoys and lights. It'll be daylight then, so we won't need the lights so much.'

Three hours' power nap had sharpened her. 'Let's not get ahead of ourselves,' she said. 'Did everything go all right through your watch?'

'Yes, Captain. Nothing to report.'

'Good. Go and get some rest now, Straightline. I'll want you on top of things when we go into Nancau Hangdao. And I'd be grateful if you could stay handy even if they send a pilot out to us.'

'Even if it's River Pilot Grandfather Chang, Captain?'

'Especially if it's Senior River Pilot Chang. And, now I think of it, if you see Steadyhand, tell him I want him sharp and fresh and on the helm for the forenoon watch as well.'

'Yes, Captain!' Straightline doubled off the bridge and Chang heard him clattering down the companionway towards his bunk. Then she crossed to stand beside the helmsman's right shoulder and stared out along the narrow, illuminated pathway of shipping lane C5 which would take her straight to the Nancau Hangdao channel and into the mouth of the Yangtze itself.

As Chang Jhiang Quing stood on the bridge of her command looking through the ghost of her reflection towards the mighty river that had been the mother, father and protector for generations of her family, she thought back to what she had told the *gwailo* Goldenhair. She liked the Western woman and had honoured her with her reminiscences. But she doubted that even her daunting husband the Goodluck Giant – who seemed to have unusual insight into the workings of the Middle Kingdom – would have really understood. The lengths that even an architect might sometimes have to go to get her buildings completed. The need to do such things when the Green Gang controlled the labour market now in much the same way as it had done in the 1930s. But the need to get the job done and the wages in to pay the extra fees for the brightest girl in the best school in Shanghai.

The terrible cost in loss of face to the captain of a big river boat and sometime coastal trading ship to find himself no longer master and commander – employed as a mere ferry captain. Like a Formula 1 racing champion forced to drive a bus. The way that face was only partially restored by becoming a river pilot. Even one whose name *Grandfather* seemed to signify affection and respect.

How much affection and respect would there be between them if he did come aboard *Yu-quiang* later today? she wondered. For, unusually among her generation – or so it was said of the self-centred Little Emperors who had risen from the One-Child policy – she had a lively and sympathetic understanding of what it had cost her parents to make her what she had become.

And what Shao Xiao Chang Jhiang Quing had become was the very thing her father had loved and given up to make her dreams come true: the captain of the most beautiful ship in all the world.

How could he ever forgive her for that?

Poseidon entered the inbound lane of the Nancau Hangdao channel early, before the forenoon watch was called. With the rising sun exactly behind her, she cast a long dark shadow across the channel as it angled away between the well-marked shallows of the sand-banks reaching out astride the main river-mouth called Nancao Shuidao. Nancao Shuidao was the southernmost of the three great routes through which the Yangtze came down to the sea. From

Changjiangkou Beijiao point in the north to Nanhui Zui in the south, the mouth of the great river was nearly eighty miles wide. But the broad, all too shallow flow was split into three by two great islands. The southernmost, little more than a massive mudbank revealed by the river's faltering outflow, was Jiuduan Sha. The northernmost was the much higher Changxing Dao, which extended eastwards into Hengsh Dao, separated by little more than a muddy gutter of a channel.

Richard and Robin, both refreshed, showered and shaved as appropriate, came on to the bridge just as the rising sun revealed the great brown whale's back of the Jiuduan Sha mudbank away on the starboard forward quarter. It seemed to be alive with birds, which made columns of dazzling white brightness against the deep blue of the sunrise sky. To port, away across the muddy wash of the river itself, long gold searchlight beams illuminated the feverish workings of the Hangzhou Bay Port Facility, which was still being constructed but nearing completion now. A trick of the light made the southern channel and the banks that contained it remain in shadow further upstream. A low mist made the still-dark backdrop behind the birds and the building works unsettlingly insubstantial. Even the ships sailing in line ahead like an ancient wooden-walled attack formation seemed to dissolve into the spectral greyness.

'Spooky,' said Robin, straining to see further into the shadows, following the vanishing hulls ahead until they became pale glitters of fading light in the distance.

And out of that strange grey distance, seeming to solidify out of darkness like a special effect in a horror movie, a helicopter appeared. It pulled itself out of the mist like a vampire bound for its coffin at dawn, swinging wide enough to scatter the column of birds, then it zeroed in on *Poseidon* and began to approach in a determined line that Straightline would have heartily approved. Broadband stuck his head out of the radio shack. 'River pilot coming aboard,' he said. Then he repeated, 'River pilot.'

'Is it usual to send a pilot out this far?' asked Richard amid the bustle that Broadband's announcement stirred.

'We're getting special treatment, obviously,' answered Chang curtly.

Richard turned to Robin. 'See?' he said. 'I told you that report was enough . . .'

But he stopped when he caught sight of Robin's frown. She was looking at Chang and on second glance, Chang looked worried too.

'What?' he asked.

'Something's not right,' Chang answered. 'The pilot is too early. There's really no need to send us a river pilot if we're just going to dock in Shanghai. The routing system will take us to the mouth of the Huangpu. If we need piloting down to Shanghai or Pudong from there then that's where the pilots should come aboard.'

'So?' asked Richard.

Chang swung round to face him squarely as the Port Authority chopper swung out of the lower sky behind her, heading for the helideck. 'If they send us a river pilot now, then maybe they do not want us in Shanghai.'

'If not Shanghai, then where?'

She glanced through the clearview at the dull grey ghostliness ahead. 'Upriver,' she answered.

Their interest piqued, Richard and Robin joined Chang on the helideck for the formal little ceremony of welcoming the pilot aboard. On the way down from the bridge they passed Straightline coming up with Steadyhand at his shoulder. 'Everything must be perfect,' ordered Chang.

'Perfect. Yes, Captain,' echoed Straightline.

'I will bring the pilot to the bridge as soon as he has come aboard. You will have signed on the log, even though we are a little early.'

She threw this last instruction over her shoulder as she hurried down the corridor, with Richard and Robin at her heels. The three of them came out on to the helideck as the chopper touched down. Richard and Robin stood casually, with only general anticipation and with no sense of foreboding at all. Chang was settling and twitching her captain's uniform into the closest to perfection she could achieve, as though she were going to meet the chairman, not the pilot.

Richard had expected the Port Authority helicopter to almost hover there, ready to swoop away the instant the pilot stepped on to the deck. Such vehicles were expensive to run and consequently kept as busy as humanly possible. But no. The chopper settled, squatting on its undercarriage as its full weight came down. The rotors began to slow.

The side door opened and a slight figure emerged, his almost boyish form clad in the most perfectly pressed uniform Richard had ever seen. Shoes that would have flattered a Guardsman on parade brought him swiftly but unhurriedly across the deck until the pilot faced the captain. They were oddly identical in height. The peaks of their formally squared caps almost touched. It was a wonder they did not knock each other's headgear off when they both saluted, with movement and timing so identical they might have been each other's reflection. To Richard – even with his insight into the workings of the Middle Kingdom – their Han faces looked remarkably similar. They could almost have been brother and sister, he thought.

'Welcome aboard, Pilot,' said Chang.

'Thank you, Captain,' said the pilot.

Chang turned. 'May I introduce you to the owners?' she said in her most fluent and perfect English. 'Captain and Mrs Mariner, this is Senior River Pilot Chang.'

Now there's a coincidence, thought Richard and he opened his mouth to pass a remark as the pilot reached out to shake his hand. But Robin kicked him in the ankle and managed to shut him up.

'Shall we go on to the bridge now, Father?' asked Chang hesitantly as Robin shook the pilot's hand and Richard blinked the tears out of his eyes.

'Not yet, Captain Chang,' said the pilot, his voice crisp and formal, lacking in any emotion. 'I must first deliver a message. Captain Mariner, Mrs Mariner, the helicopter is waiting for you. Would you please prepare yourselves to fly over to Shanghai. You have a meeting scheduled in a little more than an hour's time.'

'A meeting!' said Richard, stunned. 'A meeting with who?'

'I believe it is with the Deputy General Commissioner of the Institute of Public Security,' answered Senior River Pilot Chang.

TWENTY-SIX
Security

'The Deputy General Commissioner of the Institute of Public Security! And who the hell's he when he's at home?' demanded Richard ten minutes later, as he buckled himself into the passenger seat of the Port Authority helicopter. His tone was almost dismissive, almost angry; and perhaps just a little apprehensive.

'More to the point, my love, is *why does he want to see us*?' added Robin. Her tone was lighter on dismissiveness, heavier on worry.

The Port Authority helicopter swooped across the lines of vessels moving relentlessly into and out of the Nancau Shuidao and climbed up over the shoreline above the building site that was soon to be the updated Hangzhou Bay Port.

'I don't know,' said Richard, tightening his seatbelt with a jerk that put both his white uniform trousers and his starched shirt at risk. 'Maybe it's a bit of both. *Who* is he? *Why* does he want to see us?'

'I don't see that it can be anything good,' worried Robin.

'Don't be silly! What have we done that could possibly get us into any trouble with anybody? They probably want to give us an award for saving their submarine. Medals, maybe, like in the Olympics. Like they gave to the aid workers who helped clear up after the earthquake in Olympic year.'

Robin did not say *Get a grip!* But she thought it. She tightened her own seatbelt, but less severely than his. She had changed into her one good semi-formal outfit and she didn't want to crease either the high-waisted blue linen trousers or the cream-coloured brushed silk of the blouse. She patted the cream lapels of the collar and wondered whether she might have gone too far with the plunging neckline and the power-cleavage below it. From this angle she could see the lace of her bra cups, low-cut though they were. But she could not envision any Chinese official, even the Deputy General Commissioner, getting close enough to catch an eyeful. Then she ran her fingers through the short-cropped riot of her golden curls and looked out of the window beside her.

After the ants'-nest activity of the nascent port facility, the countryside of the Shanghai Shi seemed flat and dull. The chopper climbed over green fields fighting a losing battle with urban sprawl and crossed the coast road to Huangwan and Hangzhou at a height that made the traffic look like Dinky toys. When he swung north, the reason for his care became obvious – they were crossing the flight path into Pudong International. Looking south and west the sky had seemed as empty and featureless as the plain that stretched away into the hillock of She Shan with its oddly out of place Catholic basilica. As soon as they turned, however, the sky seemed to teem with planes settling towards Pudong Airport like the seabirds whirling over Hengsha and, more distantly on the far side of the city, Hongqio.

The ground also bustled. The long line of the Maglev running in from the international airport seemed to heave with trains skimming in either direction far faster than the chopper itself – or most of the aircraft rising or falling above them. Grey lines of urbanization followed every road or railway, making spider webs against the green. Some houses in the outskirts, but mainly factories that sucked in what the great freighters on the Yangtze brought and poured out the goods they carried away again.

The chopper swept over Zhoupu, settling a little as it did so, with the ring road ahead and the colossal Shanghai–Hangzhou expressway teeming with freight traffic away to their left. She had read somewhere that two-thirds of China's foreign trade came through here one way or another. The road ran north as well, she knew, hopping along the increasingly precipitous shoreline of the river up to Nanjing.

Beyond the ring road, Pudong itself reared in the early morning brightness as though an entire city could be Disneyland. In no time at all they were among the fairy-tale towers, weaving between the high points of the Jinmao Tower, the Oriental Pearl TV Tower and the Shanghai World Financial Centre. 'Where exactly are we going?' Richard asked the pilot in Mandarin as they swooped over the heaving Huangpu River and over the Port Authority Building itself.

'I have been ordered to take you directly to the Central Police Administration Building,' answered the pilot.

'Did he say the Central Police Administration Building? That can't be good,' called Robin.

'We'll soon see,' answered Richard bracingly. 'I'm sure it's nothing to worry about.'

There was a helipad on the roof of the Central Police Administration Building and as they approached it, Robin looked down. She was just in time to see a squad of armed guards form up. There were half a dozen of them and they seemed to be carrying Kalashnikovs. 'Richard,' she called nervously.

'That's nice,' he said drily. 'They've sent an honour guard. Look at those Type 56 assault rifles. You can hardly tell them from the old AK47s, can you?'

Before she could actually scream – more with frustration at her husband than in fear of their situation – the helicopter touched down. Richard snapped his seatbelt loose and hit the door. 'Chin up, old thing,' he said, sounding to her exactly like one of the doomed English officers in *The Great Escape*. Wishing fervently that she had Steve McQueen at her side, preferably with that sodding great motorbike of his, she snapped off her own seatbelt and followed Richard out.

Stooping under the whirling rotors with the down-draught making a riot of her hair, she half ran towards the wall of armed men. After a few steps she followed Richard's lead and began to straighten, aware that the chopper had barely touched down before leaping back into the air once more. So it was that they were fully erect and walking shoulder to shoulder when they reached the line of stone-faced guards.

No sooner were they there than the guards split into two well-drilled lines and formed up with Richard and Robin in between them. They marched across the roof to a door, speechlessly, only the rhythmic crunching of their boots breaking the quiet of the air above Renmin Park. As they reached the door, the leader of the line on the right reached forward to open it and Richard and Robin were ushered through into a sizeable lobby. They found themselves facing a pair of lift doors which squealed open at once as though the lift had been waiting especially for them.

They stepped in automatically. The soldiers stayed outside. The doors closed and the car began to sink. 'Bloody hell,' said Richard feelingly. 'This is really getting a bit . . .'

The lift stopped. It had gone down only one floor. The doors wheezed open. Richard and Robin found themselves faced with a sizeable office. Opposite the lift was a window, which gave a panoramic view across the treetops in Renmin Park right across to Tomorrow Square and the stunning skyscraper whose uppermost floors comprised the JW Marriott Hotel. On the right there was a double door, currently closed. On the left a wall decorated with degrees and certificates, photographs and framed newspaper stories. The office was modestly if practically furnished. There was a desk, a small suite comprising a settee and a pair of armchairs. The desk had a leather-backed swivel chair behind it and a pair of less comfortable chairs in front. The suite was gathered round a lacquered table which currently held a tray that contained two teapots, a milk jug, a sugar bowl, four teacups with saucers and spoons. Four little tea plates. And, of all things, a platter full of biscuits.

Apart from that, it was empty; and, apart from a distant murmur of traffic from far below, silent. The slight mustiness of an office airspace was overlain by the fragrances of chocolate and ginger. And of tea.

Richard stepped forward, his eyes drawn to the platter at once. 'By Jove,' he said, sounding irredeemably English. 'Those look like chocolate digestives.' He sniffed appreciatively. 'And I'll be damned if those others aren't gingernuts!'

He had taken perhaps two steps towards the gingernuts when the door opened. At first no one entered. There was a quiet drone of conversation from outside, and then a little silence. Richard and Robin stood, also struck dumb. When the lift doors hissed shut behind them they both jumped.

'Hello?' called Richard. 'Anybody there?'

The door opened wider, and a tall figure strode in. He was dressed in a white uniform more formal than Richard's. Epaulettes and buttons gleaming. He crossed the room smiling, his hand held out.

'My God,' said Richard. 'Lieutenant Commander Tan. What are you doing here? This Deputy General Commissioner chap hauled you in off your destroyer into the bargain?'

'The Deputy General Commissioner has asked me to assist with enquiries, yes,' said Tan, shaking Richard's hand heartily. He swept the taller man away past the table full of gingernuts towards the window. 'But you must call me Xingjian, Richard. It is my Chinese name. We are not on duty aboard our respective vessels now . . .'

Robin was left standing alone, feeling strangely isolated, almost threatened, between the coffee table and the lift. Richard and Tan were over by the window, looking out at Renmin Park and People's

Square. Tan was babbling something hearty and inconsequential. A dreamlike sense that this was not quite real swept over her.

And the feeling suddenly intensified out of all control and it really seemed to her that she was in the grip of a dream – if not of a nightmare. The lift doors wheezed open behind her. A breath of cold air seemed to roll through the room and claim her. The short hairs on her neck prickled. Her heart thumped almost painfully. Her breath went suddenly short. Her flesh rose in goose-bumps and her nipples hardened into flinty peaks beneath the soft swells of her silk blouse.

She turned and he was standing immediately behind her, almost close enough to touch her. 'I am the Deputy General Commissioner of the Institute of Public Security of the People's Republic of China. Thank you for coming so swiftly, Robin,' said Daniel Huuk. And his eyes seemed to expand as though they were trying to swallow her whole.

TWENTY-SEVEN
Game

D aniel Huuk had calculated everything about this moment with the precision of a chess grand master constructing an endgame. Everything except what the effect of the plan would be upon himself.

He planned to separate Richard and Robin from each other, for he knew of old what a formidable team they could be when they were working together. He wished to control them individually for he had plans for each of them within the larger plans that he had been drawing up since he arrived. They had positioned themselves by luck – if by nothing else – right at the heart of every aspect of what seemed to be going on. They had released the *Romeo*. They had found the treasure ship. They had recovered at least one artefact worth a fortune. They had destroyed the communications cables. They had bested the pirates and the men in the Cigarette who might be more pirates or who might be something else, as described by the late Mr Ang, whose name would have been changed from Flatface to Armless had he not been found floating in the Suzhou Creek like the corpse of an old-time beggar family seeking water-burial in the Huangpu.

Deputy General Commissioner Huuk had garnered all this information from several sources, primarily from Shao Xiao Lieutenant Commander Tan Xingjian, but also from Shang Wei Lieutenant Leung, both of the *Luyang* class destroyer. Some also from the reports of ship's acting political officer Shang Wei Straightline Jiang, and not a little from *Poseidon*'s boatswain, Non Commissioned Officer (Fourth Class) Steadyhand Xin. Though to be fair, Jiang reported the barest minimum, embarrassed by a position he strove to keep secret; and Xin thought he was reporting to a minor collector and enforcer in the Green Gang in furtherance of clearing a debt for his younger brother who gambled unwisely.

It didn't for the moment matter that Richard and Robin had saved fifty lives. That they had succeeded where generations of treasure-seekers had failed. That they had behaved so wisely in the face of such temptation – and had earned the gratitude of the curator of the Shanghai Maritime Museum at the very least. That the cables they had apparently destroyed had been all but irreparably damaged by someone else with a far less noble end in view. That the pirates deserved what they got and had been lucky to have been allowed to live. The same as the men in the Cigarette.

As a consequence of all this, the Mariners, old friends though they might be, could be used as camouflage to cover up his actual plans. As distractions to draw attention away from what he was really doing.

As bait.

But now he found himself standing gaping like a schoolboy, stunned into a strange lassitude by the simple impact of her. The tumble of her gleaming hair. The shocked wideness of her fathomless grey eyes. The slight flush of her cheeks. The way her slightly parted lips revealed a gleam of pearly teeth. The way her white neck plunged into the valley between breasts as pale as swan's down. The swell of them. The way their points lifted her cream-coloured blouse. The way the rose-pink flush of her cheeks became the crimson of a blush when she recognized his face and whispered his name, '*Daniel!*' It made him wonder if she had been thinking of him, after all, in the way he had been thinking of her.

It was Richard who broke the moment. 'Daniel!' he called, from the window. 'Well, I'll be damned. Daniel Huuk!'

'Deputy General Commissioner Huuk,' said Tan to his huge English companion in a tone that carried the hint of a warning.

Richard was neither stupid nor insensitive. He remembered well enough that his old friend – and sometime adversary – now had an important-sounding title. And knowing Daniel Huuk the elevated-sounding position wouldn't be either window-dressing or some kind of sinecure. This was now an extremely important man. He remembered also, a ruthlessly focused man. Perhaps a murderously ambitious man – better held close as a friend rather than an enemy. And Richard instinctively understood all this, even though he had not the slightest inkling about Huuk's position within the Invisible Power Triad.

With Tan in tow he crossed the room, stopped at Robin's shoulder and reached out to shake Huuk's hand. The handshake he received in return was firm and cool. Huuk's skin dry, almost papery. There was a lingering hint of physical power there, however, reminding Richard of Huuk's whipcord strength and the unshakeable, indomitable will that went with it. It was only when Richard released his grip that he registered the fact that Huuk hadn't yet looked at him at all – he had been staring at Robin. And he continued to do so now as he offered her his hand in turn.

And when their fingers touched they both flinched a little as a powerful spark of static electricity passed between them.

'You know Deputy General Commissioner Huuk?' Tan asked Richard, as much to break the moment as anything else.

'Oh yes. We're old friends. He shot me in the head the first time we met.'

'But only with a baton round,' said Huuk, releasing Robin at last and switching his gaze to Richard. 'And it doesn't seem to have done you any permanent damage. Unlike whatever – or whoever – hit you in the face more recently.'

Richard a little sheepishly stroked his wounded cheek, his eyes hooded and speculative.

'What does a deputy general commissioner do, Daniel?' asked Robin gently.

Huuk switched his full attention back to her. He gestured to the table. 'Please be seated and we will discuss the matter,' he said gently. 'Over tea. It is English Breakfast – your favourite, as I recall. It is by Jacksons, one of the founders of the China tea trade, I believe. Do they still have their emporium on Piccadilly?'

Huuk and Robin shared the sofa so Richard and Tan took the armchairs. With a mounting sense of unreality threatening to swamp his lively sense of suspicion, Richard found himself delegated as 'Mother'. He took the strainer – no teabags for Daniel Huuk – and began to pour. Tan passed the biscuits round, but regarded them more than a little askance. Robin and Richard took a little milk. Tan and Huuk took lemon.

Settled on the sofa with a cup of tea, a gingernut to dunk and a digestive thick with milky chocolate, Robin repeated her question, 'What does a deputy general commissioner do?'

'Perhaps,' answered Daniel at his most inscrutable, 'you have read stories of the great Judge Dee?'

'I have,' said Richard. 'I read *The Haunted Monastery* by Robert van Gulik when I was a kid. Went on to lots of others. Judge Dee was a sort of oriental Sherlock Holmes. A Tang Dynasty magistrate who travelled around seventh-century China solving murders and mysteries. I've an idea somewhere in the back of my mind that he may have been based on an actual historical character . . .'

Huuk sipped his clear amber tea, savouring the lemon. 'Richard, you never cease to amaze me!'

'Is that what a deputy general commissioner does, then?' Richard countered. 'Travels around China solving mysteries?'

'Mysteries,' replied Huuk, nodding gently, 'and the occasional murder. Real and attempted.'

'But what has that to do with us?' demanded Richard.

Deputy General Commissioner Huuk put down his cup of English Breakfast Tea by Jackson's of Piccadilly, and used his most pellucid and persuasive English tones to explain his answer to that very question. He also used a carefully edited series of half-truths prepared – with not a little rehearsal in front of a mirror in the JW Marriott Hotel – for just this situation.

'You are aware, perhaps, that there have been problems with the Internet recently?'

'Yes,' said Richard, frowning, his tone uncharacteristically uncertain as he tried to work out the relevance of the information.

'It went down a hundred and twelve hours ago; coincidentally at the exact same moment as the submarine you rescued yesterday became trapped.'

'Coincidentally,' echoed Richard, taking Huuk's bait.

Huuk allowed a little silence to lengthen as he watched Richard weighing the implications. What he had to remember, he said to himself, was that Richard was himself an extremely gifted player of these games. He would see any trick too carelessly presented; any trap not perfectly concealed. And, like the tigers that used to roam the inland mountains, he was no less dangerous just because he had been caught in a little trap – quite the reverse, in fact.

'You are right, of course. We believe that the trapping of the submarine and the closing of the Internet were no coincidence at all. On one level, they were a part of the same incident. It appears that it was the cables that carry the Internet traffic that fell over the cliff and trapped the submarine. They did this when the submarine itself blundered into one and broke it, bringing several others down on top of it.'

Richard looked at Huuk narrow-eyed. 'But you are clear that it was the submarine that caused the damage to the cables? It was the *Romeo*-class submarine *Huangpu* that killed the Internet?'

'Certainly. You may put your mind at rest. The Internet was down for the whole east coast of my country before you blew the cables up. Your action there was heroic, not . . . ah . . . *culpable*.'

'OK.' Richard was mollified, if not yet quite convinced.

'But leaving that aside, consider the impact. Most of our population, all our major cities, two Special Economic Zones and at least one international stock exchange struck blind in an instant. The first instinct of my masters in government was to conceal the truth while they investigated. You remember how the Hang Seng Stock Exchange in Hong Kong was closed in the Olympic year by adverse weather conditions, though it survived the earthquake, of course . . .'

'That sort of story wouldn't last for long!'

'Effectively for forty-eight hours. Within another forty-eight I was assigned to investigate.'

'Investigate what? A sub had accidentally damaged some deep-sea cables. Big deal. You needed the standard repair scheme. There are ships out there that do little else but dredge up broken cables and splice them back together . . .'

'Indeed. A fleet of such vessels is on its way. From Nagasaki, I regret to say. It is a pity Heritage Mariner is not yet involved in this cable-mending market. I would have far rather kept the situation in-house, so to speak.'

'OK,' allowed Richard once again. 'But there's at least one element missing here. At least one aspect that you haven't mentioned. And an important one. A crucial one.'

Huuk sat back with the ghost of a smile – a tutor using the Socratic method to guide an outstanding student towards a truly brilliant insight. 'Can you work out what that missing element might be?'

'That it wasn't an accident,' he answered decisively. 'You must have received some kind of credible information that the cables were cut on purpose.'

'Cyber-terrorism taken to a different level,' prompted Huuk.

'There were questions asked back in 2008 when the cables off Alexandria were cut and everywhere from Israel to India lost most of its bandwidth for a while . . .'

Huuk smiled and nodded – each an infinitesimal gesture. By coincidence, his left arm had fallen into the space between his body and Robin's. The back of his hand was less than a hair's length from her thigh, so close that he could feel her heat. But he must not allow her to distract him now. This was the most cunning trap of all – allowing his tiger to tie himself up in nets of his own devising.

'But it must have been something pretty convincing. And it must have been backed with pretty solid proof.'

Huuk thought of Flatface Ang on the phone screen in M on the Bund. And the chopper-wielding professor who had featured so horribly in the clip and on the street afterwards. He particularly remembered the way the back of her skull had blown out into the Guangdong Lu gutter like a section of shattered eggshell. And the tattoo on her little finger of the character that signified *Green*. It had been a mistake to kill her, of course. But not even the Deputy General Commissioner can be perfect all the time. He moved the hand that was not lying beside Robin's thigh and eased the Rohrbaugh Stealth 9mm pistol in its chamois-leather holster in his waistband.

The unsettlingly vivid flash of memory assisted Huuk in remaining silent and seeming distant as Richard continued to wrap himself in nets of speculation. 'So it seems logical to suppose that whatever sort of a message you or your masters received must have come from an accredited source with some kind of established provenance as well as enough supportive proof to make it stand up convincingly. When the cables off Alexandria were cut, Muslim extremists came into some people's thinking because it was done in their own back yard. And, I guess, through your Olympic year there were Muslim extremists up in Xinjiang fighting for the same cause. And there were the Tibetan monks, of course. But still and all, it's a long way from Kuga and Lhasa to the Ryukyu Trench . . .'

With a pang of regret Huuk moved his hand, leaned forward and took a small bundle of papers and magazines from a shelf beneath the tabletop. He moved the cups and saucers, then placed the bundle in front of Richard. The topmost magazine was *Go Shanghai!*. It had been opened and folded back to reveal the restaurant section. Several entries had been circled in black. Richard read *Uighur Cuisine. Fancy succulent lamb, spicy kebabs, mouth-watering chicken, singing, dancing and Xinjiang black beer? Try Shanghai Xinjiang Restaurant or Tian Shan or, of course, Kao Quanyang named after the signature dish* . . . He glanced up. Point taken.

'Read on . . .'

How about chatting over those long Tibetan treks? Settling down to fondly remembered dumplings and choila while you admire the prayer flags all around? . . . Nepali Kitchen, Momo and Lhasa House are for you . . .

'OK,' he allowed. 'Long way from Xianjang and Tibet. Not so far from Julu Road and Yishan Lu. But even so, how the hell are Tibetan or Uighur separatists going to get right the way out to the Ryukyu Trench? And when they get there, how the hell are they going to know where to cut the cables?'

'Perhaps you would like to read the second bundle of papers there. I have marked a rather self-congratulatory piece from the *Shanghai Daily*. Read it aloud, from where I have marked, if you would be so kind.'

'"The treasure-seekers are by no means local people. Although their captain Shao Xiao Chan is of Han descent and from a long-established Shanghai family, there are officers and crew aboard from almost every part of the People's Republic. There are men and women of Mongol background, which, considering their mission, is extremely apt. Less foreseeable is the presence of at least two crew-members from the roof of the world: Tibetans Submariner (Fourth Class) Tzu and Submariner (First Class) Zhoigar are joined by Zhuangs and Uighurs from as far afield as Kunming and Turpan."'

Richard looked up.

Huuk gave a smile that was little more than a grimace. 'It seems unfair to make you do all the work, Richard. So I will tell you that the next piece of paper you have there is part of a report by Captain Chan of the submarine *Huangpu*. It details the loss of an emergency radio beacon which was jettisoned by accident almost immediately before they heard the sound that began the avalanche that trapped and incapacitated them. A sound which seemed to all aboard to be very like an explosion . . .'

'So, someone on the sub, apparently by accident, sent a signal that marked where the sub was. At just the moment it came up to a major junction of undersea cables. Cables that were then almost immediately blown up – leading to the near-loss of the sub itself. So you believe it may have been done on purpose. As there were, it seems, people with possible motivations in all the most important areas of your scenario.'

Richard sat back. Robin watched him narrowly and reached for more chocolate. She pretended not to notice Daniel's hand lying like feather-down beside her thigh. Tan thoughtlessly reached for a gingernut. Chocolate was not to his taste. But ginger was.

'But this could only work if there was a third element in play, surely. There had to be something with a bomb already onboard waiting for the sub to get into position. A big boat, maybe. Logical in one way but hard to get hold of; difficult to hide. Impossible to get away in.'

'Or?' Huuk returned to the Socratic method. The end of the game was very close now. He could feel it. Or the end of this particular phase of this particular game.

'A small but enormously fast vehicle, alerted a little earlier to get into the area. Something that could get over to the emergency beacon, get it aboard and disable it then drop their bomb and get out of there at a really incredible speed. If it wasn't for the waiting around you could do it with a chopper. You could even pull it off with a chopper rigged with floats, I suppose. But it was still a bit choppy after the typhoon for anyone to be sitting in a float-plane.'

'And choppers are so expensive. So hard to fuel – and such a lot of fuel needed. And they're so easy to track. One might even need to file flight plans and so forth. So much unnecessary trouble in a city surrounded by water and teeming with all sorts of boats, don't you think?'

'A boat as fast as a chopper? I don't think . . .' Richard stopped. Mouth open, eyes almost shut.

'Ah,' said Huuk, the satisfied teacher seeing the right answer arrive in his student's mind.

'The Cigarette,' said Richard. 'They could have done it with the Cigarette . . .'

'Precisely,' whispered Huuk, grand master of the game. 'And there is only one man in Shanghai who can supply Cigarettes.'

'Well, you have to talk to him!'

'I do. I am going to see him now. Would you care to accompany me? Only you, Richard. I'm afraid poor brother Ang is not in a fit condition to entertain a lady . . .'

TWENTY-EIGHT
Head

'Cigarettes have so many interesting associations, don't you find?' asked Huuk quietly.

Richard nodded, forcing his mind off thoughts of Benson and Hedges, Players and British American Tobacco on to extremely fast speedboats. The police car whose back seat the two men were sharing was faintly redolent of the Double Happiness brand so it had brought the other kind of cigarette to mind. In Hong Kong someone had once told him Double Happiness got their name from a little extra opium mixed in with the tobacco. Urban legend, he supposed – like the apparently mythic, all too accurate, story that there had once been cocaine in Coca-Cola.

'I read somewhere, probably on the Internet while we still had access to it,' Huuk continued with a dry chuckle, 'that the original Cigarette was designed for smuggling tobacco, heroin and so forth between Havana and Florida. Or maybe tobacco across the Great Lakes between Canada and America. That it was designed to be too fast for even customs cutters to catch, supposedly for a member of the American Mafia. And that the man who designed the original was gunned down in a car park. Conceivably as part of a Mob war. And the head of the Mob was also slaughtered soon after him. One can see how boats with a provenance like that would fit right in to certain sections of our waterfront here. And, sadly, right into the history of our country into the bargain. So much history. So many ghosts.'

Richard was happy to let Huuk chat on, pleased to have prised him away from Robin – for the time being at least. And, to be fair, as Huuk had observed at the outset, steady though Robin was under most circumstances, the idea of introducing her to what was left of Flatface Ang really did not appeal.

Ang, or what was left of him, was currently resident in a cold drawer in the basement of People's Hospital Number 1, situated up in Hongkou on the corner of Wusong Lu and Wujing Lu. It was well on the far side of the creek where he had been found floating, but it was the closest convenient morgue. And as it happened both the morgue and its occupant were on the way to Ang's boatyard down on the little river island that lay off Liping Lu further out in the Yangpu district.

Huuk did not introduce the taciturn pathologist who met them at the mortuary door and conducted them to the post-mortem area. 'You will have to trust us on a couple of matters here,' said Huuk to Richard as they crossed towards the examination table. 'First, that we identified him from fingerprint and DNA records. Rather than dental ones. And secondly that his name, Flatface, was particularly well chosen.'

By the time they reached the corpse Richard had worked out from Huuk's apparently inconsequential words that the head was still missing. The head at the very least.

The pathologist pulled a heavy rubber sheet off what was left of Ang. Richard did not flinch, even though the stench of preserving fluid left him almost breathless. It was probably sweeter than the natural odour of the waterlogged, grey and bloated flesh, he guessed. He had seen his share of corpses, and enough of them in mortuaries, to be expecting the huge Y-shape of incisions brutally stitched shut between the throat and the groin. The telltale hollowness beneath the diaphragm. The jars containing organs – the big brain one, obviously, empty. Less ordinarily, the left arm ended mid-forearm, as neatly severed as by a surgical procedure. Ridiculously, Ang's corpse suddenly made him think of one of his son's computer games. Zombie Apocalypse or some such.

'Cause of death?' snapped Huuk. 'Have you established it beyond doubt?'

'Beyond doubt, blood loss and shock.' The pathologist clearly lacked a sense of humour – or any desire to play games with Deputy General Commissioner Huuk of the Institute of Public Security. 'Probably due to decapitation.'

'Probably?' Huuk's eyebrows climbed his high forehead.

'It could conceivably have been brought about by the severing of the lower forearm on the left side. Particularly as I guess this is the standard triad questioning technique. Fingers first. Then hand. Then forearm. Then elbow and so forth,' the pathologist explained in a dead voice. 'The first three chops are usually the limit in these matters. Unless some kind of drug has been used.'

'And was there?' purred Huuk.

'No.' The pathologist shook her head decisively. 'But to be fair it is unlikely he was dead of shock before his head came off. If you find the murder site you'll know. If he was alive when the head came off there'll be blood on the ceiling. Not that we can assess too much from the corpus delicti itself through the blood loss because it's more or less total in any case. Almost every drop of blood is gone – on to the murder site or into the water. And the natural points of egress – the severed veins and arteries – have all been damaged through immersion.'

'What else?' demanded Huuk shortly.

'The deceased's last meal was lamb. Roast lamb with noodles. He had also eaten a salad of cucumbers, tomatoes and red onions.'

'Any drink? Black beer, say?'

'Water, I would guess. Nothing else obvious in the stomach or intestines. But he was a drinker – the liver shows that. And a smoker. His lungs were a mess; strongly pre-cancerous. Whoever did this may even have done him a favour in the long run.'

'No,' said Huuk feelingly. 'No, I don't think so.'

'And you have recognized the triad mark on the back of his right hand there?'

'Oh yes,' said Daniel Huuk. 'I saw it and recognized it at once. He belonged to the Invisible Power Triad.'

On the way down to Ang's boatyard, Richard discussed the coincidence briefly with Huuk but the deputy general commissioner was less willing to talk all of a sudden. Richard abruptly felt a little nervous. Perhaps because he saw that there was more going on here than he really understood. Perhaps it was the way in which Daniel Huuk seemed to have changed since their last meeting in Hong Kong. Perhaps it was the fact that he realized the car he was sharing with his old friend was at the heart of a little motorcade. Security cars in front and behind. Motorcycle outriders. It all seemed to emphasize, with unexpected force, just how much Huuk had changed now that he was the deputy general commissioner. How much more powerful he had become. 'I know the Dragon Head of the Invisible Power Triad, though I have never had any dealings with him or his organization.' It was Richard's turn to babble a little. For the life of him he could not remember whether Huuk already knew all of this or not. Both silence and openness could hold potent dangers if they put him on the wrong side of the Deputy General Commissioner of the Institute of Public Security. Like pissing off the prime minister, he thought. 'Man named Twelvetoes Ho. He used to work on one of my ships. Then he became dragon head after he retired to Hong Kong. I know his daughter Su-Zi as well though I haven't seen her in years. Is Ang's membership of the Invisible Power Triad all that important?'

'Yes,' said Huuk. 'Yes, I'm afraid it is.'

Ang's boatyard was little more than a big battered shed on a semi-derelict riverside with a couple of rickety piers thrusting dangerously into the Huangpu's muddy flow. The shed itself would normally be a dirty, dull and dingy place, thought Richard, full of shadows and secrets. Not today. Today it was taped off, solidly secured, bustling like a beehive and lit up like a film set ready for principal photography. All it seemed to be lacking was someone to play James Bond – or Sherlock Holmes.

Richard followed Huuk into the heart of the investigation, eyes narrow and ears pricked. He could see where Huuk's thinking seemed to be leading and he was desperate to make sure it wasn't going to lead him – up the garden path. But his interest was thoroughly piqued now. That apparently gratuitous visit to the mortuary had thrown a new light on things. Up until now he had thought this was all about political separatists – Muslim Uighurs or Buddhist Tibetans – damaging the Chinese Internet access and threatening to do it again unless some of their demands for liberty were met.

But now it was maybe about triads. Triads damaging the Chinese Internet access and threatening to do it again unless . . . What? What would triads want so badly they would shut down the Internet to get it?

But knowing what he had learned about triads during his time in Hong Kong – a good deal more than he had admitted to Huuk so far – suggested to him that if any triad would be willing to take the terrifying risk of making just that threat, the Invisible Power Triad would be the most likely culprit.

'Anything?' Huuk barked at a man in a police uniform. Richard was pretty confident with badges of rank in the People's Liberation Army Navy but he didn't recognize any in the police as yet.

'We have the murder site. It's like a slaughterhouse in there. Blood on the ceiling.'

'It was the head coming off that killed him, then,' said Richard quietly without thinking.

'I know,' answered Huuk in a whisper hardly louder than a breath. 'I have seen the whole thing. Someone filmed it on their cellphone.'

Then why give the pathologist such a hard time? Richard wondered. Then he thought, *Because you don't want anyone to know you've seen it.*

Then he wondered, with a tingle of shock, *Then why are you confiding in me?*

'Are there any body parts in there?' Huuk was demanding, striding across to the room the policeman indicated. There were what Richard assumed to be the Chinese equivalent of scene of crime officers all over the place. Men and women in white spacesuits, armed with fingerprint kits, ultraviolet torches, plastic bags and tweezers. Huuk went through them like an icebreaker through brash.

Richard stayed back. Skirting the scene of main activity, he wandered round the edge of brightness out on to the river's foreshore. Under the misty smog of a morning that threatened yet another stultifying Shanghai day, the piers leaned crazily against the Huangpu's steady stream. Surprisingly close at hand, a bewildering range of ships from freighters to sampans bustled by while the thrusting outskirts of Pudong opposite seemed to crush them against this bank. It was a miracle the piers hadn't been ripped off by a passing ferry and washed away in the wake.

It seemed almost insulting to find a second Cigarette moored there, like a brand-new Bentley in a scrapyard, like a beautiful young starlet with a clapped-out old millionaire.

This one was red. The kind of red you usually only find on Ferraris and Ford Mustangs. Red fibreglass hull with a stiletto point on one end and a couple of raked windshields at the other that seemed to have been taken from a 1950s racing car. Red leather seats in the cockpit. Two big fighter pilot's bucket seats at the front, bench seat at the back – like the inside of a top-of-the-range Lincoln Continental Sportster. Red leather handles to the engine controls. Red leather trim to the steering wheel.

As far as Richard was concerned, it was love at first sight. The Cigarette was the exact opposite of everything he had ever coveted. His beloved Bentley Continental was metallic battleship grey; his venerable E-Type Jaguar was black and so was his Heritage Mariner Company Chairman's corporate Rolls – as black as the Royal family's. The Turbo Mulsane and the massive Discovery he used as family cars were British racing green – a colour he rather thought that Bentley had invented.

He owned a launch which he hardly ever used – it was a stylish but conservative Slipper with painted wooden sides and varnished wooden decking as shiny as the dance floor at the Savoy. The raciest vessel he had ever sailed was the elegant white multihull *Katapult*. But here was something he had never experienced before. It simply knocked him sideways. He felt a little like the bookish academic Arthur Miller being introduced to Marilyn Monroe.

So when pandemonium broke out in the shed behind him, Richard was uncharacteristically slow to react – unwilling to tear himself away. But when he went back through into the dazzling brightness, he found himself on the edge of an utterly unexpected situation. The media had arrived. A camera team with a young producer clutching a clipboard and a redundant lighting man stood in the doorway to the boat shed. Away on the kerbside a van with CCTV on it was parked in front of another that, bizarrely, read Shanghai Couriers – Your Local Fed-Ex.

On this side of the film crew, her surprisingly curvy bottom pressed against the police tape, stood Bridget Wang. Behind them, out in the gathering brightness of the morning, Richard could just make out the familiar shape of Robin, with Tan beside her. Now what on earth are they doing here? he wondered.

Richard started to ease his way round the outer walls, hoping to get to Robin before any further complications emerged. Ideally he wanted to get the pair of them out of this and back to *Poseidon* – if not back home to London. But he had a sneaking suspicion that Huuk was by no means finished with them yet.

'What's all this about?' he asked Robin the moment he reached her side.

'I'm not exactly certain. Bridget Wang showed up at Police HQ twenty minutes ago asking for Huuk and saying she had important information for him. Someone told her where he was. She came straight down here still looking and we followed.'

'Why does she want Huuk? Triad murders aren't the sort of thing she normally covers. Aren't the sort of thing that gets on CCTV at all, in fact.'

'There's something more,' said Tan, suspiciously. 'She's had this information but she won't say what it is to anyone other than Huuk. Someone's setting something up.'

'Better warn Huuk, then,' said Richard at once. 'He won't want to walk into anything unexpected.'

Tan was just moving towards the tape, reaching for his ID card, when Huuk himself appeared. The deputy general commissioner strode forward into the camera shot behind the reporter, apparently deep in thought. As he approached, Bridget Wang was talking earnestly into the camera. 'This is Bridget Wang speaking to you live from Liping Lu . . .' At a sign from her producer, she turned. 'Deputy General Commissioner Huuk,' she began. 'This station has received exclusive information that—'

Precisely what information Bridget Wang was talking about she never said, for as she spoke, the door of the Shanghai Courier van slid open and a young delivery man climbed out carrying a large cardboard package. He walked swiftly and confidently over to the reporter, pushed past the ineffectual arm of the producer and handed it to her.

Bridget Wang was holding a microphone and a clipboard. She was not expecting to receive packages mid-interview. As the delivery man turned away, she tried to pass the package to her producer. Who dropped it. The package burst open as it hit the ground and something the size of a football rolled out.

Richard knew it was going to be Ang's head even before the shocked face with its wide eyes, gaping mouth and flat-squashed nose was revealed. It was the cloth that it was wrapped in that gave him pause. For it was a ceremonial dragon flag, not unlike a Tibetan prayer flag. But there was no doubt as to the creature depicted in gold and red on the cloth that unrolled like a carpet and sent the last of Flatface Ang to rest against Daniel Huuk's perfectly polished shoes. And it spelt a disturbingly simple message for anyone to see. Dragon. Head.

TWENTY-NINE
Cigarette

'That could have been a bomb!' snarled Tan. 'Where the hell are all those security people? Two cars' full. And he just strolls right in!' He looked around, his face twisted with outrage and suspicion. The interview was over. The live broadcast done. Bridget Wang was still screaming. The flag and the head were surrounded by white-clothed scene of crime officers. Daniel Huuk had disappeared. As had his police guard, apparently.

'I don't know about a bomb,' said Richard, still thoughtfully. 'Bomb*shell*, certainly. That's one hell of an accusation to make, live on CCTV.' *Dragon Head. That'll take some thinking through*, he thought.

'They'll cut it. It'll never see the light of day,' said Tan uncertainly.

'But it was *live*,' repeated Richard. 'Didn't you hear her say?'

Bridget's screams were quietening now. The film crew were supporting her back to the CCTV van. The Shanghai Courier van was long gone.

'It was a declaration of war, wasn't it?' asked Robin quietly. 'Someone just declared war on Daniel Huuk?'

'Who would dare?' demanded Richard. 'Tan. Who would dare do this?'

'I don't know,' answered Tan frowning. 'Uighur separatists or Tibetans might well attack the deputy general commissioner. He held them under tight reign particularly after the earthquake and then later in Olympic year. Remember the suicide bombings in Kuqua? American woman arrested for photographing a Tibetan demonstration during the closing days – and then released almost at once. Both situations controlled before any more publicity could be generated, you see? He has done much to frustrate and outmanoeuvre them . . .'

'The closest Ang got to Uighurs was eating in their restaurants,' grated Richard. 'And that may look like a Tibetan banner wrapped around the head but I don't think it was. It's all just camouflage. This is triad-related, isn't it?'

'How would you expect me to be able to comment . . .'

Richard's hand struck like a king cobra. Tan was taken utterly unawares. Before he could snatch it back, Richard held the naval officer's right hand in the brightness of the augmented sunlight. There was a tiny tattoo on the back of it. An Invisible Power Triad tattoo. 'Poor old Flatface had one of those,' Richard grated. 'On the hand they didn't chop off in sections. Is this what it's all about? Some enormous triad powerplay?'

'Yes,' said a gentle voice. They all swung round to find Daniel Huuk standing in the space left by the hysterical, fainting Bridget Wang. 'Yes, I'm rather afraid it is. You see, Flatface was one of my most trusted and fruitful Invisible Power informants – because he lived undercover here in the heart of Green Gang territory and seemed to be playing both sides off against each other. A kind of double agent.'

Because they were all facing Daniel, they all saw what happened next; and perhaps it was as well they all did see – for had any one of them seen it on their own, the others would never have believed. And the one lonely witness would in time have come to doubt their own memory. Perhaps their sanity.

Just as Bridget had been moved away, so had the dragon flag and the head. The bright cloth was now being folded into a plastic bag and beside it a spacesuited forensics officer was preparing to put the head back in the damaged box which stood on a table in the middle of the boathouse. Taking it respectfully by the temples, fingers spread over the ears, the officer lifted the head as though to examine it face to face. Exactly as Huuk would have done had the box not dropped. Had he been the one to open it. Had he been the one suspiciously unwrapping the football-sized bundle in the dragon flag.

Two jets of smoke suddenly erupted from the wide-squashed nostrils. And, before the officer even had a chance to react to the unthinkable horror, the whole thing exploded. The force of the blast simply obliterated the officer and the officer with the flag beside him. A deadly sphere of flame and force spread out through the ramshackle boathouse at the speed of light. It lifted the roof off above and sent smoking shreds of it raining far and wide. It blew the table into blocks, batons and splinters and hurled them far and wide. It burst the floor beneath, pitching several SoC officers into the unsuspected cellarage. It blew the nearest – inland – walls into Lipang Lu, leaving only the strengthened riverside walls and the doorframe standing. And it blew Daniel Huuk into the arms of Robin Mariner so that they both hurled backwards into the littered roadway.

As Richard flew through the air, almost inevitably, his unfortunate sense of the ridiculous brought the old saying to his mind: *If brains were dynamite, he wouldn't have enough to blow his nose* . . . On that scale, he calculated, Ang was up with Hawking and Einstein. He hit the ground and rolled, wondering distantly just how much C-4 you could get into an emptied brainpan, leaving room for some sort of detonator too. Quite a bit, obviously. He lay for an instant doing a mental check on his body. Nothing seemed immobile or broken. So he started pulling himself to his feet.

Tan was there, on his feet already, and looking like he hadn't been blown over. His uniform no longer immaculate. The rest of the pavement seemed to have been blown clear, like a Kansas cornfield after a twister. 'Captain Mariner,' he called far too loudly as Richard came erect. 'Are you all right?'

'A couple of kilos,' said Richard.

'*What?*'

'Ang's brains,' he explained. 'Poor sod's done a hell of a lot of damage. I think we're the only ones up and about. My God! It's even blown Bridget's TV van over. She won't be happy about that!' He staggered over and grabbed Huuk's splayed body by the shoulders. 'Trust Huuk to find a soft landing,' he said, lifting mightily to reveal Robin.

Robin rolled free, groaning.

'Are you hurt, darling?' Richard asked her.

'I'll live. Are you OK?'

'Better than I look if I look anything like Tan.'

'How's Daniel?' She raised herself on one elbow, leaning on the pavement like Cleopatra on her couch.

'Out for the count. Pulse seems OK, neck and wrist. Bloody great welt across the back of his head. Pupils react to light, though. Shoulders peppered with what looks like buckshot.'

'That'll be bits of Ang's brainbox,' wheezed Tan, staggering unsteadily closer.

'My God,' said Robin. 'I hope he's had AIDS shots!'

'And rabies,' added Richard feelingly. 'Lucky Ang wasn't looking the other way, now I think of it.' He met Tan's gaze and explained: 'Teeth.'

A few moments later, the two men were standing with the

insensible Huuk between them. Other blast victims were beginning to stir. A stream of semi-audible invective came from the back of the CCTV van. Bridget was clearly up and about.

Robin picked herself up at last. 'My God,' she said again. 'Look what he slipped me!'

'He'd've had to have been bloody quick to slip you anything in mid-flight,' said Richard. 'What is it?'

'It's the smallest handgun I've ever seen in my life!'

'Hang on to it,' said Richard, looking around at the carnage narrow-eyed. 'We may need it! What d'you reckon, Tan?' As he asked, the first sirens started sounding in the distance. That was quick, thought Richard. Until he remembered how upset the Shanghai police had been at the slow response time shown in *Mission Impossible III*.

'We have to get him somewhere safe,' said Tan. 'This is the second attempt on his life. He didn't want you to know, but he was attacked and nearly killed yesterday evening. By the people who did that to Ang.'

'Do you think we can get him back to Police HQ, then?' asked Robin. 'Sounds like the cavalry's on its way!'

'I really don't know. Can we be certain of appearances at the moment? What looked like a delivery van brought a head in a box. What looked like a head was a bomb. Who knows what a couple of men that look like policemen might be! And I certainly don't know how safe he would be even if we did get him to HQ or hospital.'

'May be a case of third time lucky, eh?' said Richard. 'Well, if you don't know anywhere he'd be safe until he recovers then I do. We just have to get him there, that's all!'

'Where?' demanded Tan. 'You're a stranger to Shanghai. How would you know anywhere that's safe?'

'Because it isn't anywhere in Shanghai!' replied Richard. 'I'm talking about taking him to *Poseidon*.'

'But *Poseidon* is somewhere out on the Yangtze between here and Nanjing!' said Tan. 'Even if we could get in contact with her how on earth would we get him out to her?'

'Easy,' said Richard expansively. 'Have you met the new love of my life?'

They laid Huuk along the Cigarette's bench seat. Robin sat beside him and took his head on her lap a little grudgingly; she was by no means immune to the powerboat's obvious charms and felt that she had served as a mattress for the wounded man quite often enough for one day. But the Cigarette was a boys' toy par excellence so Robin let the boys have the bucket seats and the fun.

The mostly deceased and injured scene of crime officers had been over her earlier so everything was secured and labelled. The keys were in a clear plastic forensics bag on the driver's seat. It was the work of a moment for Tan to slip her mooring lines and stow the cockpit entry steps. When he eased himself into the second seat he found that there was a full three-way 'Deathproof' shoulder and crotch set of safety straps. It was like settling into the co-pilot's seat on the space shuttle.

She coughed a little modestly when Richard tried to start her for the first time. 'Come on, *Marilyn*,' he said. 'Wake up, old girl.'

'You sure she shouldn't be *Rita*?' demanded Robin, her finger on Daniel's neck pulse, her eyes on her watch. 'Rita had red hair.'

'Miss Hayworth had her moment of glory in *Shawshank*, as I recall,' he answered airily. 'I knew at first glance that this was *Marilyn*. Because . . . is she ever *hot*!' And on the word the massive 662SCI Mercury racing engines fired up with a deep-throated roar.

Richard drifted the 12-metre length of Ferrari-red dreamboat away from the rickety pier and out into the Huangpu's thick muddy stream. Easing the throttles forward, he slid her two-and-a-half-metre width along the shallow shore, eagle-eyed for obstructions, wary of other shipping. But after ten minutes of new-owner caution he realized that *Marilyn* was as easy to handle as his big V12 E-Type Jaguar. More powerful and even more nimble. He shoved the throttles wider, feeling her settle down to work as the long nose started to rise. The wind sighed past, the speed of it beginning to attain a little wind-chill. The outflow of a stream on their left pushed *Marilyn* out a little further. Richard went with the flow and began to weave in and out of the lumbering river traffic, growing more confident by the second. 'First thing is to go below and see what we have aboard,' he called to Tan. 'Then we'll need to check the GPS and get the radio fired up. See if we can reach *Poseidon* and swap relative positions.'

Tan nodded to show that he had understood. Richard reached for the switch marked CABIN DOOR and flicked it up. The hydraulics kicked in. The door slid up. Tan went below.

'You OK?' Richard asked Robin.

'Fine. Or I will be when I get over this insane attack of jealousy!'

'You want to drive?' he offered, his voice dripping childish disappointment. 'I'll nurse your comatose boyfriend . . .'

'Not for the moment,' answered Robin, refusing to rise to his bait. '*Marilyn*'s your girl. You two need to get acquainted.'

He gave a shout of delighted laughter. 'Have I proposed to you recently?'

'Not in some time,' she answered in her most maiden-aunt voice.

'Remind me to do so. You'd make one hell of a wife!'

'Why thank you, kind sir. Now you'd better watch your speed. I'll bet there are limits on this river.'

'Why should I?' he continued in his excited-little-boy vein. 'There's no one will ever catch *Marilyn* and me!'

But even as he spoke, a helicopter swooped into the air just above the river's misty smog and began to follow them.

By the time Tan came back up from the cabin, Richard was sailing more sedately between banks where buildings were fewer and further back from the stream. The river traffic itself was a little thinner. The ferries were gone. The city cruises had stopped at the last bridge, where the helicopter had also pulled away, and only the long-range tour boats also bound towards the Yangtze still followed them. Otherwise the river was bustling with what looked like deep-water traffic. Oil tankers, freighters and container ships; coasters and big-river boats – they seemed to Richard to vary between ten thousand tons and a hundred thousand. The supertankers and the new-generation supercontainers at quarter-million to half-million tons were probably out in the anchorages *Poseidon* had come through last night when he and Robin were tucked down. But these ones looked more than big enough to him, sitting down at the waterline in a twelve-metre craft. Like the driver of a sports car negotiating a motorway full of pantechnicons. But of course they were unwieldy, slow and lumbering, while *Marilyn* could duck and dive like a mosquito among an elephant herd. Almost without conscious thought he eased the throttles open a little wider.

'Anything down there?' he asked as Tan climbed back into the cockpit.

'Nothing much,' answered Tan. 'What were you hoping for? Smuggler's arsenal? State-of-the-art guns and so forth? Rockets? Grenades? Enough plastic explosive to fill a few more heads?'

'They might have come in handy,' answered Richard. 'If the

going gets tough. But now that you've completed inventory, why don't you check on the GPS and get the radio working. And while you're doing that, then maybe you can tell me just how tough the going is going to get.'

'Triads are territorial for the most part,' said Tan as he worked. 'Some of them spread into particular enterprises – the White Powder Triad tries to run the cocaine and crack industries everywhere. But they're always running into trouble because there's always a local triad who wants a piece of the action in Shenyang, say, or Kunming or Changsha . . .'

'OK, I can see that. Like the Green Gang and Shanghai. They've been like coffee and cream since the thirties. But then what are you doing here? The Invisible Power Triad is centred in Hong Kong – and maybe Macau.'

'That's where Invisible Power is different. Like the White Powder Triad trying to control the whole market in cocaine country-wide. Except that Invisible Power deals in just that – power. And I don't mean electricity or gas. Political power. In the thirties if you wanted a contract with Shanghai City Hall you went to Big-Eared Du and the Green Gang swung it for you. Even in more recent times. There are stories about contracts in Pudong . . .'

'OK. I see that. But that was then. What about now?'

'But now, the way it works is this – Invisible Power runs City Hall, and if you want anything done, even the Green Gang comes to us. Invisible Power runs City Hall everywhere from Harbin to Kunming, Ningbo to Urumqui.'

'Just not in Shanghai.'

'It seems not. Pudong has made an almost incalculable difference. The amount of money it has generated . . .'

'Money being power, of course . . .'

'And the cutting-edge technical advances . . .'

'Meaning that even thick-ear triad footsoldiers have cellphones with built-in cameras, Internet access and a great deal of knowledge about such things as well as expertise in employing them. And what the footsoldiers know is as nothing to what the upper echelons can get their heads round; and their hands on. Yes, I see . . .'

'Who is Zhang Tong when he's at home?' demanded Robin suddenly.

'Where did you hear of Zhang Tong?' asked Tan, suspiciously.

'Zhang Tong is Dragon Head of the Green Gang. If anyone is responsible for starting a triad war against Son of Dragon Head Huuk and the Invisible Power Triad it is him. Why do you ask?'

'Well, Daniel's still out cold. I don't think he's actually coming to, but he's muttering things in his sleep. Zhang Tong is all I can make out and he keeps saying it over and over.'

Richard shoved *Marilyn*'s throttles wider. She tossed her head and leaped forward playfully. The river swept away to the right on its final reach. Richard could see the schematic on the GPS screen. And, more colourfully and more vividly, he could see it straight ahead. The wide brown watercourse of the Huangpu swirled away to a low horizon. Beyond the creek approaching on their left hulked the city of Wusong, the grimy grey opposite to soaring Pudong. Behind it, away upriver towards Nanjing, the banks of the Yangtze gathered themselves into cliffs undreamed of in this flat confluence of estuaries. Beyond Wusong, along the lower sky above the low marshy land on the left, lay a thick brown line, as though a strange sort of squall was threatening the sunny peace of the afternoon. It was the Yangtze River itself.

Son of Dragon Head, thought Richard. *Son of Dragon Head Huuk*. Curiouser and curiouser . . .

But then his thoughts were overwhelmed.

Robin called across from the back seat. 'Hey, Richard, I don't know if you have a rear-view mirror or anything like one up there, but there's a couple of nasty looking speedboats have just swung out of the Wusong Creek behind us and it looks like they're coming after *Marilyn*!'

THIRTY

River

oseidon came past the mouth of the Huangpu just as Straightline took over technical control of the bridge for the afternoon watch. His control was theoretical for three reasons. Firstly the ship was under the control of River Pilot Grandfather Chang. Secondly because the captain, Chang's daughter, was also there. Thirdly, because Straightline had been on the bridge in any case since Grandfather Chang arrived aboard. Just as the captain had been there, standing foursquare at her father's shoulder. And Steadyhand Xin had been seated at the helm.

Still, the arrival of midday and the beginning of his official watch seemed to revitalize Straightline and reawaken his mind and senses. He seemed to leap awake to find himself standing at the far right of the bridge, just in front of his chart room. The pilot stood midships, with one steady foot planted on the port side and the other on the starboard, like someone at the equator standing with one foot in each hemisphere. Just beyond him, Captain Mongol Chang stood like a rock behind Steadyhand. Father and daughter might have been a pair of matching statues, he thought.

As the bell-like tone of midday and change of watch sounded on the tannoy, Lieutenant Straightline Jiang jumped a little, therefore, and began to look around himself with lively interest. He had never been this far up the Yangtze, for they were now beyond the point at which, on previous voyages, his ship had always turned to port under the guidance of the Shanghai port pilot and entered the Huangpu River. If he looked past the Changs, father and daughter, he could see the mouth of the Huangpu slipping sedately past, with its bustle of shipping coming in and out. If he looked right, he could see the last of the vessels in the anchorage waiting patiently to move on up or down, in or out.

And then, beyond them, the reach of the great river itself, broken only by the mudflats upstream of Changxing Dao Island. It was still tidal – still rose and fell according to the dictates of the China Sea and the Pacific Ocean beyond – but it was losing much of what the great waters meant now; it was becoming riverine. Ahead on the starboard quarter, the view was beginning to widen – though he knew the sea lanes in the water itself narrowed for a while. He stood watching, entranced, as the view expanded before him as though someone were opening curtains made of mud, hill, shore and shipping. There was a river smell that was seeping on to the bridge now, too. Something very different from the sea smell Straightline was used to. It was more feral, more personal, more immediate. A smell of mud and humanity, sweat and excrement. Potent, unsettling; oddly timeless.

'Come to 320 degrees,' growled River Pilot Chang, clearly positioning *Poseidon* to take the northernmost, upstream course in the last of the local management system.

'320 degrees,' echoed Steadyhand at the helm.

Straightline, excitement welling quite unexpectedly, found himself reaching for the binoculars and wishing he was up on the flying bridge – or, better still, up in the crow's nest halfway up the mast. Even from his current position it was possible to see the way the river was widening out. *Poseidon* took her place at the north side of the channel and adjusted her course once more, 'Come to 300 and hold her on that,' growled Grandfather Chang.

'300 degrees,' confirmed Steadyhand.

Motors eased in their pounding, *Poseidon* settled back. Time slipped past like the deep brown water.

Straightline jumped out of another little trance and pressed the binoculars to his eyes. There was nothing to starboard now but modest river junks, sampans and more modern small boats. Everything from laden barges to rowing boats and very occasional pleasure craft. *Poseidon* seemed quite sizeable beside them. For the first time in her life, perhaps, a big fish in a small pond. Straightline was able to see over the top of them towards the far bank. It looked the better part of fifteen miles distant, though the automatic rangefinder was thwarted by the clearview so he couldn't be certain. He spent several happy moments sweeping them back and forward over the view. Then several moments more. Even at this slow speed, it seemed to him that everything he could see was constantly changing. Much more so than it ever did at sea, where only the movements of the sun, moon and stars, only the restless boiling of the clouds on the back of the fickle wind and only the height and rhythm of the waves might slowly vary, day after day after day.

'Steady on 300 degrees. Match your speed to nearby shipping.'

'Steady on 300 degrees. Matching speed.'

The motors eased fractionally again.

It was not all wide views and frenetic bustle, however. If Straightline looked past the two matching statues – father and daughter – to his left, there was a wall of big ships to port outbound, whose high sides and huge cargoes cut great chunks out of his view of the busy southern shore. All he could really see of it was that it was higher, steeper, gathering into cliffs on occasion. And road traffic bustled along the top to match the river traffic below.

Dead ahead, his view was blocked by the stern of a much larger freighter in whose wake they were comfortably positioned. Whose heading they were so precisely following. Whose speed they were so carefully matching. She was the *Golden Harvest* of Nanjing. Where, no doubt, she was bound.

The river pilot caught his eye and said, with unexpected courtesy, 'There are three of them. They always sail together to and from Nanjing. *Golden Harvest*, *Golden Hope* and *Golden Happiness*. They are the biggest vessels that travel this section of the river and they have to ride the tide. Especially as the Yangtze itself is so low this year, even with the river management in place because of the mighty Three Gorges Dam upstream. They said it would not affect the flow down here, nearly a thousand miles away – but I think it has. Consider. When the planned water level of a hundred and seventy-five metres above sea-level was achieved the year after Olympic year, the reservoir covered more than a thousand square kilometres and stretched some six hundred and sixty-three kilometres along the upper river. The reservoir has flooded more than six hundred square kilometres, turning a fast-flowing river into an enormous lake. Imagine the volume of water it holds.' There was a brief silence as the two men considered the implications. Then the pilot continued, 'Nearly forty cubic kilometres of it by all accounts. Forty cubic kilometres. No matter how well they manage the outflow, we feel the effects down here. Therefore the *Golden* sisters must be very careful or they will never get into Nanjing. Or never get out.'

Where are you taking us, Father? Surely not all the way up to Nanjing! wondered Captain Chang. *Why not to Shanghai?* She simply could not work out what was going on here – and she was not a woman who reacted well to uncertainty. But she suddenly found herself distracted by wondering what the sight of the *Golden Harvest* might mean to her father. The words he had so unexpectedly shared with Straightline made her speculation all the more poignant. The battered but sturdy freighter was everything she remembered of his own ship; but younger, stronger, more modern. And her two sisters *Hope* and *Happiness* were probably just the same. Like thousands upon thousands of ships sailing the Yangtze. Did it break his heart each time he looked at such a vessel – knowing he would never be her master – from the bridge of someone else's ship that he was merely piloting to safe haven?

She stole a glance at him, but could read nothing in the solid stance of his square-set body, legs slightly astride, hands clasped in the small of his back. Nor in the profile of his set face, with its jut of jaw and square-set cap seeming to conceal his eyes. The cap was an irritant, she suddenly thought, mutinously. She did not normally allow caps to be worn on her bridge. And yet she was wearing her own cap out of respect for his unspoken wishes.

She took it off and slid it under her arm. She clasped her hands in the small of her back. Spread her feet a little.

'Steady on 300 degrees. Watch your speed,' growled the river pilot.

'Steady on 300. Watching speed,' echoed Xin.

'Send all hands to lunch, Shang Wei Straightline,' Chang ordered, suddenly realizing she had missed the usual lunchtime and was running nearly half an hour late. She felt a shiver of disquiet. Would her father realize that the crew normally ate at 12:30, not at 13:00?

'Pilot Chang, watch officers eat on the bridge,' she informed him, her voice made more formal still by the nervousness she felt. 'Would you consent to join us in *mai*, sir?'

'Thank you, Captain. I would. A little rice would be very welcome.'

She glanced across at him. His cap was off and under his arm. And it suddenly occurred to her that he had kept it on out of respect for *her* unspoken wishes. She opened her mouth to say something further, something more personal and filial. But Broadband stuck his head out of the shack and said, 'Captain, I've a message coming in. It's pretty garbled, but I think it's from the owner.'

Richard came out of the mouth of the Huangpu and on to the Yangtze proper pushing *Marilyn* up to thirty knots. It was as fast as he dared go in the circumstances, even with a pair of speedboats riding ever closer in his wake. However, *Marilyn* reacted well to the change to more sealike conditions, seeming to ease over the bigger waves no matter where they came from. And they came in all shapes and sizes from every direction at once. True to the spirit of an era the better part of twenty years before her birth, she really was a rock-and-roll girl, thought Richard, as she corkscrewed lightly through the Huangpu's outwash with all the aplomb of a princess getting out of a sports car. She didn't show even a glimpse of lacy spray.

It was an odd sensation, controlling such a vessel in such conditions. The power of the lesser river pushed out into the flow of the greater one. But unlike in the sort of coastal estuary Richard was more used to, the great river had a powerful flow as well, where the sea of course did not. And one flow cut across the other almost perfectly at right angles. The Yangtze's relentless push down towards the East China Sea bent and twisted the current of the Huangpu thrusting out into it, in spite of the fact that the Yangtze was unnaturally low this year. Perhaps it was the Three Gorges Dam; perhaps it was global warming. But there was still enough flow to make things very tricky. And of course it was further complicated by the fact that the rivers were tidal – and the tide was near the crest now, and powerful, sending millions and millions of tons into the narrowing estuary.

The western lip of the Huangpu's mouth thrust east in a hook of mud made by the eastward flow of the greater watercourse. And *Marilyn*, turning upstream round the point of it, found herself crossing an area of whirlpools, cross-currents and sharp-edged waves where the powers of the rivers were at war and the tide was making matters worse. And she loved it. Ducks taking to water were not a patch on her. Which was just as well. Whoever was at the helms of the speedboats all too close behind her knew the river – and knew what their own craft would do. Richard pushed the throttles forward another few inches. At least the wild water scared off some of the shipping, he thought, powering up to forty knots and watching out for a whole new range of hazards.

The first set of problems were presented by the flotsam and jetsam on the water by the point. In the Huangpu and the main channels of the Yangtze, Richard suspected acutely, the traffic would keep the waterways fairly clear. That was not so true in the restless almost circular flow of the backwater here. 'Tan,' he called. 'Robin! Keep an eye out for anything in the water.'

Then he was spinning the red steering wheel over to his right, sending *Marilyn* dancing out into the next series of hazards, looking over his shoulder to see the two black speedboats powering round the mud-hook hard on his heels. The next series of hazards were the incoming vessels on the southern-bank route which were sailing down from places closer than Nanjing and using the inner east-bound channel hard against the shore. Like a racer going the wrong way up a one-way street, Richard jinked *Marilyn* left and right, cutting under the low bows of little coasters of ten thousand tons and less – and skipping over their wakes like a flat stone skimmed at the seaside.

Then he was out into relatively quiet water, with two sets of traffic coming relentlessly counter to his course on either side of him. The southern course of the midstream channel was also a downstream course, like the one on his left by the shore. It was on the far side of the oncoming ships on his right hand, he calculated grimly, that *Poseidon* would be heading up towards Nanjing some-where up ahead. With the water under *Marilyn*'s bows looking relatively clear, he pushed the throttle hard forward. *Marilyn* tossed up her head, wiggled her hips and got down to a serious show of speed.

'Jesus!' bellowed Tan, half falling back into his bucket seat and reaching for his straps. 'A little warning would be welcome!'

'Christ!' shouted Robin from the back seat. 'I nearly dropped poor Daniel on to the back of his head. I assume you don't want us looking out for hazards any more!'

'Sorry!' bellowed Richard.

But the instant that he said it, his apology became redundant. The first bullet cracked past. Just in the position Tan had been half standing, looking for hazards in the water. They could tell because it gouged a short shoulder-height channel in *Marilyn*'s uptilted fore-deck just in front of his windshield.

'Can this thing go any faster?' demanded Tan feelingly.

'Not if I'm going to keep any kind of control of her,' answered Richard grimly. 'But they're only shooting at us because we're getting away.' He took his hand off the throttles and used both fists to spin the wheel hard over, sending *Marilyn* into the canyon-narrow gap between two oncoming vessels. Water washed aboard for the first time and poured over the freeboard beside him as he sent her under an ivory hillock of foam above the propellers of the first one, seemingly under the overhang of her poop and scant inches away from the flaking, rusty blade of her rudder. He swung hard over the opposite way and Tan was hurled towards the racing brown froth of the big ship's wake.

Tan thought for a moment he had escaped a soaking – until *Marilyn* went under the forecastle flare of the following ship and the bow wave at her cutwater came aboard in a dirty little waterfall.

'Thanks a bunch!' bellowed Robin. 'That's a new outfit you owe me, Richard Mariner. And as for Daniel . . .'

The first of the black speedboats burst into the middle channel on their wake. But he misjudged the turn. The hillock of propeller foam threw him off and the second ship's cutwater clipped him, sending him zooming crazily across the little stream that existed like the central reservation of a motorway, between the hulls of the huge vessels. He only just saved himself from turning turtle but his wild attempts to save himself made him cut up the second speedboat when it burst through the gap just behind him. They both floundered there for a moment, their way lost. Whoever was shooting at them tried again but the bullets went high and were nothing to them but the distant echo of the gunshots.

Even so, Richard pushed the throttles forward into their final notch. 'See if you can get hold of *Poseidon* on the radio, would you, Tan?' he said. 'Things should be a bit more quiet for a moment or two now.'

One of the many things about Richard Mariner that already fascinated Tan was his idea of 'quiet'. And here was a perfect example. The Ferrari-red Cigarette was powering forward at full throttle under the mad English giant's hand. The noise it was making, trapped and amplified between the reverberating hulls of the shipping on either side, was deafening. The throttle setting did not just generate noise – it meant they were pounding upstream at eighty knots. Eighty knots relative to the counterflow of the downstream current. They were doing this unheard-of speed in an all too narrow channel between two sets of black steel cliffs – like modern Argonauts trying for a water-speed record between the Clashing Rocks.

The ships whose sides represented the rocks were all travelling – albeit at a much slower speed – upriver or down. Each of these large, lumbering vessels was throwing out not one wake but two. One from the bow and one from the stern. The water between them was therefore criss-crossed by overlapping undulations like the blades on a diamond file. But that was only the beginning. For the ships on their right hand were going upstream against the current while those on their left were coming downstream with the current. The double wakes that one set of ships was throwing out, therefore, were nothing like the waves generated by the others. The variation was not predictable in any way. And this was compounded almost beyond calculation by extraneous factors such as the size of the ships in question, their power and their lading.

As long as he lived, Tan was never quite able to work out whether it was the good nature of the amazing vessel they were riding in or the simple genius of the man at the helm. Or, on the other hand, almost unbelievable luck. But *Marilyn* seemed to weave her way through the nightmare waters like an American football quarter-back or a British rugby fly-half of unmatchable skill. She ducked, she dived, she jinked and she flew. But she never lost momentum or velocity. And she got them upriver at a speed the black boats trailing in her wake could never hope to match. But, to be brutally frank, she also made it almost impossible for a man to use a radio effectively.

'*Poseidon*? This is incoming vessel. Flame-red Cigarette with owner Richard Mariner at the helm. We are being pursued and may need assistance. I say again this is incoming vessel with your owner at the helm . . .'

'Look out, Richard!' bellowed Robin. 'They're back!'

There was no hanging fire this time. As soon as the two black speedboats got into the choppy channel behind *Marilyn*, the men aboard them opened up, seemingly with everything they'd got. The range was long. Neither the target nor the firing platform was anywhere near steady. The shots that reached *Marilyn* did so by luck. And they ricocheted harmlessly off the massive hydraulic engine hatch that kept her steady aft. But even so, there was too much risk for Richard. He glanced sideways. Huge bows flared above him. How could a ship this size actually get upstream? he wondered briefly. He registered the name *Golden Happiness* and *Marilyn* dived for cover. Swinging right under the cutwater, she actually seemed to pause for a moment under the crest of the bow wave as though she were a surfer, and then she was through.

Richard span the wheel hard left and raced forward along the flaking Plimsoll line painted on the hull of the next ship forward. Another huge freighter. Then he went hard left and left again. *Marilyn* burst out from under the leading ship's bow and came screaming back down her length, bows high, nothing showing but enormously strengthened V of fibreglass keel. The black boat imme-diately behind was just about to swing right, hoping to follow him beneath *Golden Happiness*'s bows. Whoever held the con hesitated, simply shocked by the sudden reversal. The speedboat dived right, out of the charging Cigarette's way – but just that little bit too slowly. *Golden Happiness* ran her down relentlessly. As *Marilyn* powered past, Tan had a horrified flash of the long black hull rolling over and over like a log, spewing black-clad bodies; see-sawing under. Breaking apart.

Richard, on the other hand, leaned out until his harness creaked, looking for the second speedboat.

'Richard!' bellowed Robin again.

'What?' demanded Tan, fearing that the madman at the wheel might actually look back in answer to his golden-haired demon wife.

'This!' she spat. And handed Tan the Rohrbaugh Stealth 9mm that Huuk had given to her in mid-air. 'Give it to him. Just in case.'

And there it was, thought Richard, straining out of the cockpit, oblivious to the conversation going on behind him. It was already wavering off-line, as though shocked to see the terrible fate of its sister. But there was almost no room to come off-line at all. Richard had a view of half a dozen shouting faces. Someone was brandishing a gun, drawing a bead on the fast-approaching *Marilyn*. Tan's hand came down on his shoulder, distracting him almost fatally, but then the PLAN officer and triad member was pressing a little black pistol into his fist. He took it without a second thought and pulled the trigger without really taking aim. It was enough. The gunman in the other boat jumped out of the way, crashing into his colleague at the helm. Leaving the black boat floundering helplessly just for the vital instant.

So that when *Marilyn*'s keel smashed like a dull blade into the rearmost section of the speedboat's hull, she did so almost painlessly. There was a twist on the wheel – which Richard was expecting and controlled, one-handed, as he pulled the Rohrbaugh back inboard. There was a lurch to the left – countered at once by the wake of the *Golden Hope* and the almost immediate bow wave of the *Golden Harvest*. The second speedboat simply stopped dead in the water. Its whole aft section, weighted by a pair of massive Yamaha outboards, was already at the bottom of the river – and the rest of the hull was about to follow suit. Then the Cigarette was back on-line and suddenly charging under all too familiar bows while Tan and Robin were both bellowing, 'That's her! That's her!'

Richard spun the wheel again and throttled back as the Cigarette turned. Then he was coming in under *Poseidon*'s counter, already losing speed. *Poseidon* was turning to starboard as the *Golden* ships ahead of her slowed and prepared to drop their lifeboats. *Poseidon* had different priorities, however. She moved up the outside of the lane as the men in the water were recovered, like a racing car edging off the track to slip round a pile-up ahead.

'Tell them to drop *Neptune*'s recovery lines,' ordered Richard, throttling back further and forcing his pretty thoroughbred to the pace of a lumbering dray horse.

Tan broke into a conversation between River Pilot Chang and the Port Authority reporting the men in the water and the action being taken to recover them. Then it was the work of ten more minutes to drop and secure the lines – double to *Marilyn*'s stiletto-sharp bow and one each to the points on her slim-hipped stern. Then, with the four of them still aboard, the Cigarette was winched aloft until she was level with the deck.

Even the august river pilot, it seemed, was happy to come down to the weather deck and help them climb aboard now that his report was made and his course deviation agreed. It was Grandfather Chang, in fact, who took Huuk's shoulders as Robin carefully handed him aboard.

So that the first thing that Son of Dragon Head Huuk of the Invisible Power Triad saw as he blinked himself awake at that very moment was a tiny tattoo on the smallest finger of Pilot Chang's left hand in the character that signified *Green*.

THIRTY-ONE
Ghosts

As soon as everyone from the Cigarette was safely aboard, Richard ran up on to the bridge as swiftly as he could, exchanging introductions with the pilot as he ran. Pilot Chang came up to the bridge beside him, leaving Tan and Robin to look after the still semiconscious Daniel Huuk. And, from the look of him, thought Richard grimly, poor old Huuk still needed a good deal of looking after.

While *Marilyn* was being recovered, Captain Chang had guided her command round the outside of the narrow shipping lane, past the three big *Golden* vessels and back into place ahead of them. Only the confidence of her father, the accuracy of the echo-sounder and the incoming tide like the crest of a wave under her counter gave her the confidence to risk the five-metre shallows that rose into the massive central mudbank all too close to starboard.

'I'll need to complete detailed reports for all the relevant authorities,' Richard said as he arrived, looking back at the confusion he had left in *Poseidon*'s wake, then across at the mudbank where a few of the survivors from the first speedboat were crawling like prehistoric amphibious life forms. 'But the deputy general commissioner's countersignature should keep me out of trouble, with any luck. Now, tell me, exactly where are we bound for?'

Captain Chang looked across at her father, who was standing solidly in the middle of the bridge once more, hands clasped determinedly behind his back. 'The river pilot has orders, apparently . . .'

But before he could vouchsafe the orders, Broadband called again. 'Message for the pilot. Can the pilot come to the radio room, please?'

'Keep her steady,' said Grandfather Chang to Xin. 'Course and speed. Navigator Shang Wei Jiang, I would be grateful if you could continue to keep an eye on the depth, please. We no longer have the big *Golden* vessels ahead ensuring we are in the optimum channel and the mudbanks here are notorious . . .'

'Haven't you asked him where he's taking us?' demanded Richard when the pilot had left the bridge. 'It's incredible that he hasn't told you! I'll get the Port Authority on my cellphone if I can get a service and talk directly to them.'

'Leave it a while, please,' asked Captain Chang. 'Give him a chance . . .'

Richard shrugged accommodatingly.

But the pilot's return cleared everything up. 'I apologize for the confusion,' Grandfather Chang announced as he came back on to the bridge, his face folded in a thoughtful frown. 'But we have been ordered back to Shanghai. The Port Authorities, in cooperation with the police, the Department of Antiquities and of course the Museum, have arranged secure and suitable anchorage and accommodation.'

That one little speech seemed to settle all Richard's immediate Who? Why? When? Where? and What the hell is going on? questions. There was even a number at the Port Authority for him to contact in the event he required any further information or guidance as owner. And a name. Port Authority Officer First Grade Bing Yuesheng.

But Big-Eared Bing remained undisturbed as Richard got involved in the sort of ship-handling he hadn't done in years. Moving a sizeable vessel from lane to lane to lane in a crowded waterway. The manoeuvring for the U-turn was potentially quite complex. Richard watched with growing admiration as the pilot required *Poseidon* to slow until clear water had opened up for some distance ahead. There was clear water behind because the *Golden* vessels had effectively blocked the waterway during their rescue of the men in the river and on the mudbank.

Surrounded by clear water, therefore, *Poseidon* swung to port across the flow, crossing the empty channel between the inbound and the outbound traffic. Then she swung to port again, carefully matching her speed with the line of ships heading out towards the sea, with the flow of the river behind them and the top of the tide running counter. After a little negotiation with one or two respectful junior colleagues, the pilot was able to slot *Poseidon* into the outbound line by swinging her a degree or two more to starboard. But she joined this sedate procession only temporarily.

No sooner was she settled on the 120 degree course downriver than the pilot was ordering that they swing away to starboard once again, even as the confusion around the three *Golden* vessels came into view, and move across to the outbound channel closest to the southern bank. The ships there were all bound for Shanghai and would soon swing hard a-starboard, round the hook of mud that

Richard had last crossed in *Marilyn* at thirty knots, and into the Huangpu River. Once again the pilot began his negotiations to break into the outbound line.

It was late afternoon by the time all this delicate manoeuvring was completed and *Poseidon* was casting a long shadow forward as she finally settled on to her eastbound course towards the Huangpu and Shanghai. The midday bustle of shipping had eased and the big ships had started to head for deep-water anchorages as the tide started ebbing away. There was still enough water in the Yangtze for the mid-sized craft like *Poseidon* but even she had to take care. Not only was the tidal water from the China Sea falling backwards, pulled away by the distant, invisible moon, but the slight but significant damming effect of the counter-flow also made the river itself run thinner at the ebb. As though the fact that it had to run further to get down to the sea now stretched it out like rubber and made it lie shallower above its treacherous bed.

Straightline stayed beside his depth gauge and warned the pilot of any shoals that had shifted into the channel since his last voyage here. 'The riverbed is never still, never at rest,' Grandfather Chang informed Straightline, to whom he seemed to have taken a liking. But, Richard observed acutely, the old man always talked loudly enough so that the captain, too, received the benefit of his wisdom. Precisely when he worked out that they were father and daughter he never really registered. But in the end he wished he had worked it out more quickly and taken action sooner. 'It is a living thing,' Pilot Chang was explaining, 'a kind of ghostly dragon, and it is not always well-disposed towards the ships that ride above it. If you become in the least distracted, it will catch you and try to destroy you. It is like life in that respect.'

'But the banks are becoming steep, sir. Look, the cliffs ahead will easily top our mast; would even have dwarfed the big ships – the *Golden* sisters. Where the banks rise in such cliffs, surely there are always deep waters at their feet.'

'Sometimes,' nodded Grandfather Chang. 'Sometimes not. You will see.'

Dusk seemed to gather rapidly, thought Richard a little wearily, spreading up from the ocean like a tidal wave as the sun sank slowly behind them, somewhere far west of Nanjing, up by the Three Gorges Dam. And the effect of the gathering gloom was accentuated by several factors. The bank close on their starboard did rise high, as Straightline had observed. It wavered into little bays and promontories. Here and there the road that ran along the cliff-top leaped out on bridges from headland to headland and little tributaries ran under them, trying to push *Poseidon* off her course. The bays and valleys seemed to be filled with inky blackness, and, like the little rivers, this also flowed out into the Yangtze itself. Switching on the bridge lights only seemed to make the outside world darker, more gloomy. More haunted.

Then there was the mist. What lingering brightness there was, out late like a child after its bedtime, seemed to be soaked up by a grey and ghostly layer of vapour. It billowed on the evening breeze, thickening and thinning unexpectedly, without rhyme or reason. It was never quite where you expected it to be, but it was always where you didn't want it to be, dousing lights and hiding hazards. As though it had a wicked will of its own. The will-o'-the-wisp, maybe, except that there were no sparks of light within it. It was as though the Hungry Ghosts of the autumn festivals were out and abroad a little early. Generations of dead parents dissatisfied with what their living offspring were doing in the bright, brief world of flesh and blood.

Then there were the birds. It seemed to Richard that every bird in the massive estuary had taken flight. They milled across the sky, obscuring the last of the high blue brightness like monstrous thunderclouds. Even in here, cocooned from the outside by the bridge windows and the clearviews, with the engines pounding and the alternators throbbing, their screaming seemed disquietingly loud.

It was the bird calls, in fact, that masked the thudding of the first helicopter's approach. So that it came as a shock to Richard – enough to make him jump, in fact – to glance out of the port-side window and see the chopper hovering almost level with the bridge, seemingly close enough to touch. And even as he opened his mouth to ask the pilot what he thought was going on, another chopper joined it. The pilot suddenly saw them too and swung round, his face working, as though he had been as shocked as Richard to see them.

But before either man could say a word, the bridge door burst wide and Daniel Huuk was there. His head was bandaged. He was naked to the waist. His back and shoulders were speckled with yellow disinfectant that covered every little wound made by shards of Ang's exploding skull. The antiseptic was the only colour above the black belt binding Huuk's trim waist. Otherwise he was almost deathly white as though he too had become one of the Hungry

Ghosts. Behind him, Robin and Tan filled the narrow companionway leading down to the next deck.

'Where are you taking me, Pilot?' demanded Daniel hoarsely.
'Where are you taking us all?'

'To Shanghai . . .' The pilot suddenly seemed hesitant, almost
taken aback. Guilty.

Richard went cold, looking out at the helicopters again. They
were unmarked. As black and anonymous as the speedboats. And
there was another thing. Another surprise almost strange enough to
make Richard jump. There, at the inner edge of the darkness, as
dark as the shadows and as ghostly as the mist, an enormous junk
was pulling across the ebbing river, its ribbed sails as black as her
spectral hull, on a collision course with *Poseidon*. As though the
Great Khan had launched his ghost ship and come back in person
to recover his treasure.

Captain Chang saw the ghostly vessel too. And the danger it
represented. 'FULL AHEAD!' she ordered.

'No!' countermanded the pilot.

But when it came to a choice between the Mongol and the
Grandfather, Steadyhand Xin knew which one to obey. 'Full ahead,'
he echoed.

Richard felt *Poseidon* leap forward at once.

'Don't rely on him!' called Huuk, striding forward again. He
grabbed the pilot's hand and pulled it into the bridge light. 'He is
Green Gang!'

'Father,' screamed Captain Chang, her heart seeming to break
between the syllables.

The pilot tore free of Huuk's grip and took one step towards his
daughter, his face working and his mouth wide, its corners pulled
down like a tragedy mask. He would have taken another step, but
Straightline was there in front of him, protecting his quivering
captain.

Which is why the navigator was not at his post beside the echo-
sounder depth gauge when *Poseidon* drove full-tilt on to the
mudbank.

THIRTY-TWO
Downfall

T he mudbank was a long, soft wall reaching out like an under-water dam from the foot of a little promontory backed by a tall cliff. The cliff came out into a tall black blade of earth, like the prow of the ghostly junk's giant cousin. Between this and the next headland downstream, across a little deep-water bay with a shrunken stream behind it, was the first and largest of the bridges that leaped from headland to headland, carrying the main shore road west from Wusong and Shanghai up towards Nanjing.

Poseidon rode up across the back of the mudbank, see-sawed forward, settled down and stilled. Like everyone else onboard, Richard was staggered by the speed and totality of the disaster. Literally. He was thrown forward and almost fell to his knees. He collided with the pilot and all but skittled him over. The pair of them hit Straightline and made a sort of human three-legged stool which steadied as the ship began to settle. The captain was thrown against the back of Steadyhand's chair but she managed to keep her feet, which was fortunate, as she provided yet another soft landing for Daniel Huuk.

Chance brought Richard and the other two with him up against the starboard clearview so he was able to see that *Marilyn* swung mightily, but stayed safely secured. As, indeed, did *Neptune*, un-worried, sitting solidly in her cradle, no more worried by this than she had been by the typhoon. There were shouts of complaint from below, but no sounds of serious damage, for everything was still well secured after the storm and the sea chase. Not too surpris-ingly, thought Richard, tearing himself free and going to check on Robin; there had hardly been an opportunity to do anything other than to leave everything aboard squared away and shipshape.

The helicopters were gone, snatched away into the shadows ahead by the unexpected stopping of the ship. Even the huge junk was now no longer on anything like a reciprocal course. But it was angling its massive ribbed sails to whatever wind there was over the estuary and turning back towards them.

'You did that on purpose!' snarled Huuk, swinging round to face the pilot. 'You've left us with nowhere to run. On purpose. You know if they get onboard they will kill everybody.' He swung back and included Captain Chang in his outrage. Swung back again to face her still gasping father, *'Everybody!'*

'Then we have to stop them getting onboard,' said Richard decisively from the bridge door. He looked down at Robin and Tan, standing ready on the steps below. He felt in his pocket for Huuk's lethal little Rohrbaugh. 'Captain Chang, where are the keys to the gun locker?'

The captain reached into her uniform trouser pocket, took them out and threw them to him. Richard caught them one handed as he was turning, ready to clatter away down the companionway. But as he did so, the helicopters came thudding back through the lower air and hovered nose-down like a pair of vultures inspecting a likely looking carcass. So, instead of going himself, he threw the keys down to Tan. 'Anyone will show you where it is,' he called. 'The guns are loaded, primed and zeroed. Tell Chef to break out the galley equipment too. If it comes to hand-to-hand fighting then carving knives, cleavers and choppers will do just as well.' Under his breath he added, *As anyone who's ever seen Gordon Ramsay at work will know . . .*

The last, blissfully inappropriate comment got him back into the middle of the bridge. Huuk and the pilot were back on face-to-face confrontation. 'Yes, I am Green Gang,' Chang was shouting. 'I have not made the decision or the sacrifices willingly or lightly. But *this* . . .' He held up his hand, fingers spread to show the tiny tattoo. 'This has allowed me to rebuild my life and my family's life!'

'Well, the cost may well be escalating now,' snarled Huuk. 'It is likely to cost you a daughter. Even if she survives, it will have cost her her command. And if I survive it will have cost her her freedom – and you your freedom too. If I get back to Beijing, you can expect to be spending the rest of your miserable existence fixing roadways as far from flowing water as I can arrange! Have you no idea what you are caught up in here? Dragon Head Zhang Tong hopes to hold even the Supreme Government to ransom! Like one of the ancient warlords whose ghosts still haunt this place. To make Shanghai as run by Green Gang a virtually independent state! He has taken the ideas put forward by the Tibetans and the Uighurs following in the footsteps of their other independent brother countries in the West and applied it to triads! Don't you see? Shanghai and Pudong together generate more capital than half of Europe! A prize worth playing for indeed. And such a clever game – to use Uighur separatists as a cover to destroy our Internet access – and threaten to do it time and time again unless we acceded to his demands. To throw up a smoke-screen of half truths, lies and murder while he plays his hand out in Beijing.

'And Shanghai is only the beginning! He has also learned all too well from the Brotherhood of Invisible Power that it is possible to spread influence at the highest level, far beyond traditional triad limits. If his plans bear fruit, there will be Green Gang officers in the People's Liberation Army, Navy, Air Force. In the police and detective services. In the Institute of Public Security. In all the professions. All the universities. In the local government councils of every major city, state, area. In Beijing itself!'

'As the Invisible Power Triad already has!' huffed Chang, but he sounded less certain now. 'It is one tiger fighting another tiger for the right to raid the biggest herds. The goats themselves will never know the difference.'

'No!' spat Huuk, with almost manic force. 'Invisible Power is a brotherhood of the brightest and the best. It exists to protect and to better the lives of all Chinese. The goats as you call them *would* notice the difference if the Brotherhood of Invisible Power remained supreme. They would be safer. They would be happier. They would be fatter! Tell him, Chang Jhiang Quing. Tell your father what we have promised.'

Captain Chang turned stiffly and stood in front of her father. She pulled up the left sleeve of her uniform and snapped off the watch she always wore. There, on her wrist, under the circle left by the backplate, was a tiny tattoo. 'It is as the Son of the Dragon Head says, Father,' she confirmed quietly. 'The brightest and best for the greatest good of all. It is what we swear when we drink the black cock's blood.'

'What have you done?' cried the pilot, reaching round to grasp Huuk by his shoulders. 'What have you all done to us?'

And the clearview exploded inwards. A bullet whipped through the bridge to shatter against the aft wall beside the bridge door. On the way it passed through the pilot's hand and the deputy general commissioner's shoulder it was holding. Both men span away shouting with shock and pain, each spraying blood from his wounds. Robin, returning with a heavily armed Tan in tow, ran to the staggering Daniel. Chang ran to her father. 'Pappi,' she called, a child once again, 'Pappi, are you hurt?'

The river pilot rolled over and held up his shattered left hand. 'I seem to have resigned from the Green Gang!' he said with a hysterical laugh. His little finger was gone, chopped off from the knuckle by the bullet. His daughter made a very strange sound indeed and wrapped him in her arms.

Richard was crouching in the splintered glass with his head just under the windowframe. 'That came from the nearest chopper,' he said. 'Why do they want our heads down?' Then he popped his head up over the parapet for an instant and hunkered down again as another volley of shots came in.

Straightline doused the bridge lights. 'What is it?' he asked.

'It's that big junk,' answered Richard, risking another glance out in the darkness. 'She's pulling into the little bay dead ahead. She's preparing to lower boats as soon as she's steady, by the look of things. Getting ready to board us, I suppose. The choppers are sitting in the air immediately above her. That's where the rifles are, at a guess. Though they may have sharpshooters in the rigging too.'

'Christ,' said Robin feelingly. 'It's like the Battle of bloody Trafalgar!'

'And Nelson's never handy when you need him!' observed Richard.

'HUUK!' came a great booming voice. 'DRAGON HEAD HUUK!'

'I'm here,' answered Huuk, pulling himself towards the shattered clearview. His shoulder was oozing blood from where the bullet had pierced it. Not spurting. No damage too fatal, then, thought Richard and slid the Rohrbaugh across the deck towards him. At least not yet.

'I'm gone,' said Richard. 'Keep him talking, whoever it is. Captain Chang, Steadyhand . . . Someone, give him the microphone and switch on the ship's tannoy.'

'I'm here,' repeated Huuk a second or two later, his voice massively amplified by the ship's address system. 'Is that you, Zhang Tong?'

Richard was therefore able to listen to the conversation as he dragged Tan down the companionway. Straightline and Steadyhand followed him and the four had a brief council of war at the foot of the steps. Chief Engineer Powerhouse Wang and several of his men joined them before Richard had finished his planning, and Electrical Engineer Zhong Wei brought a tough-looking team of seamen with him. Chef appeared with two Sabatier carry-cases full of the most terrifying kitchen implements Richard had ever seen – and a bunch of battle-ready stewards willing to wield them. Broadband Dung appeared breathlessly and was sent back to the radio room with an ancient Russian CZ52 automatic and orders to start broadcasting general Mayday signals. Just as he turned away, Richard called, 'Wait!' and passed him two old but indestructible Tokarevs. 'For the captain and the pilot if she thinks we can trust him now.'

The others were sent off to repel boarders. Richard and Tan took a couple of geriatric but well-maintained Simonov assault rifles to the high ground. 'You might as well give up,' Zhang Tong was saying to Huuk. 'In only a moment or two more we will be able to relieve you of your powers and your treasure both at once. If you surrender now we will let you live.'

'Now where have I heard that before?' wondered Richard.

'He's playing for time until they get the big junk into position,' said Tan. 'Then he'll just board us, kill everybody and take what he wants.'

'He wants old Genghis in one piece or he'd have used rockets again before now,' said Richard. 'Unless they went down in the powerboats. Probably wants Huuk in one piece too – for a while at least. Then he'll want him in pieces,' he added, thinking of Flatface Ang.

Then another thought struck him. 'But why's Zhang Tong come out here himself?' he asked Tan. 'It's a bit of a risk. Not much of one, I grant you, but still . . . More risky than sitting at home in Dragon Head House giving orders.'

'It's a matter of honour,' said Tan. 'Of *face*. He will be the victorious general reducing a once-honoured opponent to nothing. There will be nothing he cannot achieve. It will be as though he has eaten Dragon Head Huuk's heart. His luck. His very soul.'

'Well, let's hope we can blow the smile off his face, at any rate,' snarled Richard, in position to do so at last. 'That looks like the only way forward for all of us now.'

The view from the front of the flying bridge was eerily breathtaking. An almost impenetrable bank of fog sat low on the river seeming to pick up and diffuse any light nearby. The hull of *Poseidon* herself seemed eerily invisible. *Neptune* rose like a reef half covered, *Marilyn* seemed about to set sail on the cloudy white surface of the stuff. The channel dead ahead was awash with misty darkness. Only the span of the road bridge far above seemed to hold any brightness, the pallid concrete almost aglow against the utter moonless, starless velvet of the sky. Outlined flat and black against it, their cabins lit by dashboard lights, their exhausts like dragons' nostrils, hung the choppers. One high and one lower, nose angled down, allowing Zhang Tong to talk to Huuk.

And there, underneath it, the huge junk was feeling its way into the cove, visible only because it was blacker even than the night. Its decks were thronging with amorphous gloom, from which came the occasional steely glint. One or two figures, however, were individually visible. Richard nudged Tan. 'Look,' he said. 'That explains a lot.'

'What?'

'They've got a leadsman in the bows taking soundings,' added Robin's voice, so close behind them that they both jumped. 'We could have done with one of those coming up to that bloody mudbank.'

Richard realized that Robin had been able to get so close to them because of all the noise going on. Huuk and Zhang Tong were both speaking through megaphones. Two choppers were hovering in a confined space under an eight-lane highway bridge that was full of traffic, judging by the constant background roar it added. And the birds were adding further to the bedlam, utterly invisible now but seemingly ten times as audible. 'What is the matter with those bloody birds?' demanded Richard, dropping his cheek to the stock of the Simonov and drawing a bead on Zhang Tong's chopper, knowing that a perfect shot was the only chance they had and knowing that it was really no chance at all.

And the answer came at once.

It began with an intensifying rumble, as though the traffic on the bridge had somehow become much larger and heavier. The cliffs began to judder. Loose earth and stones started sliding seemingly soundlessly into the river. Within five seconds the trembling had become so strong that clumps of solid earth and rock were beginning to tear themselves free. The individual explosions they made as they plunged into the river became audible, like a stick of bombs being dropped in the distance. A deep bass note entered the air as though every molecule within it was beginning to shake as well.

Poseidon began to judder hard enough to make Richard slide across the deck, the Simonov simply jerked right out of his hands. Instead, his hands found Robin and they clung together as the noise and the vibration continued to increase. The water was beginning to writhe now, so that the junk was tossed from side to side. The leadsman tumbled off the heaving bow into the foaming water. It seemed incredible to Richard that the helicopters could still hang apparently immune, in the reverberating air. *Poseidon* was really heaving now, her long, strong hull pitching and tossing, rolling and reeling as though she were back in the terrible typhoon. *Marilyn* broke free then, leaping off her twisting hangings as though she were jumping for safety. She vanished down into the mist like a duchess deserting the *Titanic*. She must have made some sort of noise as she hit the water but it was lost in all the rest like a whisper in a whirlwind. *Poseidon* reared and heaved, but she was designed to do so. Designed to be thrown about – by great storms, not by seismic shocks. But even so . . .

The junk was not so lucky. The storm she found herself trapped in ripped her rigging to shreds. Her masts began to reel and topple. The ribbed sails tore free and collapsed like decks of cards. The threatening army of triad pirates was turned in those twenty seconds into a routed rabble throwing itself into the boiling water to escape the terrible rain of struts and spars.

But that was as nothing to what followed.

Thirty seconds into the earthquake the Wusong Bridge began to fail. It had been twisting and writhing above Richard's stunned view far more dangerously than he could begin to comprehend. The first thing he knew about it was when a massive block of masonry soared silently down into the waist of the junk where the tallest mast had so recently stood. He looked up, horrified, actually rolling on to his back, legs spread in a vain attempt to hold still, with Robin wrapped around him like the giant squid round *Neptune* at the beginning of all this. The underside of the bridge was undulating. Great waves of force were running along it, making it flap like a long grey pennant in the grip of a high wind. A streamer suddenly webbed with black like a Tibetan batik banner. More massive blocks of concrete started falling. The third one hit the furthest helicopter. Like the hand of some wanton God swatting a fly, it simply smashed it out of the air. To become part of the destruction raining down on to the junk. A ball of flame with a block of concrete the size of a pantechnicon at its heart.

Forty seconds in, the Wusong Bridge's back broke. The span failed utterly and the whole structure tore itself in half. Articulated trucks, family saloons, lorries, buses all came hurtling down like hail, their headlights blazing, lighting up the scene as the last of the masonry fell among them. Zhang Tong's chopper simply vanished into the maelstrom of cascading steel. It added its own brief flash of dying light to the lake of petrol that flamed and died on the instant.

The largest of the ring of waves generated by the utter destruction was enough to wash the heaving *Poseidon* back off the mudbank and into the deeper water upriver where she continued to heave and pitch – but at her own bidding, no longer gripped by the terrible writhing of the land.

After fifty seconds it was over. Or the first part of it was at least.

Poseidon sat safely on the outer edge of Armageddon, all aboard her shocked and utterly overcome. And lucky to be alive.

Chang Jhiang Quing clutched her father to her breast and he held her as hard as his damaged hand would allow. 'There's work for your mother the architect, if she's still alive,' he whispered. And she nodded, unable to speak.

The door to the radio shack burst open. Broadband came staggering out, his face as pale as ivory.

Daniel Huuk pulled himself erect and leaned on the solidity of Steadyhand Xin, who had not needed to use his cleaver after all. Any more than Daniel had needed to use his Rohrbaugh Stealth 9mm. They looked down on the utter destruction of Daniel's enemies. The demise of the briefly resurrected Green Gang. 'That bloody Goodluck Giant,' said Steadyhand. 'He's saved the whole bloody lot of us.'

'I'm not sure that he has,' gasped Broadband, turning towards his captain.

And on the flying bridge above their heads, Richard rolled over, sat up and tried unsuccessfully to pull himself erect. 'Looks like *Marilyn*'s gone,' he said sadly.

'Yes, my love,' said Robin. 'I think you'll find that Marilyn left us in August 1962.'

And before Richard could think of anything like an adequate reply the ship's tannoy boomed into life, seemingly very much louder now that everything except the screaming of the prophetic birds was still.

'The Three Gorges Dam has burst,' announced Captain Chang, her voice expressionless, flattened by shock. 'The epicentre was apparently up there in Hunan Province and the whole construction's come down.'

Richard stopped worrying about *Marilyn* then, and about Daniel Huuk, triads and treasure. He slid his arm round Robin and hugged her fiercely to him. As he began to try and calculate what forty cubic kilometres of water would do if it was all unleashed at once.

Acknowledgements

The title of *River of Ghosts* comes from the breathtaking book *Red Dust* by Ma Jian (Vintage, 2001), which describes the author's epic journey across modern China in much the same way as Tim Butcher's *Blood River* tells of his journey across Africa in H. M. Stanley's footsteps. 'River of Ghosts' is the heading of the section in which Ma Jian comes down the Yangtze. It seemed so apt to me as a title for this book because I had centred the back-story of the Chinese characters in my tale so very carefully on the river. I did this not only to prepare the reader for the final sections of the story but also as a way of trying to control the massive amount of information that flows like a tidal wave out of China's recent history. It was only a short step to move from a river full of memories to a River of Ghosts, and *Red Dust* provided the bridge.

Although general research for the story goes back over ten years to my earlier novels *The Pirate Ship* and *Tiger Island* – with which it shares some characters – detailed research for *River of Ghosts* really began during my family's first visit to Sharm El Sheikh in the summer of 2007. Here I read Tom Bradby's novel *The Master of Rain* (Bantam, 2002), set in the Shanghai of the 1920s, and, in spite of the fact that I was at that time actually working on the book that was to become *Benin Light*, I was entranced. At once Shanghai became a character in the new story as a companion to the Yangtze itself. Research continued much more pointedly in England later that year and was deeply influenced by *National Geographic*'s Special Issue on China in May 2008.

Other printed sources included *Countries of the World: CHINA* by Carole Goddard and *Country File: CHINA* by Michael March. Needless to say, with Shanghai and the Yangtze so much in mind, I consulted *The Lonely Planet Guide to Shanghai* and the *Time Out Guide to Shanghai* as well as the *Rough Guide to China*, which returned to Sharm El Sheikh with me in summer 2008. So did Eliot Pattison's simply awesome *The Skull Mantra* (Century, 2000) and Charles Cumming's towering *Typhoon* (Michael Joseph, 2008), both of which have informed the narrative in many ways, I suspect. *Typhoon* not only added some details of modern Shanghai but also dealt with the plight of the Muslim Uighurs in the north – as *The Skull Mantra* dealt with the Tibetans south and west. The more modern facts underlying both of these dazzling fictions were added by *The Week* magazine, an invaluable source. All through the spring and summer *The Week* carried details of Buddhist monks disrupting the passage of the Olympic torch abroad and the immolation of the Uighurs at home – including news of China's first suicide bombing.

On returning from Egypt I had turned at once (as I have for more than twenty years) to the chart division of Kelvin Hughes. Thanks must go to Mike Kelly and to Bob who discussed matters at length with me, then sent me the charts I needed to navigate *Poseidon* from the Ryukyu Trench, through the Yellow Sea, past Shanghai itself and on up the Yangtze.

As ever, colleagues at The Wildernesse School were only too willing to help and special thanks must go to Jenny Fenn and Gwyneth Higgins, librarians extraordinaire. And also to Ed Cookson who gave me several recent copies of *International Ocean Systems* and much insightful advice which enabled me to describe the remote AUV *Neptune* with so much more authority and, I hope, accuracy. *Poseidon* herself owes more than a little in terms of internal structure and layout to the *Hammersley*, the corvette at the centre of the excellent Australian TV series *Sea Patrol*; though the characters who command and crew her are of course my own creations.

It was the Internet that supplied the rest, from the ranks of officers in the Chinese People's Liberation Army Navy – and the vessels to be found beneath its flag – to the Chinese signs of the Zodiac and the character traits associated with them. From Chinese helicopters to Chinese armaments. It was here that I found seismic details of the Ryukyu Trench, estimations of the capacity of the completed Three Gorges Dam. Here I found a bewildering variety of speculation about triads (though neither of the two I mention is, to the best of my knowledge, current). Here also I found the wonderful Cigarette speedboats – with which, like Richard himself, I fell all too easily and probably not too wisely in love.

Peter Tonkin
Sharm El Sheikh and Tunbridge Wells, 2008